Prior

Repercussions

A novel by

Timothy LaBadie

Dedication:

I wrote this for my wife Eva who not only breathes life into my characters but into my world as well.

Acknowledgement:

I want to recognize the Fiction Studio for all the hard work in editing and bringing this fiction into your hands. Lou Aronica was there with me from start to finish, from storyboard to final draft. The editing of this work is superb. Thanks Lou, I couldn't have done it without you.

1

A dirty bundle lay on the concrete sidewalk to the left of the front entrance to Doug Sirius's office building with a sign that said, "Anything will help." Doug glanced long enough to see the body within. She was pregnant. The soles of her feet were cracked and knobby. Though weathered and crusty around the mouth with a fuzzy upper lip, she was probably a teenager.

Doug looked away.

Using his badge, he entered the building, his dog Constant (as in constantly a dog) heeling close to his side. In his right hand, he carried a walking stick. Placing his left hand on the shoulder of the building's security guard, Doug leaned close to the man and, nodding out the window toward the bundle, said, "Have that removed. I don't care where. Drop it in Hunter's Point if necessary."

On his way to the elevator he thought about the authorities already being paid enough that they should at least be able to keep the streets clean. He looked up at the security camera mounted on the wall above the elevator doors. These were accessible online so that he could monitor the entire building, even from home.

Doug's development and construction businesses occupied the two top floors of the building. In the elevator, he held his badge to a scanner getting access to his floor. Though it looked like an old freight elevator, all the hardware was the slickest high tech. Something he had personally designed, it managed to be harmonious in style to San Francisco's SOMA district, yet still one of a kind. Even the squeaks and rattles, the sound of chains and pulleys, he heard on the ride up were recorded.

Constant sat patiently by Doug's left foot as they rode to the top floor. Doug patted his dog's head twice without looking down, though he knew that Constant's curl of a tail would wag once. Doug often amused himself by imagining what dog thoughts Constant might be having. *I don't know how humans can make different places appear beyond this door*, Doug considered the dog thinking now. *They go into this little room, the door closes, they press some buttons and when the door opens they're someplace else. If I had hands I would press the buttons for the park.*

After the elevator shook to a stop, they stepped through the doors in unison and turned right. Doug first took in the light green cubicles comprised of five-foot walls that didn't obscure the breathtaking view from the floor-to-ceiling windows surrounding them. Scattered around the ceiling were similar security cameras to the one in the lobby. Then he heard the orchestral sound of his endlessly busy staff: fast ten-keys and keyboards, and whispering voices; pencils on paper, the slapping, high, crisp notes of plastic straight-edges, the higher sound of protractors with rubber erasing; and of course the crinkling and shredding of periodical paper blunders.

Doug smiled as he passed through. This was the sound of serenity for him: the sound of progress. The only sound that surpassed it for him was the sound of construction itself.

Doug stopped near his assistant Jasmine's desk, telling her to join him in five minutes with her project list.

"There's a woman waiting for you in the lobby," she said. "I'm surprised you didn't see her on the way up."

"What does she want?"

"She has a package for you."

"Well, have her leave it at the front desk."

Using his thumb for the biometric lock on his private door, he entered his inner sanctum. Within, two walls were the light green of lima beans – the same as the cubicles – and one was dark green. The fourth was glass looking out over the city.

Constant was a skinny gray-and-black grizzly mutt of a dog, maybe forty or forty-five pounds with a tail that curled like a black cinnamon bun. On his dogface, abundant gray and white whiskers stuck straight out from his semi-pointed fuzzy snout. He walked directly to his bed under Doug's enormous white oak desk facing the door in the farthest corner, probably thinking in dog-thoughts about taking a nap since nothing exciting was likely to happen around here.

Doug leaned his walking stick in the corner. He turned on his computer, opened a desk drawer to take out his Kindle, turned it on, and after downloading the morning newspaper, placed it on the empty surface of his desk. Also in the drawer was a bottle of

Seroquel for his bipolar disorder that he had not taken yesterday nor would he take today. He didn't want the side effects to diminish his performance should he get lucky this evening after the show. Before his computer had fully booted, his phone rang displaying the name of his assistant.

"Yes," he said after closing the drawer and hitting the speaker button.

"The woman down in the front lobby?"

Doug scowled. "I told you to get rid of her."

"She insists on delivering the package personally."

"So? Do I know her?"

"Her name is Evangelina Guzman and she says that she is willing to wait as long as it takes, even if that means catching you on your way home."

Guzman? Doug thought. It sounded German. He imagined some stocky, masculine delivery woman.

Thinking of incompetence in general and Jasmine's specifically, Doug thought about slapping his assistant with a sarcastic response. Instead, he simply said, "Very well. Send her up and show her in." He decided to use this time to demonstrate to his assistant how things needed to be done.

Checking his e-mail he opened an attachment, a CAD-generated diagram showing the electrical changes he had requested yesterday. He was pleased. He had started his career as an electrician, later becoming a contractor and finally a developer. Each part of his success had become a corporation in its own right.

All named after himself of course: Sirius Electrics, Sirius Plumbing, Sirius Tile and Bath, Sirius Construction, Sirius Developers etc. He loved his name, it sounded like "serious," but he spelled it like the name for the Dog Star. Doug's grandfather had chosen this name to avoid creditors back when birth certificates were not a requirement and not so easily traced. This had been the last of a long list of names his grandfather had used. Doug no longer remembered what his original last name had been, if he had ever known.

A door chime sounded and Doug pressed a buzzer to release the lock on his office door. Jasmine entered, followed by a Filipino woman dressed in light tan business attire, a stretch synthetic material that hugged her features smartly. Doug stood so quickly that his chair scooted out from behind him and hit the wall. Underneath the desk, Constant hurried to his feet and came out and around to the open space, at first in a protective stance but relaxing quickly. He stretched his back by dragging his hind legs and lifting his chest and pointing his head to the ceiling.

Jasmine backed out, closing the door behind her.

The woman's dark bangs were cut straight along her brow, but her hair was long and thick and flowed past her shoulders onto her chest. This was definitely not what he'd expected this woman to look like; he was astonished to find this beautiful woman before him, all five-foot-four of her. He studied her for a moment while he tried to gather his thoughts.

"Mr. Sirius? I am so sorry to interrupt. I'll make this as brief as possible."

Doug found himself nodding.

"My mother said it was imperative that I give this to you today."

He watched her closely. Her movements were elegant, her demeanor confident, her words articulate. Her eyes never left his. She was stunning.

She held the package out to him. He stumbled around his desk and took it mechanically, the fingertips of his other hand resting on his desk for balance. The allure of her scent was subtle and swift.

"Well, that's it, I guess," she said. "Thanks so much for seeing me." She smiled and turned to go. Before she did, though, Constant nuzzled his head into her hand with unexplainable familiarity and she stopped to scratch him almost absentmindedly behind his left ear. Doug assumed Constant was thinking, *aaah, right on my favorite spot.* The woman bent her knees and took Constant's head in her hands smoothing back both ears, and looking him in the eyes.

Finally finding his voice, Doug said, "I should open this." Both of his hands dug into the brown wrapper.

The woman – Jasmine had said her name was Evangelina, right? – stood up straight, leaving Constant sitting attentively. She rested a small tender hand, fingers soft and warm, upon the two of

Doug's, stopping him. "Oh, no, please don't. You're not supposed to do so until I'm gone. Please?"

"I'm not?" He studied the depth in her eyes, so different from anyone he knew. The lids were thick, flat, and smooth. With all the Asians in the City, he'd surprisingly never seen the eyes of one up close. Was this feature common among them?

"Please don't."

He relaxed and uncurled the fingers that had been digging into the paper wrapper. He moistened his lips and kept staring at her eyes, so fascinating, so enchanting, so mysterious, yet earnest and playful. "But...won't I see you again?" he blurted before he realized how awkward his words sounded, how conspicuous, how crass.

"I don't think that's what my mother had in mind. I don't think she'd approve." She whispered the second sentence and then lifted her hand from his. Glancing about the room, then making a sweep of his desk, she said in a tone that might have buried some sarcasm within, "Impressive office, by the way." She paused to swallow and looked him in the eye. She turned forty-five degrees and walked up to a painting, measuring its essence for a moment. "I don't know anything about art, but I like this, the playfulness of it, the feeling of not taking oneself too seriously."

The painting was the first he'd done, painting being a recent hobby. Before this, he'd generally considered the practice of art to be a waste of time. Now he stared at this abstraction on the wall that was more similar to a child's line drawing than any solid shape. He supposed it could be a caterpillar, or one of the giant sand worms from *Dune*, with the head large in the foreground and the tail twisting off to the horizon. He'd done it with his niece, whom he'd lovingly nicknamed "Bug" as in snuggly bug because she was so evenly tempered and cuddly when she was young. The name remained, as did her temperament, though her hugs for him seemed to be a thing of the past.

Evangelina's appraisal seemed genuine, and her openly admitting her ignorance of art impressed him. She smiled and cocked her hips subtly to one side while placing a hand there.

"Thank you," he said.

"You're welcome." Getting close enough to read the signature she said, "It's yours? You painted it?"

"I did, with the help of a most wonderful teenage girl."

"Teenage, hmm?" she said with mischief in her eyes. "Awfully young for you. Or might she be your daughter?"

Doug took a step back and placed the small package on his desk without looking, his eyes enjoying Evangelina. "No children, I'm afraid. Never married."

Evangelina seemed to consider that for a moment and then dismiss it. "Well," she said, nodding toward the painting, "I like it."

For the first time, Doug felt a sense of pride in this creation of his. "It's my first, actually."

"You should keep it up. It gives a nice contrast."

Again, she glanced around his office. Doug wanted to say, "In contrast to what?" but he didn't get the chance. Evangelina lifted her hand to shake, and he clasped hers in his. She shook once, staring into his eyes, then after a pause shook once more with finality. "Thank you again for seeing me, Mr. Sirius."

Doug continued to hold on to her hand. "The pleasure was mine, I assure you. And please, call me Doug."

"Yes, well, getting the package to you seemed rather important to my mother, so therefore it was important to me."

"Your mother?"

"You see, it was a last request, before..."

"I'm sorry," Doug said, feeling suddenly awkward.

"Oh no, she's not...." She said this while trying to retrieve her hand from his. Noticing, he finally let go. "She's in a coma, at Kaiser Hospital over on Geary. In fact, I should be getting over there."

"And you're quite sure I can't see you again?" Again, the words slipped from his lips without thinking. Something about Evangelina made him do things out of character. He didn't like the way he must have come across to her. She was talking about her mother, and he was hitting on her. "I mean, would it be okay if I visited your mother and thanked her myself for the package?"

Evangelina moved to leave the office and turned back to him with a hand on the doorknob. "Right now she's in the ICU, so only family members are allowed to visit. But one never knows. Goodbye Mr. Sirius."

She smiled and then she was gone.

To the empty room, Doug repeated in a whisper, "You can call me Doug." Then he stared at the blank door, feeling somewhat displaced. Her soft scent remained in the room, silently haunting him. He recaptured the vision of her soft hands upon his, her left lacking a wedding ring. Oh yes, he had noticed. But how had a woman such as her avoided marriage?

Walking around his dog who still sat staring at the door and then at him, Doug said, "Yes, I know, if you had hands, you'd open the door and follow her. Well, I liked her too." Constant jumped up toward him, but Doug grasped the dog's front paws before they landed on him. Holding the paws, Doug danced a circle around his dog. This was something they did together quite often. It was a form of playing that they could do indoors. Then Doug released Constant and walked to the glass wall. He gazed through the windows at the cityscape before back to his spotless desk. He sat in the chair, scooting it forward.

The package lay still unopened. His computer had gone to sleep mode. The silence surrounded him, and he felt alone, a feeling quite new for him.

Constant came over and rested his head on Doug's lap. Doug stroked it gently, looking up at the painting of the caterpillar that Evangelina had liked so much.

2

Doug's cell phone vibrated on his belt. After looking at the screen, which was full of 0s and 1s, he decided it was on the fritz and answered even before it had a chance to ring a second time. "Hello?"

"Is this Doug?" The woman on the phone spoke softly. Her voice was child-like, frail.

"This is Doug Sirius. Who is this speaking?"

"You can call me Charlie." English was clearly this woman's second language, but Doug could not place the accent.

"Strange name for a woman."

"Look who's talking. Yours sounds similar to dog, or dug as in digging a grave."

"Whatever. Listen, I don't know any woman named Charlie, so get to the point. What do you want?"

"You're right. We've never met before, yet. But this universe is a strange place. One never knows what might happen next."

The oddity of what she'd just said confused Doug for a moment. It sounded as though she were saying that *someday* they might have met *before*. He chose to ignore the conundrum.

"Okay, I'm going to hang up now."

"Wait, this is important. I've called to warn you and maybe to help you. It all depends on what you want to do."

"Help me? How?" Doug turned to the next page of the newspaper on his Kindle to discover an advertisement for the concert by Quantum Flux that he would be attending this evening. He even had a date, which was why he wasn't taking his medication.

"A moment of choice is quickly approaching. Each moment in time can change the future, some more profoundly than others."

"Oh, aren't you all melodramatic."

A message appeared on Doug's monitor. Jasmine was asking if she should come in now with her project list. He typed back that she should give him a minute.

"This is serious." Charlie said, drawing his attention back to the conversation on the phone. She paused. "The choices you make will affect many people's lives, not just your own."

Another message from Jasmine: "Okay, just tell me when you're ready."

Doug pressed the Next Page button on his Kindle and saw an article about the dramatic increase in the death rate this year of the homeless in the City. He couldn't understand how people could sink so low: Why couldn't they or wouldn't they just get a job?

"Might you be involved with the San Francisco Historical Society?" he asked.

"No, I'm not." Then she raised her voice slightly. "Would you put that thing down and listen!"

Shocked, Doug looked around the room and then out the window. This was the one room without security cameras. He calmed himself, as he realized that this was just some elaborate prank. He waved to whoever was watching him through the window. Yet, the thought that someone was spying on him – and could have been for who knows how long – caused his spine to tingle. Picking up the remote, he closed the blinds.

"Okay, you got me. Ha, ha. Now tell me who put you up to this."

"Nobody put me up to this. This isn't a joke."

"Right," said Doug while turning the still unopened package Evangelina had delivered a few minutes earlier. It was about the size of a Rubik's Cube, and he held it in both hands ready to remove the brown paper wrapper.

"Listen, please. Put the box down and just listen."

Doug dropped the package to his desk as if it were electrified. Now he was truly spooked. He felt a rush come up from his tailbone to his neck. He realized he was holding his breath.

"You need to consider the consequences of your newest project in the Tenderloin on the lives of the people who live there. Your decisions will affect not only the future. It works the opposite way, too. We wouldn't want to repeat the disaster your prior project had in the Fillmore."

Doug let out his breath and turned defensive. "Disaster? What was wrong with my building in the Fillmore?" The project had been his first as a developer and had catapulted his success. He had leveled a whole block on Beideman Street and replaced it with one big office complex. It was not as big as the high-rises he now regularly built, but it was quite substantial for the district.

"To begin with, you bought two Victorians there very cheaply. I take it you were the one that had the zoning changed."

That was true. He had helped get the zoning changed so that anyone purchasing a building there was required to retrofit the foundation to current building codes.

"That retrofit project was for the safety of everyone." He couldn't understand why he was defending himself to this woman. It had something to do with the fear he already felt of being watched. Anger was better than the fear.

"And the result was that property values declined because it was so costly to upgrade the buildings. You were able to buy that whole block for pennies."

"But I cleaned up the neighborhood."

"My, my. Aren't you so altruistic? Once buildings were purchased and remodeled with new foundations, the rents increased. And as they did, everyone who lived there had to move to Hunter's Point outside the city proper or onto the streets homeless. I'll bet your office complex sold for a small fortune."

Doug found himself getting angrier. "And what does this have to do with you?" The city government was happy because the district was no longer an eyesore or an embarrassment. They had also prospered from higher property taxes. Doug moved the two Victorians on Beideman that he had been required to save to Hunter's Point, where the zoning didn't require the retrofit. All was right with the world as far as he was concerned.

"I don't want you to repeat the same mistake," Charlie said, her voice getting distant.

"Are you kidding me? The Tenderloin is the armpit of the city, the red-light district, where the homeless crash and junkies score, where street gangs from all over the city congregate for war." The Tenderloin was positioned with the financial district and Union Square on one edge and the Civic Center on another. It was a dangerous place and even the police were leery about strolling there at night. Doug didn't need to change the zoning for this new project because the properties there were already priced as low as they would go. His company purchased prime locations cheaply. He was planning on raising the surrounding property values by developing one major office high-rise. Then he could start building condos on the rest of the land he owned. There was only one minor problem, a State Historical Resources Commission proposal that the eighteen-block area that comprised the Tenderloin be recognized as an historical site. This proposal was twenty years old and nobody had worked on it in years, though. Therefore, according to his attorneys, it would be easy to overcome. The city once again would be on his side. They had retrofitted their own City Hall for ten times what it would have cost to build a new one, so the city knew the historical proposal would be too costly.

Doug realized that Charlie was probably a "tree-hugger," always getting in the way of progress, declaring some altruistic motive that was all hogwash. There was always a selfish motivation behind people's actions.

So who was she, anyway? For the first time since he'd taken the call, he looked at the small screen on his phone. What it said caused his spine to tingle once again. No number was displayed, just one solemn word: deceased. How could a line be deceased? "Unlisted" made sense, or "unavailable." But "deceased?" What the hell did that mean?

When he returned the phone to his ear Charlie was saying in her singsong voice, "Why don't you just build a giant grave at the end of town and dump all the inhabitants of the Tenderloin into it? You do know that Hunter's Point is still somewhat radioactive from all the garbage used for landfill there, right?"

Doug considered the radioactivity in Hunter's Point to be similar to the rumor of alligators in the sewers of New York. He'd grown tired of this woman's screed. "It sounds to me like this conversation is going nowhere," he said and made ready to hang up.

"Wait," Charlie snapped. Then more softly she said, "I'm sorry. I didn't mean to rant. I want to help. There must be a way. I'm connected now." Doug heard her giggle softly to herself. "You think about it. I'll be in touch. Maybe you can profit without such a cost to others. You have decisions to make that will affect so many lives. I hope the next time we talk you will be able to see more clearly." Then the phone went dead.

Doug felt ridiculous having carried the conversation as far as he had. With his foot, he lightly tapped Constant under his desk to stop him from snoring. Doug pressed the Prev Page button on his Kindle to turn the newspaper back to the article about the increase in the death rate of the homeless and read the details.

His office phone rang and he saw on the tiny screen that it was Jasmine.

"Jasmine, get security up here. I need my office swept for cameras and microphones."

"Cameras?"

"Yes, miniature hidden things. Bugs." Sounding paranoid even to himself angered him. He was in the building development business for God's sake. Who would be spying on him? And why?

"Yes, sir. There are three men waiting who represent some sort of business association. They'd like to see you."

"Put them in the conference room and I'll meet with them while security sweeps my office."

"Regarding my project list…"

"Yes, we can squeeze that in between this meeting and my meeting with Andy this afternoon."

* * *

Closing the conference room door after Constant followed him in, Doug said, "Gentlemen, how might I help you?" Constant leered around the room, eying the men there. He sat at attention on his cushion in the corner, waiting to protect Doug should the need arise.

Three men stood up from the far side of the long white oak table with the window to their backs. They were dressed in business suits off the rack. Doug shook hands with them and they exchanged business cards. The two on each end served as a support group, nodding as the gruff man in the middle talked.

"Mr. Sirius, we're an association of some thirty-odd businesses that would very much like to clean up the Tenderloin. As you well know, most people do not venture into our district and we would like to see that change. Most people don't even think about our little part of the city unless they happen to park there during a show at the Orpheum or Warfield theaters or if they wander too far from City Hall. San Francisco is a beautiful city, yet it has this ugly spot right smack dab in the middle."

"And of course," Doug said, getting to the point, "Cleaning up the Tenderloin will bring more consumers into the neighborhood for your businesses." They all sat down. Doug's nose struggled with an antiseptic smell laid thinly over the pungent aroma of boiled cabbage that he figured must have been wafting from one of the men, if not all of them.

At first the two on the ends wiggled in their chairs as if accused of some minor sin. However, the round little man in the

21

middle seemed happy to be understood. "Precisely," he said. "We're here to give you the opportunity to join us"

"And why would I want to do that?"

"Well, for the safety of your clients who will work and live in the area. The lowlifes there might give resistance to you wanting to overcome the Historical Proposal. We could get petitions signed for you or any such efforts necessary."

"So what do I offer you?" asked Doug. "Are you men familiar with my project?" Though he knew that all his purchases would be a matter of public record, he didn't think that the plans he submitted to the San Francisco Planning Commission for the office building were yet available to just anyone.

"You have been buying property in the center and eastern edge for some time now. You must have something big in mind. Let me ask you this: is it all one project?"

Doug ignored the question and let the silence in the room expand.

The man in the middle leaned forward to place his elbows on the conference table and continued softly in a conspiratorial manner. "Your reputation precedes you. You worked on the Fillmore and then the Soma district. The improvements had wonderful results. We'd of course like the same to happen in our own neck of the woods. Everyone will benefit. Even those who live there."

"Everyone will prosper no doubt," Doug said sarcastically while thinking of the conversation he had just had with the

22

mysterious woman named Charlie. "I think I will do just fine without joining your little association, but I thank you gentleman for the offer." He stood.

The expression of the man in the middle turned dark as he placed his knuckles on the table and lifted his bottom off the chair, leaning his face even farther across the table. His smirk was knowingly presumptuous and threatening. "You will help us Mr. Sirius. I have no doubt of that. We just thought you would like to take this opportunity to take our side formally, to move, so to speak, to our end of the table."

Doug felt there was some hidden agenda here. Constant must have felt it too, for he stood in his corner and growled softly, almost a purr.

"Thank you again gentlemen, and good luck." Doug didn't bother to shake hands; he just walked out of the room leaving the door open behind him. Constant followed while never taking his eyes off the others.

Walking back to his private office through the open bay, Doug glanced at the security cameras on the ceiling. For the first time, rather than make him feel protected, they somehow gave him the creeps, as if someone else besides security might have online access to them, as if someone might be watching him even now. He quickened his step and Constant hurried to catch up.

* * *

With his foot, Doug nudged Constant in his bed under the desk to stop the dog's muffled barking, which was probably caused from chasing rabbits in his sleep. Constant's legs were extended in the air and jerking spastically, paws looking for traction until he rolled onto his side. Doug returned to writing notes on his computer.

The door chimed and Doug buzzed his assistant into his office. She placed a printed 8" x 10" sheet into the wooden in-box on his desk. He looked at the list of her projects, while in his periphery he saw her nervously changing her weight from one foot to the other. After a description of each item, she listed her progress.

"What's this item at the bottom marked 'Charities'?"

"There has been a flurry of charity requests in your suggestion box. I wasn't sure if you wanted me to research each one or if you already had some in mind for the coming year."

"My position on charities is that the majority are a crock. If the employees actually care about certain ones, I highly suggest they volunteer on their own time." "Nonprofit" usually didn't mean that people were not getting paid exorbitant amounts. The one charity he did contribute to every year, of which his company actually was the leading contributor, was the school district's art program. He had donated once at his niece's request and had continued to do so ever since.

"I'll look over this list on the weekend and we'll talk about it on Monday."

Jasmine, whom he had to struggle to refer to as his assistant rather than his secretary, stood for a moment, staring at him as if her employment had just been terminated. Doug was in fact planning to do exactly that on Monday, which was considered the preferable day of the week for terminations rather than Fridays. He had had it with her lack of self-motivation and her shoddy follow-through. She hesitated as if to say one more thing, then turned and scuttled away.

* * *

Andy already sat across the desk from Doug, Constant sitting beside him receiving attention in the form of long strokes over his head and down his neck. Andy, an only child from Atlanta whose father had died when he was fourteen, was meticulously dressed in a dark suit, blue shirt, and subtle tie. He had no remains of a Southern accent. Andy was the head attorney of Doug's legal department for the holding company, Sirius Concepts Inc.

"Sure, okay. I'll look into this association for you. I've just about completed the research on the historical Proposal that we are up against. I will probably have to meet with the building commissioner next week before we get final approval."

"Will there be someone in there representing this ludicrous proposal? If so, I'd like to attend with you."

"Not to my knowledge, but I'll double check just to make sure. You know, it's not that ludicrous of a proposal. Might even do the neighborhood good."

Doug stared at Andy, who, Doug remembered, had a tendency to want to help the world, do something good for others in general. "Yeah, sure, and grind progress to a screeching halt."

Jack, the president of Sirius Development, was also in attendance. He was obscured somewhat from Doug's view, sitting behind the thirty-four inch monitor to Andy's left. Now he spoke for the first time. "Actually the plans for the demolition should be approved first and the building plans will follow."

"They might be approved at the same time, but Jack's probably right," Andy said. "The demolition will likely come first."

"And?" said Doug, "Why the worried face?"

Jack, whose wrinkled brow and scrunched face made him look more like he'd eaten a bug than that he was worried, said, "I don't like using a third party. Our subcontractors have always been our own divisions, our own companies. I've never even worked with these people before."

Doug shook his head. "We've already gone over this." He grabbed the still-wrapped package that Evangelina had delivered, and leaned back in his chair while turning the box in his hands. "I'm not getting into the demolition business. It's not lucrative enough. You'll just have to get over this control issue you're having."

"Well, if something goes wrong don't blame me," said Jack.

Andy looked at Jack as though he'd lost his mind. This was not the way one talked to Doug Sirius.

Doug dug his fingers into the brown wrapper of the package and tore the edge loudly. "That's all, gentlemen. I'll expect a full report as soon as you have something on this association, Andy."

"Will do, Boss."

After they left, Constant came to his master and watched Doug open the rest of the package probably hoping it was something for him.

Doug lifted the lid on the box and found it empty. Now what the hell was this about? He glanced up to the disconnected USB wire hanging from the camera of his monitor, a device he used for long distance conferences. This had been the only device security had found in his office, so he had personally unplugged it. Yet he still felt as if he were being watched.

He shook the feeling off and grabbed his dog by the snout with both hands and said, "Hey boy, let's go see what Bug's doing. You want to go visit Bug?"

Constant wagged his approval.

3

Terra stood in the tiny prefab sound booth, about the size of an English call box, with a giant microphone that looked like it was out of some old black and white movie, though she knew it was brand new and very sensitive. It could pick up the sound of her shoes when she shuffled in nervousness. There had been many "takes" throughout the afternoon, but the man watching her through the small, thick window kept reassuring her that this was normal. Robert had made her nervous at first because he was so gorgeous, but he was gentle and friendly to her, building up her confidence. This was probably just his job and nothing to let go to her head. Besides, he was way too old; he must be mid-twenties at least. Still, she couldn't help feeling lightheaded around him. He even had the lofty title at PlanetSpin Productions of Sound Coordinator. He was somebody. He seemed to know exactly what he was doing, exactly what he wanted from her. And she had performed well, hadn't she? Enough so that he had hired her today during her audition.

As they were wrapping up the final take, Terra saw her uncle appear with his dog. She smiled at the thought of Constant being here, who heeled as usual and sat down when her uncle came to a stop. Uncle Doug waved to her with three fingers and waited a step behind and to the left of Robert. In his right hand he carried the walking stick that her mother, when she was still alive, had told her he had made when he was a teenager. He had made many and sold all but this one. Her mother had said that that was just the way her brother Doug was, from lemonade stand to paper route to mowing lawns to making walking sticks. "Always trying to make a buck," was the way her mother put it.

Terra concentrated on her lines, getting them exactly right.

When she came out of the booth, Uncle Doug, in his bland three-piece suit, starched collar, and needle tie, was shaking hands with Robert and introducing himself. As she walked up, Uncle Doug gave the command to release Constant and the dog came running to say hello. She bent one knee and wrapped both arms around his neck, his fuzzy snout tickling her.

Uncle Doug waved again and said, "Hey Bug," to Terra.

"Well that's enough for today," said Robert. "Study your lines and be back here on Tuesday after school. We'll pick it up from where you left off. Nice to meet you Mr. Sirius, especially after hearing so much about you from Ellen."

After Robert left, Terra said, "I asked you not to call me 'Bug' in public." She gave her uncle a big hug anyway. "And thanks for the job. This is great. I can't believe I passed the audition. Wait until my friends see this anime with my voice coming out. I'm not the main character of course, but it is an English dub of a real Japanese show, so any voice-over is so cool." She gave him another hug, and they started to leave the building, Constant's leash in Terra's hand. "Who's Ellen?"

"A friend of mine. Senior VP of marketing here. And sorry about calling you 'Bug.' It's a hard habit to break. But I guess the name is a touch childish for a sixteen-year-old."

"Seventeen. And I've been meaning to ask you..." They hit the street. "Well, I just passed the written test for my driver's license."

On the street was a "chicken," one of the many runaway boys who sold themselves to old men in taxicabs up on Polk Street. He was buying drugs for the night from one of the dealers who were always there.

"Wow, first you pass your driver's test, then you pass the audition. You must be mighty proud of yourself."

"Sure. Why not? It's like getting all adult in one week. A job, wheels, you know."

"So what's the problem?"

Terra tried to give him the best puppy dog eyes she could.

This registered. "Oh, I get it. Your dad doesn't have a license and you need someone over twenty-five to drive with you, right?"

"Right on the first try." She skipped one step to show her joy. Then after two steps she did it again with her other foot. "I need a certain number of hours behind the wheel. Dad already paid for an instructor to do a minimum behind-the-wheel with me. But I need like twenty-five hours. All you got to do is sit there and ride along a couple hours a week for a few months and then sign something saying I did it. What d'ya think?"

"Sounds like a deal."

"It'll have to be your car."

"My pleasure."

Blocks later through the Tenderloin, they turned the corner onto their home stretch. Loose, a young street kid of about fifteen dressed in desert-brown camouflage shorts, somewhat too cold for the fall weather, and a long green army jacket, came swaggering up to them and Terra gave him a high five. Constant was also delighted to see Loose again from the many morning walks Terra had given the dog. He lifted onto his hind paws, placing his front ones on the boy's chest. The boy hugged the dog, scrubbing his sides and back with the tips of his fingers.

"Hey Loose, what's happening?" Terra said while disconnecting Constant's leash. The dog took off down the alley, most likely to do his duty, this being his home block and all.

"Feels like a bad storm a-brewing," Loose said. "I need to talk to you." Since the sky was clear, Terra knew he wasn't referring to the weather.

"Introduce yourself to my uncle here while I help Constant out. Be right back." From her Tokidoki knapsack, she took a plastic bag and inverted it over her hand. She went down the alley where Constant had disappeared. Constant and Terra crossed paths, she to pick up his droppings and place it in the dumpster and he running back out to the street with a gait of accomplishment, seemingly quite pleased with himself and the world around him.

When Terra returned to the street, her uncle was mispronouncing her friend's name.

"Nice to meet you Louis. How do you and B...my niece know each other."

"Loose," her friend said. "The name's Loose. And we met at school, though she ain't in my grade." He shuffled from foot to foot staring down at the sidewalk, hair swooping down from left to right hiding his face. He then looked up at Terra and said, "My Dad's gone missing. Don't know where. Went to a job interview after dropping me off at school yesterday. The van's back in place but he's nowhere 'round. Have you seen 'im?"

"I started a job myself today and haven't been on the streets much. Did ya check at The Kitchen?"

"Yeah, nobody's seen nothin'. He's usually at the van when I get home from school, ya know. Two days is unheard of."

Bug reached into her knapsack, pulled out a banana and an apple, and handed them to Loose. She turned to her uncle and said, "Loose's Dad lost his job and then they lost the house. They live in their van."

"It's a camper van. Real nice, really," said Loose enthusiastically, somewhat defensively.

"You say he went for an interview yesterday morning?" Uncle Doug asked.

"Yeah, he was pretty confident too."

"Well, maybe he just didn't get the job, so he tied one on and is just sleeping it off somewhere today. I wouldn't worry too much." Uncle Doug stopped talking when he realized that both kids were staring at him. "What? What's the matter?"

"I don't need to take no crap from this old creep," Loose said. "Sorry to hear he's your uncle. Must be a real pain for you." He shuffled on down the road, looking over his shoulder. "You know where to find me if ya hear anything about my old man."

"Loose, I'm sorry. I'm sure he didn't mean—"

"Sure glad he ain't related to me," Loose called as he continued walking. Constant followed Loose to the corner. With dog-like quickness he read the situation and responded emphatically to it, looking sad with his tail curled between his hind legs. He stood and watched Loose walk away around the corner.

"Why in God's name would you say something like that?" Terra growled.

"I was just trying to help. Trying to get him not to worry."

"Don't you think he might be a little sensitive living on the street, a little defensive about his dad?"

"Listen Bug, no one ends up on the street without a reason, and the most common is alcohol or drugs. Are you trying to tell me that I'm not right? That his Dad doesn't have a problem."

Uncle Doug stepped up to their building and used his security badge and a numeric code to open the front door. Constant led the way into the deserted lobby. Bug followed, then her uncle. The place was under construction, full of drywall dust and canvas drop cloth. There was a front desk from the hotel it used to be. The only two apartments here were Terra's with her

Dad and her uncle's penthouse, because her uncle hadn't yet completed the rest of the building.

"Don't even talk to me," she said. She pulled her security card from the back pocket of her black jeans as she walked to the stairs. *Let him take the damned elevator by himself.* She tapped the side of her legging telling Constant to join her, used the card on the door, and let Constant lead the way.

In the stairwell, before she closed the door behind her she said to her uncle – who stood in the middle of the lobby looking dumbfounded, "Maybe the next painting should be a Therapy Session on your own!"

4

Doug stood in the lobby of his home staring at the door to the stairwell until he finally closed his drooping jaw. He looked at the mess around him from the uncompleted construction. He should have this place cleaned up considering they wouldn't finish these condos until after the office building project was complete. The top two floors were immaculately constructed. He always liked to live in the buildings he was remodeling. It was easier to supervise the project that way. He made a mental note to have some workers come by and make this lobby dust-free. He looked down at his suit and held up his hands, the right one raising his walking stick high into the air. As he stared at it, he noticed the three security cameras, one pointed at the front door, one toward the back, and the last looking at the elevator and stairs. His fear of being watched immediately returned to him. He could sign on remotely to observe these cameras from anywhere. He could watch his office from home or watch home from the office, and he wondered who else might have this ability, who might have hacked into his system. That would be a good explanation of how Charlie had known what he doing at his office, except that there was no security camera in his office, only the webcam on his computer. His fear turned to anger, and he shook his fists toward the ceiling, toward the heavens and challenged, "Give it your best shot."

He slowly lowered his arms. The elevator was on the left toward the end of the lobby behind a large wooden door with a small window next to the door for the stairwell across from the reception counter. Inside it was an old brass cage, open at the top, a skylight up the shaft. Graffiti heavily covered the shoulder-high wainscot. The brass plate surrounding the black ceramic buttons was frosted with scratches and a greenish-brown patina from long use and lack of polish. Doug closed the wooden door, then the accordion metal gate and pushed "11" for the top floor. He used a small key to give access to the "penthouse," or the elevator wouldn't move. The cage was small and musky. It moved upward slowly, loudly with jerks.

* * *

After eating a steak and changing into blue jeans, a dark red polo shirt, and red sneakers, Doug grabbed his brown leather aviator's jacket and walking stick and headed down one flight to Hunt and Bug's apartment on the tenth floor. Though his penthouse took up the entire top floor, theirs was only a half-floor.

"Hey there," said Hunt in a dark blue plastic smock covered in splashes and drips of acrylic interior house paint as he opened the door wider to let Doug in. He pushed his left hand through his shoulder length silver hair while a paintbrush dripped what looked like golden brown mustard onto his shoulder. Still holding the door with his right hand and placing the brush

36

between his teeth, Hunt made a sweeping gesture with his left, inviting Doug into the apartment before closing the door behind him. Taking the brush from his lips, he said, "Perfect timing."

He walked around Doug to a large four-foot-by-four-foot stretched canvas on a wooden easel surrounded by a drop cloth in the middle of the living room. Though Doug knew Hunt had a specific room for painting, occasionally, like today, he set up wherever he felt inspired. Doug stood back from the green-and-mustard-brown design depicting an ashtray with a lit cigarette surrounded by an abundance of what appeared to be empty wine bottles.

"Thought I'd do this one using the two things I like most about Planet Earth," Hunt said. "What do you think?"

"But Hunt, you don't drink or smoke."

"Not anymore." He nodded toward his daughter sitting on the couch. Bug was now dressed Goth-like with her hair temporarily dyed black and radically teased like the lead singer of The Cure. Constant sat beside her, her arm draped over his shoulders, but when he noticed Doug, the dog quickly got down before Doug could yell at him for being on the furniture.

"Dad, I don't mind being your initial motivation. Whatever gets you and keeps you off the sauce."

"You know, Bug," Hunt said, "many alcoholics keep drinking."

Bug stuck out her tongue at her father.

She was obviously still upset with Doug, for she didn't look at him. Instead she got up, placed the book she had been reading on the coffee table, and left the room. Constant sat before Doug, and looked up at him in apology for choosing Bug's side of the argument. When Doug didn't pat his head or offer any words of forgiveness, the dog followed Bug down the hall, most likely thinking the dog-thought, *Well, if you're not going to comfort her, I am.* Doug looked at the book on the table, titled, M.I.N.E.: More is Never Enough. He'd never heard of it. He couldn't find much use for science fiction, which, along with fantasy, was what Bug usually read. He had read *Dune* and *The Hobbit* when he was in college, but afterward he couldn't understand what the hubbub was about. They felt like children's stories to him.

"Did she tell you she passed the audition today?" Doug asked. "She got the job."

"Yeah she did. And that's great. But she seems awfully pissed off about something she's not willing to share with me."

Doug remembered what an angry person his sister Gail had been and hoped this wasn't beginning to express itself in Bug. Bug had always been so well balanced emotionally, such a positive person. Deep within Doug's mind lurked a memory of Bug's mother. Hunt had divorced her when Bug had been nine. He had filed for physical and legal custody and had unwittingly had her served the week before Mother's Day – to which Gail had taken the remainder of a bottle of migraine medication, another full bottle of antidepressants, followed that down with a bottle of

Vodka, and died in the hospital in a coma. Doug did not blame Hunt for divorcing Gail, or for her death.

Gail had awoken once from her coma before she died. Doug had stood at the end of the bed, Hunt and Bug on either side. Her left eye had fluttered open through a face drooping heavily to the left. Bug had leaned over her mother and said, "Mother, it's me and Dad and Uncle Doug. We're here for you." At this, the most awful grin that Doug had ever seen spread across Gail's lopsided face. She ground her voice a couple of times preparing to speak. Bug pressed her face close to listen. "No you're not," her mother said to her. "You've never been here for me." Gail coughed. "That's why I'm here." She coughed again and then fell back into a coma.

Doug spent that night praying to God to let Gail die, and feeling like a monster for doing so. But Bug didn't need to grow up being blamed by her mother for the overwhelming depression, insecurity, and drug-induced paranoia. More than one therapist had diagnosed Gail as clinically narcissistic, and the alcohol only made her worse.

Suddenly the air in the room was ghostly chill, an emptiness that was probably caused by the vivid memory. Doug was thinking of how the past kept control of the present, of how what had happened, everything that had happened, led us to where we stood today. He shook from this haunting reverie.

Hunt returned to his painting, stepped back from it, and snapped the brush to splash some small yellowish brown dots beneath the lower edge of the painted ashtray. Looking at the painting, Doug was reminded of his and Bug's first painting together, the giant sand worm that hung in his office, and about the woman who had delivered that package today saying she liked it. He could picture her standing there in his office appraising it, her beautiful brown eyes, her hair, and her small soft hands. He felt once again the pride he had felt from her comment. She liked it.

Just then the phone on Doug's hip began to vibrate. He stood and looked at the screen. It once again announced "Deceased" with the phone number "010-101-0101" underneath. "Damn," he muttered letting the call go directly to voice-mail.

"What's that about?" Hunt asked. He put the brush down and took a swig of bottled water from the coffee table.

"Weirdness creeping into my life."

"Oh, the old creeping weirdness. That explains everything." Hunt went over and placed a Quantum Flux CD into the stereo, keeping the volume low. "Aren't you the one who's always quoting Hunter Thompson, 'When the going gets weird, the weird turn pro'?" He grinned widely over his shoulder. "A man, I must say, with the most wonderful first name."

"Well, there's the weird and then there's the absurdly weird. I don't think anyone should be able to contact me and explain to me, in detail, exactly what I am doing at the time. This caller got me while I was in my office. There was no way she could have known what I was doing."

"Hmm." Hunt said. He took off his smock, hung it on a coat rack in the corner of the room, and waved for Doug to follow him into the kitchen. He wore a colorful sunburst t-shirt with a caterpillar sitting on a giant mushroom smoking a hookah, an original illustration from Alice in Wonderland.

At Hunt's request Doug had designed the tenth floor of this building quite differently than his own place. This floor had many walls dividing the space into an over-abundance of small rooms. Hunt thought it was cave-like. He painted two different colors at each adjoining wall, creating depth to the edges where wall met wall or wall met ceiling, yet somehow simultaneously flattening the three dimensional space into a two dimensional cubist painting. Each room had a distinct set of two colors, none the same as the next, almost a funhouse effect as one walked from room to room. The leftovers from these paints were what Hunt used to create his paintings on canvas.

From the kitchen table, Hunt opened a clear plastic lid from a plastic cup containing garlic roasted cashews, the essence of which immediately wafted through the room. "Want some?" Hunt asked, tipping the cup to Doug as they placed themselves into the chairs.

Doug took a few and talked around the mouthful. "Aren't you being a touch cruel with that painting out there, knowing how Bug feels about alcohol?"

"Probably," Hunt said crunching on his own cashews, tossing them in to his mouth one by one. "Listen, you and I both know I've had more than my share to drink. And I can no longer imbibe without jumping directly from the first drink to what feels like withdrawal. What fun is that? I abused the privilege, I admit. So, though at times I wish I could, I can no longer enjoy the activity. Bug needs to know that. She can't keep living with the fear that I might again drink myself into oblivion. Alcohol is everywhere; she can't hide from it. Alcohol didn't kill her mother; Gail killed herself." He covered the plastic container and placed it on the table. "Tell me about this mysterious voice that keeps calling you. What does she say?"

Doug thought that Bug's attitude toward alcohol might be a healthy one, considering her parent's predilection for addiction. He pulled his phone from his belt, displayed the last call, and handed it to Hunt.

Hunt scrutinized the screen for a moment. "I don't think there's an area code like that. And what is this? A call from the dead?" While pushing the redial button he said, "Curiouser and curiouser." He pressed the speaker button and held it up between their heads. A computerized message came on announcing that this number had never been in service and to please check the number and dial again. "Doesn't that message usually say that this number is no longer in service?"

"That's a first for me," agreed Doug.

"Hmm," said Hunt handing back the phone. "And you don't recognize the voice?"

"Nope,"

"And she knows your name?"

"Yep."

"And knows exactly what you're doing when she calls?"

"Ah, yeah."

"Are you going to tell me what she talks about?'

"Well, I'm not really sure. Beyond telling me how my name sounds like 'Dog,' she keeps referring to some event that is going to happen. It sounds like she wants to talk me out of doing something, only she hasn't told me what that something is." Doug didn't tell Hunt that it had to do with his project in the Tenderloin.

"So, she's talking as if she knows the future."

"Which is when I started thinking that this must be an elaborate prank of some sort."

"Sounds ominous." Hunt scratched his cheek leaving a splotch of paint there. "By the way, have you found someone to come along to the concert tonight?"

"Yes. Her name's Lucy and she'll meet us at the theater."

"Someone new?"

"Don't tell Bug, but I met her on the Internet, one of those dating services."

"Wow, you are desperate."

"It was rather short notice. You gave me the tickets only a week ago. I take it that was Bug's idea, the two tickets."

"Yeah, she thinks you need a woman in your life."

"How come she doesn't bother you about getting a woman into your life?"

"I don't know. Maybe 'cause I already have her to take care of me."

"She's more like your mother than anything, always picking up after you, making your meals, doing your laundry..."

"I have no complaints," said Hunt.

Doug was amazed that Hunt never talked about women for himself. Hell, he never seemed lonely or bored. Maybe for now Hunt was simply satisfied with life with his daughter. A teenage girl could definitely be a handful. And it hardly seemed as though Hunt needed companionship. He seemed to never stop entertaining himself. Life for him was a wonderland, everything a toy to be enjoyed.

"Hey, I got something I want to show you before we leave," Hunt said, getting up to walk down a hall. Doug followed through a maze to a small room where the ceiling and one wall were painted shiny black and the rest a dull battleship gray. Hunt sat down surrounded by computers and other electronic gadgetry, slapping his hands together and howling.

"What's all this about?" Doug asked while placing himself in the only other chair in the room.

Hunt stood and began to prance around the tiny space, dancing joyfully between all the equipment, lifting each knee high, one after the other, strutting and pointing each toe alternately in the air. His long gray hair billowed about his shoulders, half covering his face. Strutting backward he returned to his seat and plopped himself down, laughing excitedly.

Once he regained control of himself, he waved his arm in front of the equipment. "This here is a little something my company developed and abandoned. Both hardware and software are custom designed. And I picked it up for almost nothing because it doesn't seem to be of any use for anything other than what it was intended and they were quite resolved that it couldn't even do that."

Doug leaned forward, resting his elbows on the edge of the desk opposite from Hunt and propping his head in his hands. "And what, pray tell, might this monstrosity be intended to do exactly?" He ran one hand through his hair.

"I found the white paper for it, and it seems it was designed to... how can I say this?" Hunt paused to run his fingers across his lips. "Okay, without getting into the quantum mechanics of it, have you ever heard of the sci-fi term parallel universes?"

"Yes, who hasn't?"

"Well, there is a belief that at every juncture, at every point where each decision is made, or where every action is done, that reality splits and creates alternate realities based upon different outcomes as if both decisions or different actions had actually happened, yet we can only perceive the one result because that is the reality we're in."

"Sounds like way too many realities for me," Doug laughed. "That could create billions of parallel universes."

"Well, in a way, that's pretty much what my company concluded. You see, this apparatus here is supposed to track those junctures where reality splits. And that's where the people who developed this thing made their mistake. This thing isn't able to scan the overwhelming amounts of information necessary to find these points. But if I program it to follow a certain action and record it? Well, what I can do is take that recording and edit it so that the action or decision is different, thereby extrapolating a different result. And that's where I am right now. I'm trying to decipher whether the new result is an actual parallel universe, or whether it is just a projection that this thing creates."

"And how do you propose to do that?"

Hunt deflated somewhat. "Yes, that's the question, now isn't it? I think I need a current event in detail, something small so the data isn't so overwhelming."

"Is this like that silly Hollywood thing where people travel back in time, kill a butterfly, and the whole world changes?"

Hunt smiled. "Now that's just ridiculous. Not every moment can have such a drastic effect. Some moments have more emphasis than most. Time has to be able to absorb or adjust to minor variations. Yes, the details are important, but only a handful actually change your life?"

Doug wondered about how all of the moments of the past bring us to where we are today. Hadn't he just heard that recently? Wasn't that one of the things that the strange woman who called herself Charlie said? And then she'd said something very odd, something he hadn't really paid attention to at the time. She had said that the opposite was true also. What the hell did that mean?

Doug got up and walked behind Hunt to look at the computer screen that had nothing but programming text displayed. "Can you show me what you have so far?"

"I haven't designed a user interface yet. It's just code. I won't be able to, at least I don't think I will be able to, ever get an actual picture of the events. Theoretically, if we had a spaceship that traveled faster than the speed of light, we could travel out there and actually see what happened in the past. If we could get past the radio waves, and then stop and wait for them to catch up to us, we would be able to hear old broadcasts. The same would be for light waves and visuals of prior events. It's like looking at the stars. For all you know, that star may have died thousands of years ago. Yep, a spaceship would be extremely helpful for this project. Unfortunately, no such ship exists and if Burkhard Heim couldn't build one, I'm not sure it ever will." Hunt scratched his head and turned to look at Doug behind him, a slightly deranged smile on his face. "You think I'm nuts, don't you?"

"Well…"

"Listen, I don't know if this is doable, but it sure beats the hell out of watching TV."

"You don't have a TV."

"See, maybe I'm not so crazy after all." Hunt paused a moment, giggling, before he changed the subject. "They offered me a new position at work with much better pay traveling to different countries to set up production facilities. I could do it, but it would mean managing people. I so much prefer dealing with machines."

"What about Bug?" Doug was thinking that Hunt was about to unload her care onto him. Though he felt responsible for Bug since his sister died, he sure didn't want to have to take care of her full time. He wasn't even sure he could.

"I guess she could come along. I mean, you've helped a lot by giving us this place to live, but I really think it would be best if I could make more money. Her college education is really going to set me back. I'm not sure I can afford it."

"I'd think twice about managing people. It takes a certain personality."

"Yeah, well, I got some time to decide." Hunt hesitated with a wistful expression on his face. Then he brightened. "You want me to look into this weird phone call you got? Deceased? I never heard of such a thing. I'm sure the guys at the office would love the challenge." He looked at some paint on his fingers and changed the subject again. "How's your newest painting going with Bug? Painting is where it's at, man. Bug's right. It's a form of therapy. I call it 'the infinite process of becoming.' Each painting is just a step toward becoming a better painter. No painting is important except as part of the process... "

Doug remembered that Bug had told him that she wasn't going to paint with him anymore, that he could just do the Therapy Sessions by himself. He didn't want to discuss it. Instead he said, "Listen, I got to take Constant for a walk before we go. I'll be back in a little bit."

Doug clapped his hands and called Constant to him and they left together.

5

If she had to spend the evening with her uncle at least she would sit on the other side of her father from him. Terra plopped in her seat, landing harder than gravity could account for. Dad glanced at her for a moment and then looked back at the stage.

Lucy had met them at the front door as promised in a short, sexy low-cut red dress, definitely overkill for a rock concert. But the color matched her uncle's shirt and shoes. They were a pair. Lucy had rubbed Terra wrong from the get-go using a high southern voice to talk down to her as if she were a child. And she used the word "wonderful" to extreme; it made Terra gag. Lucy's blond hair bounced when she talked. None of this seemed to bother her uncle though. The two of them sat yakking away like high school sweethearts.

Too bad Constant couldn't have come. The dog and her uncle were like two halves of the same person, Constant being the better half, of course.

The lights went down and the crowd flicked Bics in the darkness. Her father had told her once that this ritual had started so that people could light up joints and the cops wouldn't be able to see who was smoking. Now it was just part of the tradition, though she still caught a whiff of the pungent aroma.

Although Quantum Flux was one of her absolutely favorite bands, she was still in a sour mood because of her uncle and his blatant disregard for other people's feelings. Hadn't their painting sessions taught him anything? Yet she knew that deep down he really cared about what happened to other people. He just didn't know how to express his feelings. So now she needed to apologize to Loose for what her uncle had said.

She thought of Loose and his father and she just knew that something was terribly wrong. Yes, according to Loose, his father started drinking heavily after his wife died and maybe that was the reason he had lost his job. But he always made sure that Loose had clean clothes and he drove him to and from school every day. Terra had never actually seen the man drunk. Regardless, Uncle Doug had no right to say what he did. He didn't even know Loose or his father. He could be so very crude at times. How could he possibly be so successful? Probably being cold-hearted was a requirement for success.

The band slammed into their first number, knocking all thought from Terra's head. She moved to the edge of her seat and bounced both heels up and down to the beat. The name of the tune was "Mechanical Movement in E-Flat." This was her second favorite song by them; she figured they'd save her favorite, "Parallel Places," for the encore.

At the end of that song, she noticed her uncle and Lucy talking to each other more than watching the show. Terra sat back in her seat disgusted, and folded her arms across her chest. The woman's hips were so large and shapely that Terra considered her what she termed "a breeder" and maybe that's what all the cuddly fun was all about. Maybe she was holding the hope that her uncle might be a promising donor. Didn't Uncle Doug say that this was the first time they had actually been together? Well, it certainly didn't look like it. How had they met anyhow?

* * *

Out on Market Street after the show, her uncle excused himself saying he was going to walk Lucy to the BART station. He was acting uncomfortably or maybe unsure of himself, as if he were at Lucy's doorway and didn't know whether to kiss her or not. It was fun for Terra to watch him squirm. She'd never seen him insecure like this.

Lucy said, "Doug, you don't have to do that."

"It would be my pleasure," he replied. "Besides, the Tenderloin gets a little dangerous this time of night." He took her hand in his and Terra had to turn away. She began walking southwest on Market the opposite direction of the BART station.

Her father caught up with her, and took her by the arm bringing them both to a halt.

"We live in the Tenderloin," she said sharply. "I walk the streets at night all the time and he never has to walk me home."

"No, but he makes you take Constant with you when it's late."

When she didn't respond further he asked, "What's up with you? You invited Uncle Doug to the concert. You bought him an extra ticket. And then you treat him like crap, like you're jealous of his date or something. You're the one who always encourages him to find a lady friend. What's going on with you two?"

"I just don't think she's good enough for him."

Dad seemed to consider this as they turned the corner and headed deeper into the Tenderloin toward home.

"You were acting funny earlier at the house too. Did something happen when he came by the audition?"

"No, the audition went fine."

"You don't want to talk about it?"

"No. It's just Uncle Doug being Uncle Doug."

"Hmm." Her father shivered in the damp air. The fog had rolled in and some of the streetlights were out. Terra wrapped her coat tighter around herself. They took a left on O'Farrell. "Listen, Bug; me and Doug and Grampa are the only family you got. And family is something that you'll have for the rest of your life. Some day you'll choose a husband, but he may not always be your husband. A dad will always be your dad. I know it's hard to understand but there are some things you just can't change. Doug is the way he is. I know you hope to change him with your little Therapy Sessions. But sometimes the best you can do is just love people for what they are. Sometimes that's enough."

Terra turned and stood on tiptoe to receive a hug from him at their front door. She felt tears coming and she didn't understand why. Then she realized she was missing her mom. She held her coat close to her chest within his embrace.

Terra stepped back from him and headed toward the door.

"I'm not going to give up on Uncle Doug."

"I know you aren't. I wouldn't have it any other way, sweetheart."

6

Down beneath Market Street at the BART station, Doug used the machine to purchase Lucy a ticket.

"I had such a wonderful evening," she said in her southern accent.

"You enjoyed the band?"

"They were wonderful. I'd never heard them before."

He took her by the hand as they walked to the turnstile. "I would think they'd be more popular than they are."

"And Terra, she's so sweet." Doug thought about that. Bug didn't like this woman, not one little bit. He could tell. He wondered what that was all about. Maybe she was still upset with him and was taking it out on her. But that wasn't like her.

"Yes, she's something else."

"Well, I should be going. Thank you again for the wonderful evening." Instead of moving toward the platform, she stood there, waiting.

Doug balanced his walking stick in the crux of his arm and took both her hands in his. He gave her a soft but short kiss, a peck almost, but she leaned into it. Her arms grabbed his waist. He wrapped one arm around her shoulders, and the other, the one holding the cane, on her hip. The kiss was a question asking for more, or a promise of things to come.

He pulled away first and looked her in the eyes. "It was a good evening, wasn't it?" he said.

She nodded and whispered, "Yes," sounding very sexy. Somehow he knew that the invitation wasn't for tonight, something in the way she moved away, placing the turnstile between them, but a future glimpse of things to come. He watched her as she walked away, her swaying hips an over-exaggeration.

The evening felt good. It was a success. Life should always feel this way. He waited a full minute after she was out of sight before he turned to go.

On his way home he spotted the woman from his office--what was her name? Evangelina?--walking away from him up ahead. He called to her as he trotted to catch up. She didn't respond until he tapped her on the shoulder. As she turned he realized his mistake.

"Excuse me," he said. "I thought you were someone else." She smiled and nodded without saying a word, and then walked away. Even though he'd just had a great date with Lucy, he stood there thinking of Evangelina, remembering her pose in his office, one of defiance yet innocent all the same. The allure of her fragrance came back to him. She was stunning even in his memory. The thought followed him all the way home and then some.

* * *

On Monday, going over, for the umpteenth time, the flowchart on his computer of his new office building in the Tenderloin, Doug's eyes went once again to the unplugged camera mounted on top of his monitor. Having grown up a country boy in Grass Valley, the closed blinds of his office windows left him feeling claustrophobic, but he dare not open them until he found out who had played that elaborate prank on him last week. It had to have been a prank, right? Why hadn't anyone yet taken credit for it?

In his frustration, he stood and ripped the camera from its mounting, tossing it in the trashcan behind him. He hated the fluorescent lighting piercing his retinas without any softening effect of natural light. Sitting again, he placed his fingers to his temples on each side of his face and rubbed them in a circular motion. He'd been staring too long at this monitor, following the complex timelines, and making sure everything was accounted for. There were no actual dates yet, but those would be easy to plug into the Gantt chart once the plans had been approved by the city.

Constant peeked out from under the desk and cocked his head questioningly, cowering somewhat at the commotion. He probably thought, *Is it my fault, something I did*, checking Doug's mood before he ventured forth.

"It's okay, buddy," Doug said taking one hand and patting his dog. Immediately, two happy thumps of relief came from Constant's tail banging against a leg panel of the desk. "Go lie down."

Doug thought back to the concert and the kiss it had ended with. He rubbed his tongue over his lower lip. Yes, the kiss had been wonderful. Just the thought of it made him feel so alive. He had had a wet dream that night about Lucy, and wet dreams were not something he ever remembered having. He wondered if it might have something to do with not taking the pills that sat in his desk drawer.

But then he remembered Bug. His headache and frustration returned. Bug was still so angry with him. She hadn't even come by to walk Constant since, which she normally did each weekend. He had been curious about the familiarity with which Constant had treated her friend Loose, the street ragamuffin, and the thought came to mind now that it was probably during these weekend walks that the dog and he had met. Hunt had told him on Sunday evening, when asked, that Loose's father was still missing, mentioning that the boy's last name was Silver.

His frustration with the lighting, the camera, and the headache led him to a determination to prove Bug wrong. He picked up his landline and information connected him to the Tenderloin police station on Eddy at Jones. Finding a drunk would be difficult. There were so many places to curl up and sleep it off.

"San Francisco Police, Tenderloin District," said the phone.

"Yes, I'm looking for a man, last name Silver. He disappeared sometime last Thursday."

"So, you want missing persons," stated the tough female voice.

"Actually, no. I'm trying to find out if he might have ended up in jail."

"Jail?"

"Yeah, like maybe your drunk tank."

"This a friend of yours?"

"I'm helping his son look for him."

"If he had ended up here on Thursday, he would have been released on Friday."

"Well, he's still missing."

"Was he a danger to himself and others? If so, he can be detained for forty-eight to seventy-two hours in solitary."

"I don't know. He's homeless."

There was a brief, frustrated exhale on the other end. "Listen, I'm not really allowed to give you any information over the phone. But since I don't have any information, I guess I can at least tell you that. No one was arrested on Thursday or Friday by the name of Silver. A lot of homeless don't carry identification, though. We release them anyhow once they sober up. Have you tried the hospital over on Geary? Sometimes they wander over there into the ER trying to get help for their DTs. They then send them over to the detox center."

"Withdrawals? Hmm... No, I haven't tried there yet. Say, if I brought a picture over, might someone be able to see if he was one of the unidentified homeless. See if he was released?"

"Sure; we take pictures of everyone who goes through here."

"Okay, thanks."

After calling two different local detox centers and getting the same results, Doug stood by the window and opened one shade, not caring who saw him. He looked out over the city to the north. Constant sat obediently beside him, staring. Doug placed one hand on the window frame and shifted his weight to the corresponding hip. Constant lifted his left rear paw to scratch his ear and cheek.

People checking into detox didn't even have to identify themselves.

Thinking of the hospital reminded Doug of the rapid increase in deaths of the homeless. He decided to check the ER. Figuring the reluctance to give information over the phone would be doubled at the hospital, he decided to visit in person.

Before leaving his office, he delivered Constant to his executive assistant, telling her to take the dog for a walk down by the waterfront. Constant watched his departure with droopy eyes, the tufts of gray fuzz over them scrunched down low.

Hopefully this won't be a waste of time, he thought. *Hopefully Bug will appreciate my efforts.* Doug no longer wished to prove himself right. He just wanted to find this street urchin's father, this Mister Silver.

7

Having had no luck at the ER on O'Farrell, Doug ventured downstairs to the morgue where a portly man responded reluctantly to his questioning. No, there had been no one named Silver, and yes, there had been three unidentified bodies since last Thursday. Two were women, one a man.

"You want to come into the back and identify him?"

"I don't know what he looks like."

The man looked at Doug skeptically. "You're looking for someone you don't even know?"

"For the son. The boy's father is missing."

"And what makes you think he might be here?"

"He's homeless. I checked the drunk tank, detox, ER. Thought I'd be thorough."

"There are a million places in the city for a man to be."

Wasn't that the truth! But Doug felt queasy, as if, without really wanting to be, he was on the right track, though he definitely didn't want to be the bearer of such bad news. Bug was already mad at him. He didn't need to make things worse.

As he walked through the lobby toward the exit, his queasiness turned to paranoia. Once again, he felt as though he was being watched. He stopped, grasped his walking stick in both hands, and slowly turned around. There, not three feet away, was Evangelina, the woman who had delivered the empty package to his office on Friday. He had been thinking a lot about her since the last time he had seen her.

Doug relaxed his stance and let the tip of his staff fall back to the floor.

"Mister Sirius, what might you be doing here?" she asked as she approached him.

"I might ask you the same." He couldn't remember her last name.

She looked around as if expecting someone, or not wanting to be seen with him. "I mentioned the other day my mother was sick. She's here at the hospital."

Yes, she had mentioned something about having to go see her mother in the hospital. "You did mention that. I'm here looking for a friend."

Without warning she looped her arm through his and said, "You look like you need one. That and a cup of coffee." She smiled as she led him down the hall. "I'm buying."

"Okay," Doug stammered clumsily, accepting her lead.

They walked in silence to the hospital cafeteria, the silence making their footsteps clack loudly, the thud of his walking stick adding a fifth step. Doug walked to the rhythm.

* * *

From his position on a chair with his coffee on the table before him, Doug admired the curvature of Evangelina's bottom tightly snug in a dark blue suit with white pinstripes as she folded her long black leather coat onto the chair beside her own. She placed herself gingerly down to her coffee and shortbread cookies. She must have noticed him looking from the corner of her eye, and seemed to smile to herself while staring down at the table.

"You look tired," he said.

"I've been here all night. My mother…," she cleared her throat, sniffled, and started again. "The hospital called late last night. Her body went into some kind of shock. Her lungs shut down."

"Oh my God!" Doug uttered with his cup paused halfway to his lips. He placed it back on the table.

"Oh, it's okay now. She's off the ventilator already and has been breathing on her own for about an hour. She's still in a coma, though. Still in the ICU."

"I think you mentioned in my office that she was in a coma."

"Did I?"

"Yes." He finally took a sip of his coffee, black and hot, leaving a flavor of cardboard in his mouth from the paper cup.

"To think that getting you the package may have been her last request…"

"Don't talk like that. We always need to hope for the best."

"Hope? She's seventy-two years old and has Multiple Myeloma. I don't want to talk about hope." She looked at him with moist brown eyes. "I just want my Mama back," she whispered while looking down to her lap. She was beautiful in her vulnerability.

Doug remembered that children of many different cultures, no matter the age of the child, often referred to their parents as "Mama" and "Papa," though to him it sounded childish. "What's your...mama's first name?" He felt the urge to hold Evangelina, to comfort her. But he knew she could take this the wrong way. He didn't know her well enough.

She tilted her head and looked at him sidelong. "Petra. Why?"

"Well," he said with a grin, "I'm a touch uncomfortable calling her Mama."

Evangelina forced a smile, but it didn't take. The opportunity to comfort her made Doug feel better than he had since leaving the morgue. It mystified him that her feeling bad could make him feel good, but he accepted this without berating himself.

As he reached across the table for Evangelina's hand, his thoughts inexplicably became philosophical. Maybe this is what it's all about: the chance to comfort one another, just a moment in time to be there for someone else. He placed his hand on top of hers and she looked up at him without raising her own hand from the surface of the table, leaving her palm flat, not returning his grasp but not rejecting it either. This time, though, she smiled without it being forced.

He looked into her dark eyes, seeing the innocence there, the pain, the vulnerability, puppy dog eyes. He remembered the empty box, the gift from the package that Evangelina had gone out of her way to deliver to him at his office. What did that mean?

"I don't know her, but if she raised you, I'm sure she..." he almost used past tense, "is just wonderful." The words sounded corny even to him.

Evangelina looked surprised by what Doug said and he wondered if Petra had not been such a nice person after all.

"You don't?' she asked.

"Don't what?"

"Know her?"

"Ah, no," he said, shaking his head, now understanding what her surprised look was about.

"But she gave me that box to give to you. She made it sound very important." Evangelina turned in her chair to face him, a position that forced Doug to let go of her hand.

"That's a question that's sort of been haunting me." That and the image of Evangelina. "Why would a woman who doesn't know me send me a package? And an–"

She cut him off before he could add that the box was empty. "That doesn't make any sense."

"We'll have to ask her when she wakes up."

"If she wakes up."

"Oh, come on now…"

"Sorry," she said, turning back to face the table. "You're right."

He admired her perfect posture for a moment, and then said, "That's okay. It's to be expected under the circumstances. Actually, I think you're holding up quite well."

She didn't say anything, but he could tell she was pleased with his comment, proud of herself, her strength.

At that moment Doug felt that he was making progress. Though minor, he was actually succeeding in comforting her. "One of my favorite things about life is the possibility the future holds. You just never know what might happen next." Hadn't he just heard that recently?

"That sounds scary."

"Sure, I suppose, in a way. The world could go to hell any minute. But think of all the good things that could come."

"But it's so uncontrollable. I like my life simple, predictable." She took her last bite of cookie and leaned her head back, draining her coffee cup.

"I took a philosophy course, and I remember a guy, I think his name was White, but anyway, he said something like 'I may not be able to control the framework of my life, but what I put into that framework is mine.'" Doug laughed. "It may be the only thing I got out of that course."

"What school did you go to?"

"I graduated from San Francisco State."

Evangelina's expression brightened. "Me too. And to think we never ran into each other."

"There were a lot of students there."

"True."

"Did you grow up in the City?"

"Yes and no, we moved here from the Philippines when I was eleven. You?" Evangelina rose from her chair and put on her leather overcoat.

Doug stood as well, grasping his walking stick, which had been leaning against the plastic chair next to him. "I grew up in the foothills out toward Tahoe. Just a simple country boy."

"You've adapted quite well."

"Yes, I guess I have."

She nodded at his cane and said, "I noticed that you're limping. If I'm not being too forward, could I ask why?"

Though Doug had made walking sticks to sell when he was young, he used one now because of a motorcycle accident he had been in a few years back. That memory returned.

He had run to the street in a fit of anger. Jumped on his bike, a black and silver Harley Sportster 883 Custom that he had just purchased that morning. He revved it up, popping loud and resonant down the empty late night streets and headed out of the City, north across the Golden Gate. He had had dirt bikes growing up in the mountains but today was his first experience with a street bike this heavy. He watched the speedometer increase to seventy miles per hour as he opened up the throttle on the road

68

to Stafford Lake heading west toward Point Reyes, the lights of the car following left far behind. Slowing down to forty-five and leaning in to the first banked turn, his left foot peg-scraped the road. He overreacted by bringing the bike upright perpendicular to the planet, which was stupid on a banked turn because the bike was then leaning to the right in relationship to the surface of the road, causing it to immediately turn to the right into the metal guardrail.

His right thigh crunched between the bike and the rail, breaking his femur. He felt his ribs crack, too. The bike bounced off the rail heading across the street to the left while his body continued to the right. Flipping high into the air over the steel rail, the tops of his feet shattered against the handlebars. He landed hard on his back sliding down the slope away from the road until his crotch stopped him by slamming into a small gnarly madrone bush. His breath wouldn't return as he struggled with his left hand, his right arm hanging limp, a torn bicep, to first remove his helmet and then his leather jacket, a form of claustrophobia making him panic and think irrationally that these clothes were the cause of him not being able to breathe. This would become one of his worse nightmares for months, tearing t-shirts off in the middle of the night. Once he could take a breath, a thought passed quickly though his mind about how predictable it was that God wouldn't even give him the relief of being knocked unconscious. Then all he could think about was relieving some of the pain from his broken leg and his balls by trying to scoot his butt back up the hill. Which he failed to do.

The memory went through his mind in a flash, but lasted long enough for Evangelina to be staring at him.

"A motorcycle accident," he said.

"Recently?"

"Almost two years now." He had resigned himself to living his life with a limp. Perhaps he should discard the walking stick, force himself to walk without it. Maybe that would make his leg stronger.

Evangelina stuck her hand out to shake his, saying she needed sleep after the long night.

He pulled a business card from his wallet and handed it to her. As he did so, his ears stuffed as if some tremendous suction had filled the room. He yawned and tried to pop his ears. "Maybe when your Mama wakes up, I could come and visit her." She looked at him quizzically, like he was hitting on her, so he quickly added, "So I could ask her about the box she sent me."

"Okay," she said, smiling once more while placing the card in her coat pocket. "By the way, did you find your friend?"

"Friend?"

"You said you came here looking for a friend. I figured that was someone specific, not just anybody."

"Yeah, I sort of hope he's not here."

"Huh?"

"Well, I have this seventeen-year-old niece who has a homeless friend whose father has been missing since last week. I came here looking to see if maybe something bad happened to him."

Evangelina seemed impressed with his concern. "I volunteer at Saint Anthony's soup kitchen. I could ask around. You wouldn't believe how many people they serve a day. Over half are homeless. Somebody's bound to have seen him. They're quite a close-knit community, taking care of each other. What's your friend's name?"

"Silver. Don't know his first name. His son's name is Loose."

They were now back in the lobby, walking toward the front entrance.

"Loose? Sure, I've seen him around. Nice kid. Don't remember his dad though."

"Well, I'll talk to him and get us some more information. I'd appreciate any help you could give us."

She tapped the pocket of her coat where she had placed his card. "I'll give you a call if I hear anything."

Doug was more excited by the prospect of her call than the information she might give him. Suddenly the ground felt unstable and his head became light.

Doug stood still trying to regain his balance. "Did you feel that?"

"What?" she asked.

"It felt like a small earthquake."

"No, I didn't feel a thing."

Doug shook his head, wondering how Evangelina could have possibly not noticed the tremor.

Out the main entrance on the corner of Geary and St. Josephs Avenue, they parted ways. Evangelina headed down O'Farrell toward the Fillmore District, and Doug crossed St. Josephs to hail a cab on Geary. Before he reached the other side of the street, he realized that Evangelina's name had the word "angel" right there in the middle. He decided he would think of her as Angel from now on.

His gait was light and he tapped the tip of his walking stick on the pavement to a song in his head by the band Flipsyde, "She's an angel, working on God's train."

But by the time he got in a taxi, he had changed songs to a Jimi Hendrix tune. "Angel came down from heaven yesterday, and she told me 'bout the love between the moon and the deep blue sea."

8

They run from their classroom at the sound of the bell. They pass the boiler room. The windows down here are small and dirty, placed at the top of the walls, this being the cellar. At the top of the stairs they cross in front of the gym and run out to the playground. Doug is with his best friend, Boots, who is a very big kid for a third grader, whereas Doug is small for his age. They don't play with the kids in the "normal" class during recess. Their class, the "special" kids from beneath the gym, play alone from the other children.

They circle and toss a red rubber ball textured with crosshatching a touch smaller than the size of a basketball. Three boys walk up to Boots. Maybe they're sixth graders.

"Hey retard!" one says.

"Hi," replies Boots, innocently, not even noticing the name or the tone.

"Tell us your name," says another.

"Boots," he says, pointing at the boots on his feet.

Doug knows his real name is Bruce, but the boy's vocabulary is small. Boots smiles at each boy, proud of his boots, proud of his name.

Doug runs up and pushes the first boy. "Hey, why don't you just leave him alone?"

"Ooooh," says the third boy shoving Doug from behind. "Little retard wants to play." The three circle Doug, shoving him this way and that until he tumbles to his knees. "Come on, retard. Let's play." They walk around Doug, slapping his face.

Doug tries to get to his feet and fails. If only he could stand up.

His classmates huddle together seeking safety, each squeezing toward the center of the herd. Boots, a giant of a boy, stands alone off to the side with his mouth open.

"Come on, retard; come on." Each takes a turn boxing Doug's ears as they pass behind him.

As one ear starts to bleed, Doug curls up in a ball and begins to cry. He cries not from the pain but at his helplessness. If only he could get to his feet.

Doug woke from his nightmare sitting up rapidly in bed gasping for breath. He hadn't had this memory in quite some time.

Sweat soaked his T-shirt. He forced his breathing to slow down as he looked around the room and recognized where he was. Home. His heart kept pounding. The feeling of helplessness remained.

* * *

He was dressed, showered, and shaved when he sat down at his desk. He had taken Constant for a walk, and now the dog was in the kitchen crunching dry dog food, something Constant wasn't very fond of, though it was better than not eating at all. Doug never gave him table scraps except for the occasional steak bone. Of course, the kitchen was actually part of this living room, the entire penthouse being mostly one room.

Doug whistled the Hendrix tune from the day before as he dialed Lucy's cell number. She answered on the first ring. Doug kept tapping his foot on the hardwood floor to the beat of the song.

"Hello." Her southern drawl was more sensuous over the phone than in person.

"Hey, girl, I was hoping we might get together for lunch."

"Doug?"

"Yours truly."

"Are you kidding?'

"What?"

"Can't you get it through your head?"

"Huh?"

"I made it more than abundantly clear the other night at the show. And then again in my e-mails. I never want to see you again. Please delete my phone number." And then she hung up.

"What e-mails?" Doug asked the empty room. He was under the impression that they had a good time at the concert.

Constant came around the counter looking for someone else in the room to whom Doug might be speaking. He stood with his head cocked to one side, questioningly.

Doug booted his computer on his desk and searched his e-mail. Not only were there messages from Lucy, but they were marked as having been read. He went to the one on the top, the newest, which included the entire exchange, and started at the bottom of it to follow along in sequence.

Doug: Why are you so upset? Please just take my call and we can talk about this.

Lucy: I told you. I don't even know my own measurements. I'm pretty sure none of my partners ever knew what my measurements were, and I would have been really offended if that was the way they characterized me. I need to be with someone who accepts me regardless and whose only concern with how I look is that I'm healthy and happy. I don't get that sense from you.

As Doug was reading this, he wondered how a woman would not know her own measurements. How would she get fitted for stylish clothes?

Doug: But you asked. I can almost quote you. You said, "It is important to me, given my history, to understand your needs with respect to appearance as well. I'm probably one of the most open minded, honest, direct women you'll ever meet. So I'm not afraid to talk about this in a very open way. And now I'm real curious about your take on all this. I know a lot of guys who are attracted to a specific type... certain hair, certain body shape/size, legs, derrières, breasts... you name it. Better to understand it and talk about it, than have it be under the table. So, tell me."

Doug doubted the quote was accurate. It was probably an exaggeration. But he'd made his point. He could almost hear Lucy's sweet southern voice utter those exact words, though he couldn't remember this conversation.

Lucy: I am one of the most open women, but that doesn't mean I would tolerate you degrading women in general, or categorizing me by my measurements. I'm signing off now. Please just throw my phone number and e-mail address away.

Having reached the top of the e-mail, Doug scooted his chair back from the desk. What the hell was going on here? He succinctly remembered walking Lucy to the BART station after the concert and kissing her goodnight. He did not remember any fight they might have had or these e-mails. Yet this was his home computer and the e-mails were marked as read. How could that be? Could someone be messing with his e-mails? He thought about how Charlie had been watching his movements behind closed doors at the office the other day. Was this part of the same elaborate prank? But then Lucy would have to have been a part of it, and that didn't make any sense. There must be some other explanation.

Doug reached for his phone to delete Lucy's number. Given the exchange, he was glad to be rid of her. She sounded like a kook.

As he checked the rest of his messages he began to hum the Hendrix song once again.

9

"So why are you doing this?" asked Terra while looking over her left shoulder to change lanes. The night traffic was thick here.

Uncle Doug sat beside her in the tan leather bucket seat of his 1974 BMW 3.0 csi. It was a classic and he rarely drove it, not having much use for a car in the city. She felt awfully special, him letting her drive it. Nervous, too.

"You mentioned you needed time behind the wheel," he said.

"Not that. I'm talking about helping Loose. What changed your mind?" She came to a stop at the light. When she accelerated, it was jerky. This thing had a lot more power than her instructor's little Ford Focus.

"Well, he's been missing more than a day now. What has it been, five? And you seem to care a lot about Loose, don't you?"

"Yeah, I guess." She drove out of the Tenderloin across Market. "His mom died a while back. It sort of sent their life into a tailspin. Then his dad lost his job. He just seems to need taking care of."

She turned on 24th Street heading toward the bay. "Thinking about Loose's dead mom is probably why I been thinking of my own mom lately."

"You have?"

"Yeah, I've been wondering if maybe there wasn't something we might've done to save her."

"Probably not a good idea."

"Boy, you're just full of empathy."

"I didn't mean trying to save her. I meant thinking about it. There's nothing we can do now."

"If I could travel back in time, I'd try."

Uncle Doug was twirling his wooden cane between his knees. He always twisted it when he was nervous. "You know our parents got divorced," he said. "They'd shuffle us between the two of them. When your mom was old enough, maybe fourteen, she chose to stay with our mom, your grandma. But me? Staying with one and then the other. No place to really feel like home. I kept going back and forth, staying at my dad's longer and longer as time went by. It was terrible. The divorce was bad enough but when your mom decided to stay only at Grandma's, I really felt abandoned. Your mom was the only constant thing in my life, the two of us moving back and forth together."

He was silent. He had never actually talked to her about his past before. Maybe this was a good thing. But she couldn't quite see the relevance.

He continued. "I learned early on that there are long-term consequences to our actions. You got to be responsible. I think we're all alone in this world when it really comes down to it. Some of us own up to it and just buck up; and some of us ignore it and act as if we're not. I prefer the former, but either way there's no sense dwelling on it." He sounded thoughtful. Almost depressed. He probably needed a lot more therapy than her painting could provide. Something professional.

They reached the end of 24th Street just past 3rd Street. Loose's van was parked at this dead end with a light on inside.

Terra shut off the car and handed her uncle the keys. She again thought about what a strange conversation this had been, how her uncle was talking, how he sounded so philosophical. It wasn't like him at all.

"Are you okay? You seem so…distant."

"It's nothing. Never mind," he said as they both left the car. Constant jumped over the seat from the rear to get out.

10

Bug, dressed in dark shirt and leather jacket, knocked on the sliding side door of the Volkswagen Vanagon. Her hair was brown, its natural color, and straight. It was a rare occurrence. Usually she dyed it some strange color, or black, and teased it. Doug squatted down to ruffle Constant's neck.

"Who's there?" came from within.

"Hey Loose, it's me, Terra. I got my uncle with me."

"Him again?" Loose said as he opened the sliding side door. Constant jumped on the bed in the middle of the van. It was a camper van with stove and sink. The roof had window portals running along the side edges. Doug could see one of those thick black plastic bags used to warm up water for taking showers while camping hanging in the front seat. All the comforts of home.

"Uncle Doug wants to help find your dad."

"Yeah? How come? Probably just wants to dig at my dad a little deeper. Make fun of his situation some more." Loose swung his legs from the bed out over the edge of the door. He quickly gathered his schoolwork scattered over the bed and stacked it neatly on the counter where the sink was. The sink had a cutting board covering it.

Ignoring the remark Doug said, "I take it you still haven't heard from him."

"Nobody knows nothin'." Loose wrapped his arms around Constant and hugged him to his chest. "I asked everywhere. Even Safeway where he takes his cans and bottles for money. Nothin'. Somethin's wrong. I just know it. He wouldn't just leave me."

"Of course he wouldn't," consoled Bug. She scooted herself into the van, leaving Doug standing alone on the sidewalk facing them, twisting his walking stick in his hands.

"Do you have a picture of him?" Doug said. "It might make the search for him easier."

"Starting to sound like a copper," said Loose.

Doug was a touch surprised at the word the boy used for the police. It was a little archaic. Did kids still use such terms?

"It might not be a bad idea to report this to the police," said Doug. Bug glared at him as if he had stepped in dog shit.

"Cops don't care what happens to us on the street. Just as soon have us all disappear. Same as most folks." Loose grabbed a framed photo of himself with his dad and mom fishing and handed it to Doug. In the picture, the boy held a tiny trout straight in front of him, toward the camera, while his parents looked on from either side. Looks of pride and disgust were both apparent on his face.

"Bu...Terra tells me your mother's gone." Doug had almost, once again, called her Bug.

"Yeah. A few years ago."

"How?"

"On the back of a bike," Loose said softly. Bug gripped his hand and rubbed his shoulder.

The father was probably driving the motorcycle. Probably blamed himself for the accident. Went on a drinking binge. Lost his job. The same old story.

"You're new to Terra's school, aren't you?"

"Yeah. We were originally in a boarding house over there by you guys. After we lost our home. Then we couldn't even afford that. But the van's really nice. It's got everything we need."

Bug squeezed his shoulder.

There was an obvious affinity between these two, both having lost their mothers, both taking care of their dads. But there was something more. Bug seemed to be developing a maternal instinct, something that had started with her father. She wanted to take care of this boy, like she would have if she had had a younger brother. It was a whole new level of maturity in her. And Doug noticed that she had changed into a skirt when she had heard they were going to see Loose, something more dignified, something less Goth. Maybe that's why she was wearing her hair natural.

"Can I take this?" Doug asked, waving the framed photo.

"There's more than one copy in there," Loose said, taking it back and removing a print.

"Well, we should get going," Doug said.

"All right," Bug responded. She hopped down from the open door. Constant followed. "See ya at school tomorrow."

"Right, school," Loose said, reaching over to his alarm clock.

11

Leaving the parking garage, they walked down the street with Bug on the right by the curb, Constant off his leash on the left, and Doug in the middle. There were pebbles of broken glass from a smashed car widow, which glittered from the artificial light on the street. Oil slicks reflected in purples and greens. All sound was muffled.

A group of three boys from one of the various street gangs that so commonly gathered in the Tenderloin stood in a circle. Suddenly, Constant took off and ran ahead, barking. Doug tightened his grip on his walking stick, grabbed Bug's hand, and trotted in pursuit. The boys took off, yelling and taunting the dog.

A shriveled old man was sprawled where the three hoods had stood. Beside him laid glasses and a weathered book. Doug helped the man to his feet, asking him if he was okay.

Bug handed him his glasses. He put them on, and they sat askew, creating a diagonal across his face. There was white tape on the nose bridge as if the glasses had been broken and haphazardly mended. The lenses were cut straight on the top and the curved lower edges rested into his wrinkled cheeks. Dressed in a gray woolen suit so old and worn it hung loosely around his withered frame, he gathered himself, attaining a certain air of dignity as he did so. His shirt collar was open and bare, the tie discarded long ago. Gray chest hairs curled over the top of the shirt. The remaining hair on his head was so thin there was more scalp than hair.

"I'm fine, just fine," he said.

"Fine?" Doug questioned, before he thought about whether or not he should be urging the man into conversation.

"Those boys were just having some fun with me. Ah... things are not always what they seem. People are never as simple as we would like them to be."

"They had you on the ground," said Doug.

The old man looked at the scratches on his palms. He looked up at Bug from over his glasses. She handed him his book.

Constant came back from chasing the boys away, looking proud of himself.

"I live just a few blocks from here. You've been so kind." With that he started to walk away in the opposite direction.

Bug nudged Doug and he looked down at her. She jerked her head a couple times indicating to follow the withered little man. Doug wanted to resist, but always had a hard time refusing his niece. Constant led, and the old man stopped to praise the dog.

"And what might your name be, my little hero?"

To Doug, Constant's expression said, *Don't ask me.* As if answering, Constant barked. The old man laughed.

"Constant," replied Bug.

"What's yours?" asked Doug, seeing that both Constant and Bug were accepting of the old bum.

"Alphonse," he replied. "Alphonse Duncan." He looked like a retired academic who had hit harder times.

"And what brings you out this late in the evening?"

"Ah…well, when one reaches my age, one doesn't sleep quite so well. Hard to go to sleep at night, making it hard to wake up in the morning. That's my routine. I end up taking long walks in the evening." He looked at Bug. "Cherish your sleep while you still can."

"What happened with those thugs?" Doug asked, thinking that this wasn't really the best of neighborhoods for an old man to be wandering around in the dark.

"Thugs? Not thugs really. Hooligans maybe. Just boys being boys." Alphonse laughed, which set him to a coughing fit. When he recovered, he patted Constant on the head and then resumed walking.

Constant kept running ahead, only to stop at the curb of each corner waiting for the three to catch up. He obviously liked the old man, staying beside him while crossing the intersection, making sure he was safely across the street before heading off again.

Alphonse chuckled, then sputtered and coughed, entertaining himself with his own thoughts, maybe remembering his own childhood.

He slapped his thigh and cocked a slanted smile that matched the angle of his cockeyed glasses, and took another step, wobbling like a top.

They stopped before a building that Alphonse indicated as their destination.

"You live here?" Doug asked.

"Why yes, we do. A whole menagerie of us undesirables. The place has been boarded up for a while and we take good care of it. Seems it was made for us. A clapboard village right here in the middle of town."

They were standing before Doug's building for his project – which he'd just learned was infested with vermin. Why hadn't he been told? Didn't his employees know that these people were living here? Alphonse was a nice enough man, Doug supposed, in a filthy sort of way, but he was still definitely homeless. Couldn't the city gather these people and move them off somewhere out of the way? This was prime real estate.

"Awfully nice of you two to walk me home. Hope I didn't put you out of your way."

"That's okay, Mister Duncan," said Bug. "It was a pleasure."

Alphonse stooped to pet Constant goodbye. "Take care now."

"You really shouldn't be walking these streets alone at night," said Doug.

"This is where I live, son. Don't have much choice."

12

Doug called Andy while he made circles on his screen with the pointer on the monitor. Constant finished crunching his dry food and curled up at Doug's feet.

Andy's wife Kathy answered the phone and, after some talk about how enjoyable their last dinner out together had been, she passed the phone to her husband. They lived out in the Avenues and had a couple of young boys that kept them home most evenings; going out was a rare treat for them.

Andy told him of a meeting coming up at city hall.

Doug sat up straighter in his chair and let go of the mouse. Grabbing a pen, he rolled it along his fingers with his thumb. "What's up?"

"Well, someone representing the Historical Society wants to stir things up again, make a plea to protect the neighborhood from the likes of you. The implication is that we won't be the only company represented at that meeting."

"Problem?" Doug thought of the visit he had had from the three men representing some business association in the Tenderloin.

"Don't know. Could be some new group trying to keep progress from progressing. 'Save The Slums' or some such slogan."

"You're kidding, right?"

"Yeah, it's more than likely some other company trying to make sure we're not the only ones to prosper."

"Any ideas?"

"I tried to get more, but I guess we should just be grateful that we were given a heads-up at all. Could be trouble, I suppose. Just because The City loses a lot of money supporting the homeless doesn't mean others aren't profiting. Charities can come out way ahead, for instance."

"I know how charities work," said Doug, noticing Constant's snout resting on his foot, eyes open and looking up at him.

"Well, the meeting is set for nine o'clock Monday morning."

"What have you found out about that business association that came to see me?"

"I'm working on it. It's complicated. I'm having trouble tracking down ownership of each of its members."

"Really?"

"Yeah, but I'll get it done. Give me a little more time."

"I'll be at this meeting. Is the Mayor attending?"

"I don't know. Sometimes he does and sometimes he doesn't. But the right people will be there. Decisions will be made on the spot."

"I'll give him a call just in case." Doug placed the pen back on the desk and stroked Constant's head, as the dog was now sitting beside him.

Done with the night's business, Doug and Andy talked a touch longer about a dinner club called Yoshi's that had just opened a new location on this side of the Bay. They made tentative plans to see guitarist Pat Metheny a couple of months from now.

As Doug picked up the phone to call Jack, the head of his project, a silent swoosh seemed to suck all the sound from the room. All Doug could hear was his own tapping foot. Then he stopped.

Constant's head jerked to the old coal-burning fireplace as if the sound from the room had left through there and up to the rooftop, a silent gale howling.

Hollowness remained. Rocking his foot from toe to heel, testing the timbre of each, drumming an inconsistent rhythm, Doug leaned forward in his chair. Looking around the room, he stood. His chair wobbled as if in slow-mo. Constant watched and listened, waiting for a creature that had made the noise, something to attack, something to run from.

Doug took two loud steps. The sound was more pronounced than the wood floor should have generated.

"Hello…hello," came from his phone. Whereupon all the insignificant sounds of the night – the refrigerator, the heater – came crashing back into the room.

Doug looked at Constant who was staring back at him with an expression that asked, *What the fuck was that?*

Doug didn't remember actually dialing the phone.

"Jack?"

"Doug?"

"Yeah."

"What's up?" asked Jack.

Doug looked at Constant who was settling back down.

"There're street people living in our building. Would you have it fenced off with security around the clock?"

"A fence? Only to tear it down again? It will take longer to put it up? Not to mention the cost. Why don't I just get security to roust out the vagrants and we'll call it a day?"

Was that legal? Doug hadn't done demolition before. It seemed that the place would need to be cordoned off for a period of time before the destruction. But he was hiring specialists, and they hadn't mentioned anything. He had to assume that those guys knew what they were doing.

"Okay, let's do it." As he said this, he felt a minor tremor shake the building. Constant was immediately on his feet, but cowered low, looking for a place to hide.

"Did you feel that?" Doug asked Jack.

"Feel what?"

"We just had an earthquake."

"Nope. Didn't feel a thing."

"Guess I'm just a little jumpy."

"Goodnight, Doug."

"Yeah, right. See you."

Doug turned on the news to see where the quake had been centered and how big it had been, but there was no mention of it on the news.

"Now this is a weird night, isn't it buddy?" he said walking over to Constant and patting him hard on the side. "Go lie down."

Doug sat back down at his desk and Googled "Homeless Death San Francisco," wanting to know more about the article he had read in his office. The very first link, "Homeless Deaths Rise 57 Percent" seemed to hit paydirt, but it was from September 1999 in the *San Francisco Street Sheet*. The second link was headlined, "Bronze Plaques May Mark Where Homeless Died," an article from just last Saturday by Matier and Ross in the *San Francisco Chronicle*. It seemed the Board of Supervisors had unanimously voted to have bronze plaques placed in the sidewalk, like for stars in Hollywood, marking where the City's homeless dead had been found, stating the details of their lives and the circumstances of their deaths. Though privately funded, Doug found the proposition hideous and couldn't imagine how the Board of Supervisors had passed something so morbid.

Yet, they were a committee. Doug hated decisions by committee. He started to worry about the upcoming meeting. San Francisco had town hall sessions where anyone could come in and voice their opinions. They were cumbersome and foolhardy. Group decisions were never the best decision; they were always something mediocre designed to please or placate all. Doug hated mediocrity.

94

He began to whistle the Hendrix tune again. This slowly made him feel better – until his PC screen flickered and turned that awful blue as if the operating system were crashing like the older versions of Windows did so often. Strange words slowly formed, surfacing into focus as if through a fog.

"Good evening Doug," said the words.

Doug leaned forward and stared.

"Now what the hell!"

"It's me, Charlie," said the words.

"Not you again," Doug said aloud.

"Yes, me again."

"And you can see and hear me through my computer, right?"

"Yes."

Doug reached to disconnect the microphone and camera from the computer.

"We need to talk," said Charlie on the screen.

"What about?"

"You're already headed down the same path."

"What are you talking about?"

"A total disregard for other people. It's just like the Fillmore all over again. Only this time it's worse. This time there will be major repercussions."

Doug had to think for a moment before he responded. "Those people are homeless. They're encroaching on my property. It's not my responsibility to house them. Why don't you let them stay at your house?"

"They're still people, still human beings."

"That's questionable." Doug knew he was just being flippant. People like Loose and Alphonse were real people with real problems. But did their problems have to be his? The only reason he was helping Loose was because of Bug. And Constant had been the one who had dragged him into what could have been a street fight the other night while protecting the old man.

"You need to take this more seriously. There are things happening here beyond you and me. Maybe we're not meant to understand them. But everything is interrelated. Things don't happen without affecting others. It's like a rug; pull on one thread and the whole rug can completely unravel."

Doug sat back down. Though it was frustrating, he couldn't see any harm with this conversation, and it might lead him to know who was playing this prank on him.

"And? What do you want me to do about it? How am I connected to whatever is going to happen?"

"As far as I can tell, you're at the crux of it. Look at the other night with that friend of your niece's."

"What? Loose? I'm looking into finding his father."

"We'll not get into your motivation behind that one. But think of this: here's a boy, fifteen at most, who lost his mother not so long ago, whose dad is missing, and you didn't even think twice about leaving him to spend the night all alone on the streets, probably scared to death."

"I thought we were talking about the things I do and how that affects others. In that example I didn't do anything."

"We both know that choosing not to act is an act in and of itself, with its own set of consequences."

It felt as if she were using his own words against him because he had said almost the same thing to many employees, many times. Doug stopped rapidly tapping his heel, wondering how long he'd been doing that. Constant was sleeping comfortably by his other foot.

"This conversation is sounding familiar and just as vague as the last," he said. "If you don't have something more concrete to add…"

"Your phone call to Jack has already set things in motion. You may want to reconsider 'rousting them out' as Jack put it."

"Listen, I'm not responsible for them. They'll go back to wherever it is they came from. I have a job to do and a lot of my employees depend on me for their livelihood." Doug, feeling as though he was finished with this conversation, reached over to turn off the computer. His face was very close to Charlie's next words when they appeared.

"Aren't you curious about Lucy and what happened the night of the concert?"

Doug sat back down. This Charlie woman knew too much. This just couldn't be a coincidence. They had to be connected.

Someone was playing a joke on him and he was sick and tired of it.

"So, you know Lucy, then?"

"Not personally, no."

"Come on. Talk to me."

"Goodnight Doug."

"Wait!" He stood, grabbing the monitor with both hands. But the words were gone and he knew that Charlie was too.

* * *

Later, after Doug had called Hunt and was waiting for him to arrive, he decided to call the mayor at home before it got too late. This time when the refrigerator stopped along with the air conditioning, he wiggled a finger in his ear to try to get his ears to pop as he continued to dial. Constant sat up and stared at him.

When the Mayor answered, the clarity returned to Doug's hearing. They exchanged pleasantries, Doug reminiscing about the time shortly after college, before the mayor had gone into politics, when they had transacted business together. Sensing the mayor's impatience, Doug told him the reason for his call.

"I'm sorry, Doug, I don't know about any meeting. I'm not aware of this proposal."

"Mayor, I only want to know who is attending. Just a heads up of what I'm walking into."

"Well Doug, I can certainly look into it, but if the proposal is as old as you say, I wouldn't think you'd have a problem."

Doug was hoping for more. He figured the mayor was just playing it cool, not wanting to speak the truth out loud. Nobody wants to feel or admit they can be bought.

Another tremor hit the building, probably an aftershock from earlier. Constant looked worried. Doug ignored him.

"I'd greatly appreciate that Mister Mayor. Thank you. My phone number is—"

"Just call my office and my assistant will know exactly why you're calling."

* * *

Hunt looked up from the keyboard saying, "Got it. Hand me a piece of paper. I have to write down this IP address."

"Then we can find the computer that Charlie was using," stated Doug.

"Charlie? That's this woman's name?'

"So she says."

"Hmm. I guess you did mention that."

Changing the subject, Doug went on a fishing expedition. "How'd you like the concert the other night?"

"Me? I thought it was great. That lead guitarist is fantastic. And I love his voice. Seems so weird. The voice and the body don't match. His voice is so sweet and his body is so big. And the way he and the drummer do those fast riffs together. How about you?"

"I liked it all right," said Doug, not really remembering a whole lot of the music having had his attention on Lucy.

"Well…" Hunt said, "I suppose it wasn't all that great for you, what with the fight and all."

"Fight?'

"Yeah. Her getting up and leaving right in the middle."

Doug couldn't quite wrap his brain around what Hunt was saying. Lucy leaving right in the middle? But that wasn't what happened. He remembered her there at the end of the concert. Walking her to the BART station. The kiss.

"We had a fight?"

"You kidding me, man? I figured you'd never forget something like that, the way she stormed off."

"You really remember us having a fight?"

"I'd definitely call that a fight. What would you call it?"

Doug's gears were spinning. Why was Hunt lying to him? It wasn't something to lie about. Doug had been there for God's sake. And if this were some kind of elaborate prank, then Hunt had to be a part of it. Hunt had great technical abilities, was probably able to tap into his security at work, and definitely had access to his computer. Could Hunt be fucking with him? It wasn't like him.

Hunt broke through his thoughts, saying, "Anyhow, Quantum Flux is high up on my list for a return tour." Hunt stood up from the desk next to Doug.

Feeling the need to move off this subject, Doug said, "Hey, how's that project you were working on with the abandoned equipment?"

"Oh, that. The company was right. It's worthless. I may be able to use that stuff for something else, though." Hunt stuffed the piece of paper with the IP address in his pocket. "I'll look into this and get back to you. This is a much better lead than that phone number with the zeroes and ones. That led nowhere. Even the boys over at AT&T say it doesn't exist. Not even the area code exists."

"Okay, yeah," said Doug. "Get back to me."

"Speaking of work…I turned down that international job offer. Maybe once Bug goes off to college, assuming they ever offer me something again. Either way, the time just isn't right. Besides, who knows, this may be the best decision I ever made."

13

Terra opened the front door and there stood her uncle and Constant. The dog came right in, and she greeted him with a big hug around his neck. Her Uncle Doug just stood there looking uncomfortable. And pale. He looked like he was about to throw up.

"What's the matter? Are you sick?" she asked. He stayed there in the doorway so she came and took him by the hand and guided him in.

Constant sat in the middle of the room looking concerned for his master. This scared Terra. Even the dog seemed upset.

"No, Bug. I'm not sick," said her uncle. Without letting go of her hand he sat on the couch. Terra stood directly in front of him. "I just got some terrible news."

He took her other hand so that he was holding both together yet separately. This, and the way his eyes looked into hers, told her that she wasn't going to like this news.

"I don't know if I want to hear it," she heard herself say.

"I know, honey. I'm not sure if I want to tell you."

He kept sitting there staring at her. It felt so creepy. He wouldn't let go of her hands. He looked like he was about to cry, which made her want to cry without even knowing why.

Finally she pulled her hands away, wanting to run away but she knelt down in front of him. She placed her hands on his knees. She felt so small, but something inside her wanted to comfort him. And she wanted to get this over with. "What happened?"

"It's about Loose," he said. "I found his dad."

Terra stared at his face. She didn't know what to say; too many questions were forming in her mind. Wasn't it good news if he found him? Then she got it. She felt the tears roll down her cheeks. Something was wrong with Loose's dad.

"What? Where is he?"

Constant came up beside her. His head slipped under her arm. The dog licked her face. Twice, before she shoved him away, but then she pulled him back and wrapped her arms around him.

"I was at the hospital." Her uncle kept staring at her, not looking away at all. He reached for her hands again, but only succeeded in grasping the one.

"What happened?" She could feel her hands getting cold and a rush of it ran down her back. It was getting hard to move. Her legs were cramping from squatting.

"I don't know. I don't know how it happened."

"How *what* happened? Tell me." Her throat was tightening; her voice beginning to squeak as it grew in volume, becoming frantic.

She heard her father enter the room but she didn't turn, didn't see him. He seemed to just stand there and wait.

"Uncle Doug, you're scaring the crap out of me. Tell me for God's sake." This was crazy. She imagined Loose's father getting hit by a truck. She could see it in her mind. The vision made her whole body cringe. She felt her one hand digging into the fur around Constant's neck.

"He's dead, honey. He died." He placed an open palm on the side of her face but she shook it away. She felt the skin on her face get thick, heavy, uncontrollable, gravity pulling it down. She fell to her knees and her head fell forward, gravity pulling her forward, her face pressed into her uncle's lap. "I don't know how. They don't know. He just died."

Her body was heaving out of control, big convulsive jerks. It was collapsing and heaving at the same time. And she heard herself gasping for air. The weight of her body was even too heavy for her lungs. She felt her uncle's arms wrap around her. Her fingers dug into his thighs.

"Why?" she asked though she wasn't sure who she was asking. Maybe God.

From a long distance away, she heard her uncle try to answer. "There is no good answer, Bug. Sometimes people just die. Some part of them just gives up."

She thought about Loose and what this would do to him. She felt herself slipping to the floor. She wanted to curl up and hide. To not have a parent left, what would that do to him? And she heard herself say, "I want to tell him. I want to be the one who tells him. It's got to be me."

"Okay. I'll take you."

So he drove her. She couldn't see the street through the tears, lights blurred, a streak of colors like stained glass. She tried to be strong, but her body kept shaking, drastically. She felt so cold. She used her muscles to stop the shaking, but when that didn't work she tried letting go, tried to calm herself, relax her body, and that seemed to help. *Just relax*, she told herself. *Relax.*

They entered Saint Anthony's soup kitchen after not finding Loose at his van. Uncle Doug immediately walked up to an Asian woman serving food at the buffet, calling her Evangelina, and Terra wondered where he might know her from, this not being a place her uncle would frequent. Her mind wanted to figure things out, make sense of it all.

The three of them moved off to the side and Uncle Doug updated her on his having identified Loose's father's body at the hospital. Terra could still barely believe her friend's father had died. How? Was it an accident? An overdose? Her uncle didn't know. But it wasn't a car wreck; he would know if it was. Did it really matter how he died? She was here for Loose. Loose was the one that would suffer. And that in itself wasn't fair. The survivors always did the suffering.

Terra had cried all the way over here, but now she wanted to be strong for her friend. She sniffled and looked around the open space. Her eyes were a little blurry but she cleared them with the back of her wrist and hand. People were huddled in groups everywhere. It would be hard to find a single place to sit and eat. Was it always this crowded?

Off in a corner where there were fewer people, stood the old man they had walked home the other night, with his taped and twisted glasses. Around him gathered children of all ages huddled on the floor engrossed in whatever the old man was saying. Terra saw Loose among them. She pulled on her uncle's sleeve, jerked her head in Loose's direction, and the three of them headed over.

She cleared her throat, then said, "Loose, hey Loose; we need to talk."

Placing his finger to his lips, he whispered, "Can this wait?"

"No, I'm sorry. It can't." Now she knew how her uncle had felt: the need to tell, the desire not to have to.

The old man, Alphonse she now remembered, paused for them to move off a little, and then resumed.

"It's about your dad," Terra said, getting control of her voice. But her face was still so heavy. She knew her face was giving her away.

"Yeah?" he said apprehensively, looking at the three faces surrounding him.

Terra bit her lower lip. Tears were burning her eyes. "It's not good."

"My dad, you found him, right?" Loose shuffled nervously. Constant pressed against his legs. He patted the dog's head.

"Yes. My uncle did."

"Well, where is he?" Loose was staring into her face trying to read her expression so she tried to keep it neutral until she could get the words out. But he could probably tell from her hanging face. He looked at her nervously. She wanted to cry and hug him, but she waited.

"He's at the hospital," she sniffled.

For the first time, Loose seemed alarmed. "Is he sick? Did he get hurt? What?"

She threw her arms around him and began to weep. "He's dead, Loose. He's dead. I'm so sorry." And the world became muffled, a vacuum. People moved around the room silently. She felt the motion cascading.

Loose pushed her away, his expression desperate. "No way. You're wrong."

Uncle Doug moved next to them. "No, Loose, I'm positive. There's no mistake."

Loose shook his head, as though he were trying desperately to make this conversation go away. "What happened to him?"

"I don't know," Uncle Doug said. "No autopsy's been done."

Terra sensed from his words that none would be done either. They would just shuffle his body away as if some leftover garbage. The thought made her even sadder, if that was possible.

Evangelina came over to Loose's side and hugged him. This seemed to confirm the worst for him. He turned to the woman and buried his face in her breast.

Slowly a sound emerged like a high-pitched siren. This gradually changed to an animal wail, and then painfully to human sobbing. At the sound, Constant looked up and, identifying it as a sound of distress, could not get close enough to Loose to give the comfort he must have wanted to give. Loose sunk to the floor next to the dog, his legs no longer able to hold him. He hugged Constant, leaning on him for support, his entire body shaking. Constant sat down with him and licked his ear and some of the tears off one cheek. Terra joined them on the floor wrapping her arms around them both. Closing her eyes, she bowed her head and cried for Loose's father, for Loose, for her own past losses, and for the world's blatant disregard of the turmoil it created. She cried hard and fast, their convulsions coinciding.

From outside of their circle of grief, Terra heard Alphonse walk over and ask Uncle Doug what was wrong. Terra kept her eyes closed and listened to the murmur of their voices.

"My own father died when I was in sixth grade, so I have a little experience with what he's probably feeling," Alphonse said. He coughed and hacked. "Of course, I still had my mother at the time. She lived to be a ripe old age, older than I am now actually. I remember her telling me, after the second of my three brothers died, that the worse thing in the world was outliving one's own children. Let me take the boy home."

"Are you talking about taking him to your place?" asked Uncle Doug. "Where we walked you the other night?" He named an address that Terra recognized as his building, the project he was working on. But this was a couple blocks away from where they had gone with the old man. Why couldn't her uncle remember?

"That place has been boarded up for months with security guards posted around the clock," Alphonse said. "No, no, no, I'm somewhat between places right now."

Her uncle stuttered and sputtered for a moment, not knowing how to respond to what he was hearing. Finally he said, "Loose has a van he lives in, but you'll have to take the bus."

Terra was rocking Loose back and forth, humming quietly in a low tone, almost a mantra. Evangelina was leaning over, massaging Loose's shoulder with one hand.

"Oh that's too much," Alphonse said. Terra assumed her uncle was giving the old man money. He probably thought that kind of thing could help in a situation like this. She was angry at first, but realized he was doing the best he could. Her anger was at the world itself, not at her uncle.

"Take it," said Uncle Doug. "You'll need bus fare."

"But that's way too much."

"Use it for the boy."

Terra opened her eyes, looked up, and said, "I'm going too."

Uncle Doug seemed as though he was about to object, then looked over at Evangelina and nodded.

"If you do, you take Constant with you and then you head right back home."

She traveled the buses at night by herself quite often and when she took Constant with her she had always been able to sweet talk the driver into letting the dog on the bus. She would have to do that both ways on the bus tonight, and she wasn't sure she'd be emotionally able.

"Loose," she said, "I'm here for you." And then she remembered that these were the words that she had spoken to her dying mother, and she cringed at the memory of Mom's response.

Loose clung to her, whispering in a cracked voice, "This c-c-can't be happening. It just c-c-can't be…t-t-true."

She squeezed him closer as the world disappeared. There weren't enough words, nothing would make this nightmare go away. It was like the two of them against this wicked world. And the world was winning.

"Hush, now. Hush," she said. "I'm here. We can do this. We can do this together."

And the siren sound came from him again. She rocked him, hard, trying to shake the world away, humming. She hummed in his ear, a low drone. Pressing her body against his, she wanted to get closer than she was able and she could feel him wanting the same.

His wail became sobbing once more, which was easier for her to cope with. The wail had been like that of an animal dying a very painful death. She hummed louder, rocking him, sound and motion together as one.

"I love you, Loose," she said, and he cried, weeping softly in her ear.

"You're s-s-so g-g-good…to me, Terra. So good." He scooted his butt closer to her. "They're all gone. Everybody's gone. I d-d-don't understand."

"Neither do I. And I don't think we ever will." She hummed and rocked, hummed and rocked. "But I'm here with you. I'm here, and together we'll get through this. I promise. Come on," she said as she got to her feet helping him stand. "Tell me about your trips to the lake. I want to hear all about it."

He didn't smile, but he nodded, gathering some inner strength from deep within his small frame.

"I bet those were the best of times. I bet your parents really enjoyed those trips," she said. He nodded again as they took at step toward the door, Terra on one side, Constant on the other, and Alphonse only a step behind.

As they walked out the door Loose whispered almost too soft for Terra to hear, "I miss my mom."

"Me too," Terra agreed. "I miss her all the time." After she said it, she knew it was true. And she squeezed him around the shoulders, leaned her head down, and kissed him on the cheek. He smiled as best he could and looked up at her.

14

Doug tasted the terrible brew after Angel gave him the coffee and sat down beside him. Angel wore jeans that hugged her bottom tightly, the legs straight like a chimney, what a cowboy might wear. Her blouse was short to the waist and frilly. Even when dressed down, she looked elegant, a real city girl. They talked for some time and though they sat alone, the homeless passing their table would consistently stop by, flocking, as if to the mother of some fraternity.

"...So child services will inevitably get involved," Angel was saying.

Doug nodded. "I was thinking there might be some way I could help. I should have gone with them, but Loose isn't comfortable with me." He thought of the stupid comment he had made when they had first met, a comment about the boy's father. He wondered if Loose would ever forgive him.

"Help? How would you want to help?" It seemed to Doug that Angel had a certain amount of distrust in her voice. Why did everyone think he didn't care?

"Maybe I could set him up in one of these low-cost living places."

"There are places for the poor sponsored by the city. Usually these are used for families that are coming out of recovery where someone in the household has been placed in a job. The city doesn't sponsor it totally. The people have to pay some of the rent themselves. I have information about these types of places. I could put something together if you're interested."

"Well, yeah. That sounds helpful. I could probably pay for his piece of it for a while." Doug gulped the rest of his coffee, and the heat felt good even though the taste was horrid. Angel got up and went into the back room. Doug thought she'd just grab some pamphlets, but when she returned with her purse, she gave him a personal card with her home and cell numbers.

"Give me a day or two to see what I can find," she said. She seemed to be regarding him differently as she sat down again. Was it that surprising that he wanted to help?

Doug tried to repress the excitement of holding Angel's card in his hand. While still contemplating the promises the card offered, it was nearly impossible to keep the smile off his face.

"How's your mother doing?"

Angel took a deep breath. "The same. Still in a coma. Still on the edge."

"Hang in there. You're tougher than you know. I can tell."

She offered a small smile. "Thanks."

"Give me a call the minute she wakes up. You still have my number, don't you?"

Angel tapped her purse. "Yes, right here."

He felt inordinate joy at the knowledge that she'd kept his card. "Even if you just need to talk, just call. I'm looking forward to asking her about that empty box."

A second or two passed before she asked, "The box was empty?"

"Well, yeah, didn't you know?"

"No, of course not. Why would she send you an empty box?"

"That's what I want to know."

"And you don't even know Mama?"

"I've never met her." Angel was getting upset, and that was the last thing Doug wanted.

"But that doesn't make any sense. Why would she send a total stranger an empty box?"

Angel seemed on the verge of tears. Doug was losing control of the situation, and he didn't know how to comfort her.

"We can find out together when she regains consciousness. We'll ask her together."

Angel took another deep breath. "Okay." She forced a smile.

"In the meantime, I'll give you a call to pick up the info from you."

"Would you like some help picking a place for Loose? We could go together and take a look."

Doug tried to contain his enthusiasm. "That would be great."

A woman was signaling Angel from behind the counter, and she acknowledged this with a wave. "I need to get back to work. So many mouths to feed." She placed her palm on the top of Doug's hand and squeezed it before returning to the food line.

15

At the office, Doug sat amazed at what Andy was telling him.

"The demolition and the building permits have been approved and Jack is scheduling both as we speak," said Andy.

"But what about the Historical Society?"

"I told you that wasn't a problem. I don't think it ever even came up."

"What about the meeting? They just canceled it?" Doug thought about his phone call the other night. "I talked to the mayor and maybe he intervened and got it to go away somehow."

"What meeting?"

"The one with the Historical Society."

"You must know something I don't. I never heard of any meeting."

"But you're the one who told me about it."

Andy gave him a sidelong glance as if waiting for the rest of the joke. "Right."

"Come on, Andy. Stop kidding around."

"Who's kidding who here? I never heard of any meeting."

Doug knew Andy was telling him the truth. But if there had been no meeting, then he had sent the mayor on a wild goose chase. He must think Doug foolish or deranged. Given how many strange things had been happening to him lately, maybe he was.

"Listen, I'll update you later on that association, but right now I have some contracts I need to finalize if we're going to meet Jack's aggressive timetable. So, if there's nothing else?" Andy stood and headed for the door. With his hand on the knob he turned, waiting.

Doug shook his head. "No. That ought to do it."

After Andy closed the door behind him, Doug's thoughts turned to something Alphonse had said about the security around his building being there for months. He picked up the phone and dialed Jack's extension.

"Yeah."

"Hey Jack. I wanted to know if you put up security around the building the other night when I asked you to."

"Doug, I don't have time for horseplay. We seem to be having trouble with the clearing of the debris after the demolition. Seems like we're going to have to switch dumps. Caltrans is going to have this one full of trucks at the same time."

"Jack, just answer the question."

"We've had security around the clock since we first bought the building, just like you asked for. Even put up that damn fence you insisted on."

"Since we bought it?"

"Yeah," Jack said defiantly. "Something wrong? Isn't that what you wanted?"

"And a fence? Well...yeah, yeah. No problem. Thanks. Later." Doug hung up before Jack could say another word.

Doug leaned forward, placing his head in his hands, his elbows on the desk. "Oh shit," he whispered to himself. His thoughts were racing and he couldn't keep up with them: Lucy; and Charlie; the meeting; the security; maybe even the phone call to the mayor hadn't happened.

For some reason, he had another memory of his school days then. He was in fourth grade and now part of the "normal" class with the "normal" kids. He'd been having a hard time making new friends and still hung out with his old "retarded" classmates on the playground. His mother had been tutoring him at home ever since she discovered, to everyone's surprise, Doug's amazing aptitude for mathematics. It seemed that Doug's infant sickliness, his pneumonia, his constant high fevers, had not scrambled his brains. He was simply a slow learner regarding vocabulary, his still being below that of a kindergartner's.

He and his mother sat at the kitchen table, textbooks spread out before them. They used flash cards sometimes and they even had a game that came in a big cardboard box. It had question sheets that you slid in one slot and an answer sheet you slid in another, and you punched a hole in the answer you thought was correct. It made it easy for his mother to take a break and let Doug work alone for a while, and it made it easy for her to come back and check his answers. Doug liked the game. It was a fun way to learn. Tonight though, they had been working from schoolbooks, the most boring of all the learning. Suddenly his mother pushed the books aside, her expression heavy.

"But Mom. I'm not lying."

"I didn't say you were."

"But you don't believe me."

"The school called and said you weren't there yesterday."

"Then how do I know what all the homework is?"

"You must have talked to one of your friends."

The truth was he didn't have any friends at school, not in his class anyway, not ones that could have told him what his homework was. This was so frustrating. He had *wished* he didn't have to go to school. Everyone there stared at him. He had dreamed of running in the woods, of never having to go to school again.

So maybe that's why his Mom was so worried. She knew he wasn't lying. Maybe, behind all the bolstering, she still thought he was retarded.

"I've made a doctor's appointment for you next week. It's not Doctor Krause. It's a different kind of doctor. I've already met with him. He's nice; you'll like him."

"Mo-om," Doug whined. Tears were filling his eyes. The world was overpowering him. Everyone was against him. He felt so helpless. He knew that nothing was wrong with him, but she wasn't going to listen. She never did once she made up her mind.

Though this was a memory Doug couldn't reconcile himself with once being a defenseless child. But that game...it seemed so familiar. Punching the holes in the cards and then waiting for his Mom to pronounce his answers correct. He had definitely played that game.

There in his office, he unclenched his fists and sat back. He noticed Constant sitting there staring at him.

"Good boy. It's okay," he said roughing up the dog's fur. "I'm just daydreaming, that's all."

The only acceptable explanation for all of this was that it was some kind of elaborate joke involving a handful of the people around him. He thought of Charlie as a space alien, replacing all the people around him with pod people. The thought made him chuckle. It made him realize how foolish he was being, how silly. Nothing was happening here that was out of the ordinary, that couldn't be explained. In the ultimate scheme of things, everything seemed to be going according to plan. If he just kept his mind on what was in front of him and did what needed to be done, and stopped thinking about stupid shit, then everything would be fine.

Ignoring his feelings, he got back to work.

16

Evangelina sat in the small waiting room of the ICU. The chairs were quite comfortable, but still her body ached from the extended periods of time spent here. The staff followed some kind of policy that only permitted her to visit her Mama for ten minutes every few hours. They wanted it quiet and serene for the patients, but to the visitors, it was a deathly silence, broken only by the machines keeping people alive. There was a door in this room to the hallway and another directly into the ICU. She could hear the beeping and buzzing, the sucking sounds of vacuum pumps, and the occasional alarm that set her off every time, frightened that each one might be for Mama.

A nurse came to let her in. Evangelina walked past the monitoring station, with two other nurses working there, to one of the private rooms circling the station. Mama lay there, looking corpse-like, breathing through a tube with the mouthpiece taped to her face.

Evangelina picked up the blue plastic chair against the wall and moved it beside the bed. She took a deep but shaky breath before she sat down. She maneuvered her left hand so that it would not put weight on the IV and laced her fingers through her mama's. The arm and hand were colder than she expected, probably from all the fluids being fed into her. There was no window in this room, and the one light on the wall above the bed was dim, casting shadow everywhere. She glanced at the displays on the equipment on the other side of the bed, not really knowing what all the digits and graphs meant. But they were stable and that alone reassured her somehow. She tried to ignore all the wires and tubes running into Mama's gown and concentrated on her closed eyes.

"I've been cleaning up your place for you during your stay here. You won't even recognize it when you come home. I ran into some old pictures of you and Papa back in the Philippines. The two of you looked so happy. In one of them he had on his American Army uniform. He was so handsome."

Mama's skin, though old and paper dry, was slicked with oil. Evangelina stood, took a fresh washcloth from the table, poured water into a kidney-shaped bowl, wet the cloth, and began to wipe Mama's forehead and cheeks. Her thin hair was matted, so Evangelina tried to arrange it in a more dignified manner.

"And you're still so beautiful, Mama," she said as she kissed her on the forehead. "Papa would be proud the way you raised the four of us girls on your own. I'm proud to be your daughter. Have I told you that?"

She looked her Mama from head to foot and, seeing the high-top tennis shoes there, remembered. They had told her when Mama had first gone into a coma that one of the biggest problems with recovery was atrophy, especially in the ankles. So she had showed up the next day with these high-top shoes so that Mama's feet would not be hanging forward all the time. The nurses there, though reluctant at first, thought it was a great idea.

Evangelina went to the foot of the bed and removed the shoes. She exercised the feet moving them up and down and in circular motions, a ritual she did during every visit. She needed something to do, a purpose, a way to help in a situation where she felt so helpless. The routine helped, like cleaning Mama's home.

"Roberta called me. She's in trouble again, she says. Money, as usual. I know you would help her out, would want me to help her out, but I can't do it, Mama." What Evangelina didn't say aloud was that it was serious this time. Where did all the money go? Probably for all those fancy purses she bought. She'd even borrowed against her husband's 401K without him knowing so that there was almost nothing left of it. A lifetime's savings gone. She was out of control.

Evangelina cleared her head by changing her train of thought.

"I delivered that box to Mister Sirius the other day. The one you asked me to. I'm not quite sure what that was all about." She used her thumbs to rub the pads of Mama's feet. "He's the head of a large business. It was hard to get in to see him. Security everywhere, cameras everywhere, he must be really paranoid." She pulled on and wiggled each toe. "I even had to get buzzed into his personal office. But I was able to deliver it to him personally." She grabbed both feet and squeezed them a couple of times. After that, she pulled the shoes back on and laced them up snugly.

"Being a big successful businessman, I figured he'd be used to getting his way. I expected him to be arrogant, rude, and shallow, but he wasn't. He seemed almost shy, or nervous around me. It was cute how clumsy he was. I was surprised. When I left, I thought I'd never see him again."

Evangelina sat down again, taking Mama's hand in both of hers this time. She closed her eyes and spoke softly, dreamily.

"There's this homeless boy and Doug seems to want to take care of him. His name is Loose. A nice boy, well educated. Just lost his father. I remember when Papa died. I was, what, thirteen at the time? Loose is fifteen, I think."

She rested her head gently on Mama's lap.

"I ran into Doug here at the hospital looking for someone. Now I know he was helping Loose, looking for his father. And then the next time I see him it's at the soup kitchen. You know the one where I volunteer? He was with his niece searching for Loose. They were bringing him the bad news about his father."

She brought her right arm over her mama's knees, still keeping her eyes closed.

"At first I thought he might be talking about helping Loose find a place to live as a way to impress me. But he was already helping Loose, wasn't he, before I even got involved? But it doesn't come natural to him. It feels as if he struggles with knowing how to care for someone else. I want to help him. Not just with Loose.

Sometimes I just want to help him express himself. It's almost painful to listen to him."

Evangelina lifted her head, opened her eyes, and yawned into her hand. Through her yawn she said, "I think he likes me Mama. Should I let him take me on a date? I'm so used to talking to you about these things. Talking to you whenever I have doubts. I miss you Mama." A sniffle. "Come on now. It's time to wake up."

And then she began to cry, covering her head with her arms as she pressed her head into her mother's thighs to silence her sobs. She wished that Mama would just give her some sign, a wiggling of a small finger perhaps. Anything.

17

Before answering his phone, Doug checked the caller ID. It was once again from the "deceased" line 010-101-0101. He leaned back in his chair, somewhat resigned to this strange woman, and pressed the call button on his cell to answer.

"Hello Charlie," he said, stopping in the middle of signing payroll checks.

"Hello to you too."

"What gives me the pleasure?"

"I couldn't help but notice that your building plans have been approved."

"I don't believe that has become public record yet." Doug was alternately tapping his pen on the bottom row of his teeth and tapping his foot.

"No, I don't suppose so. But I am sure you have already been notified. Have you scheduled a date for demolition?"

"We're working on it."

"You do understand that there are other ways to create without the need to destroy?"

"Maybe on the outskirts of the city. But not within the Tenderloin. We're talking about prime property that is going to waste. There aren't any empty lots there."

"You could remodel."

"Are you kidding? That would cost ten times as much as just starting over. You are one of these do-gooders, aren't you?" He looked at the larger of the two piles of checks that he still needed to sign.

"Our past is important. History has its value."

Doug was quite sure he had already had this conversation with "Charlie" and didn't want to go through it again. People were always romanticizing the past, hoping to slow or reverse progress. To him, old things became valuable simply according to supply and demand. It didn't make them better; it was just that there weren't as many old things around as there were new things. Cabinetmakers were even paid extra to make things look old by beating the surface of good hardwood to make it look rustic. It was ludicrous.

"I'm sure you're right," Doug said, trying to end the conversation.

"But you're still going to proceed with your plans?"

"Yes."

"You're still going to repeat your prior mistakes?"

"If I thought I had made mistakes with the Fillmore, and I assume that is what you are referring to, then I would probably do something different. And why are you so focused on that one project of mine. Have you seen the neighborhood lately? The whole place has been given a face-lift. It's almost safe to walk the streets at night."

"Now that the riff-raff has been forced to move out," Charlie said sarcastically.

"Listen, if the tramps and junkies want to live that way, fine! Just let them do it in some cheaper part of the city. If they want to kill themselves and each other, let them do it somewhere else. I don't really care where, just not in prime locations, okay?"

"You mean like over at that radioactive landfill called Hunters Point."

"Exactly."

"You think all those addicts and alcoholics grew up dreaming of becoming addicts and alcoholics, of living on the street some day? You think that's something they aspired to? Something they would have chosen?"

"Well—"

"And what about Loose?"

Doug sat up straight in his chair. "Huh?"

"Are you going to find him a place to live in Hunters Point? Is that your great plan for helping him?"

"Why don't we talk about who you are instead? You must be someone I know. Hunt must be helping you breach my security. I met Lucy on the Internet, so that wouldn't have been hard to arrange. Andy might go along with it. But how did you get Jack to cooperate? Good old Jack, a nuts-and-bolts kind of guy, no sense of humor really."

"I'm sorry Doug, but I don't know what you're talking about. So far, you have never met me. But I am not connected to whatever shenanigans you think are going on in your personal life. However, I am connected to you in ways you could not possibly imagine."

"Yeah, right."

"Maybe if you explain them to me I might be able to understand," she said.

"Give me a break. Why repeat to you what you already know?"

"Just try it."

"Okay. Let me see." Relaxing back in his chair and placing his feet upon his desk, he said, "They all seem to boil down to two things. People are either telling me that things that I know happened, didn't, or that things that I know didn't, did. And we're not anywhere near April Fools Day. So, you tell me: What's the joke?" Maybe things aren't really changing, thought Doug. All I have to go on is what other people are telling me.

"You are noticing these differences?"

"Of course I notice them, or we wouldn't be talking about them." Doug began to think about the earthquake he and Constant experienced the other night. The one that never appeared on the news. It hadn't been just Jack who hadn't noticed.

"Have you ever played that game where everyone sits in a circle and the first person whispers in the ear of the second person, and that person whispers the same thing to the next all the way around the circle, and when you get to the end, the last person says something that is totally different from what the first person said?"

"Well, yeah, sure. But that's not what we're talking about."

"Memories change and distort over time. What are we talking about if not memory?"

"We're talking about people screwing around with my head!"

"For the moment, let's imagine they're not. What then?"

"Then I must be losing my memory, or losing my mind, going nuts, and believe me, it's starting to feel like it. But all this started after you first contacted me. I don't believe in coincidences. And your communication has been quite mysterious, to say the least."

"You sound scared."

"I'm not scared. I'm pissed off."

"When I'm scared, I move in the direction of trust. Family, friends, people, and things that are familiar and trustworthy."

"You want me to trust you?"

"You'll just have to take my word that I am not in cahoots with anyone, nor am I trying to drive you crazy. For what it's worth, I'm trying to help everyone concerned, and that includes you." There was a pause. The line sounded hollow, almost dead, but not quite. Then Charlie continued, "Tell me. What happens during these...instances?"

"Nothing, really. Our memories just differ."

"What about immediately before or after the occurrence?"

"Like what?"

"How about a hot flash, or dizziness, maybe an unexplainable flash of white light."

"Not really, no." Doug was beginning to wonder where this might be leading. Was she trying to infer some spiritual experience? "It still comes down to either me going nuts or everyone fucking with me. Obviously you know which one I choose." Doug knew he wasn't crazy. He'd swear the whole world had gone nuts before he'd ever admit that.

"There might be a third option. Still, you shouldn't be able to recall these...disturbances."

"Disturbances? I'd say they're disturbing. But what I want to know is what I need to do to get rid of them. And don't tell me I have to abandon my project 'cause I'm not going for it." Though the words had just left his mouth, he hadn't really thought that there might be a demand on him for this, whatever it was, to stop. He considered it to be a practical joke that had gotten out of hand. But what if it kept getting worse? What if everyone around him were laughing at him behind his back? He'd never forgive them.

Doug moved his feet off the desk and back to the floor, rubbing his chin with his hand, thumb on one side, four fingers on the other.

"Just because I tell you that I'm not connected to what's happening to you, doesn't mean that these things are not connected," Charlie said.

"Oh, no. Here we go, getting all spiritual."

"God doesn't have to play into it. There are laws to the universe. I don't believe in coincidence either. Everything is interrelated, like that rug I mentioned the last time we spoke. Time and space and how we move through them is a very intricate process. A lot more complicated than any rug because each one of us is working on the same rug, weaving different patterns that create our reality."

"Really. Hmm. I noticed you said creating our reality rather than affecting."

"I did, didn't I?"

"Yes, you did."

"Do you want my honest opinion?"

"I'm not sure." Doug rather liked using Charlie as a sounding board. He was starting to like her. She wasn't just hounding him any longer. She was interested in him. Yet, something else was going on, something just beyond Doug's reach.

As a conspiracy, what was happening didn't make much sense. To be a prank it would have to include not just family and friends but employees as well. And what about Lucy? Then it occurred to him that even Alphonse had mentioned that the building that Doug and Bug had escorted him to was different from what Doug remembered. Had Bug chimed in her agreement with Alphonse? He couldn't remember right now. And what about his phone call to the mayor? Would he deny that the call had even taken place?

"You think everything is interrelated," Doug said after a long pause.

"I believe so, yes. Something you are going to do or say is going to affect those around you."

"Well, that narrows it down now doesn't it? You've said this before and I still don't understand what the hell you're talking about. Everything I say or do affects the future. Maybe not everything but close enough. And as for those effects being of any importance, I think I can safely say that you could take everyone in this city that is alive today and combined they will probably never rate much more than a couple of sentences in the history books of tomorrow."

"But that doesn't mean they didn't live and die, that they didn't have their own sorrow and joy, that their lives weren't worth living."

"But in the grand scheme of things, the cockroaches will take over the world." Doug laughed. He leaned over his desk with the phone balanced between his ear and his shoulder and started signing paychecks again, placing some aside that he had questions about. This payroll was for hourly employees and he was always suspicious of overtime. Doug had changed the workday at his company to seven-and-a-half hours per day so that overtime wouldn't happen. With California law being so strict with breaks and lunchtime, with its eight hours daily and forty hours weekly, Doug had to be meticulous or the unscrupulous could add a couple minutes here and a couple minutes there and this would add up to real money. It ended up being a royal pain in the ass not only for him but for all the other employees as well who weren't trying to milk the system, what with punching in and out more than eight times per day. "Yeah, I guess when the bugs rule the world, nobody will even care what the history books say."

"You're sounding awfully pessimistic for one who's so successful. You lose a girlfriend or something?"

"I don't have one."

"You should."

"You mean like, 'behind every successful man there is a...,' however that saying goes. Anyhow, I'm not an easy man to live with. The way I see it, I wouldn't live with myself if I didn't have to." He laughed again. The mood of the conversation was changing. He momentarily felt better just talking about all this weird stuff. When he had just been thinking about it, the thought had turned into a loop, a thought spinning with no resolution. Saying it aloud seemed to put it to rest somehow. Usually, he wasn't much prone to talking about himself, but it felt good right now, real good.

"Everyone's a comedian," commented Charlie, but she laughed along with him. "Are you telling me you've never had a girlfriend?"

"You're awfully persistent, aren't you? If you're talking about a live-in, no, I've never lived with anyone."

"And you're not gay?"

"No, I'm not gay."

"Good."

"Good? Why? You got something against gays? You, with all your high and mighty save-the-homeless type spiel?"

"No, I have nothing against gays."

"Oh, I get it. You got a little matchmaking gig on the side."

"I just think that you and that young lady should head off and find a place for Loose to live."

"I didn't mention any young lady. You mean Angel?"

"Is that what you call...I mean, is that her name?"

"Well, actually, it's Evangelina." So Charlie doesn't read minds. Doug realized that most of the stuff she knew could come from the Internet or from breaching security systems. But what about helping Loose? Doug wondered if the soup kitchen had a security system, and made a mental note to check. He doubted that it did.

"That name's Filipino, isn't it?"

"I don't know. She is, though, so it might be."

"It's beautiful as it is. You don't need to be shortening it." The woman sounded almost insulted by Doug's having given Evangelina a nickname.

But she continued before Doug could respond. "Loose might be too young to rent an apartment, and they certainly won't sign him up without a job."

"Let me worry about that." Doug had thought this through already. If he couldn't co-sign for the place, he would lease it in his own name.

Static began to come on the line, bringing Doug back to the topic at hand. "And how did we get off subject here? You were saying that I need to look for an action or decision that most affects the others around me."

"That's not really what I said." The static was getting heavier. "The moment you're looking for could seem quite mundane. But it won't be random. And you don't actually have to look for it if you always just do the next right thing."

"Huh? We could have a long conversation about right and wrong." Some of the best minds have been arguing that for centuries. How was he to know what was right?

"Just do the next best thing. Do the best you can without trying to control the outcome."

"Is this a Zen thing? Shoot the arrow in the dark? Hold it until it releases itself?"

But there was no answer from Charlie. She had disconnected. At first there was only static and then even that faded away into nothingness.

* * *

"Here is an update of my project list," said Doug's assistant Jasmine. "I thought you might want it."

He looked at the woman from the pile of signed checks he was handing her. "There are a few overtime request forms that need to be signed by their supervisors." They swapped papers. "Yes, I haven't yet completed my review of your projects." Jasmine's subtle jab, pointing out that his own follow-through was lacking, that he hadn't completed his review of her projects when promised, irritated him. "Andy was supposed to be here at two–"

"He's already waiting outside."

"Well, send him in." While he waited for Andy, Doug pulled Jasmine's previous project list from a drawer and glanced at the copious notes he'd made in the margins, none of which were complimentary. He placed the two lists, the older on top of the newer, off to the side.

Andy came in and sat across the desk from Doug taking a treat for Constant from a small plastic bag he kept in the left pocket of his suit coat. Constant sat quietly before him, not even wagging his tail while Andy rested the treat on his snout. When Andy said the word "okay," Constant tossed the biscuit up in the air and snapped it midstream before it reached the ground. Andy laughed. Walking around Doug's desk, glancing back once as if to thank Andy, Constant crawled back under the desk to devour the doggie treat.

"To simply enjoy all the simple things in life...I wish *my* life were so simple. Have you ever wondered? It's a double-edged sword, you know. The human quality of failure; we don't give up. We're never satisfied. We wake up every morning trying to get it right, trying to make it just a little better. It's probably what makes us progress, makes us successful. But it also leaves us feeling never quite satisfied with our own lives, always on edge, looking for an outlet."

"What are you babbling about?" said Doug, half jokingly.

"Sometimes a dog's life just doesn't seem so bad."

"Are you down in the mouth today or something?"

"Actually, I'm quite chipper. Except for the research you have me working on, this association thing…"

"What about it?"

"I don't think it's really an association."

"Come again? It's not like they need a certificate to be one or anything."

"These corporations are all hotels."

"Associations are often grouped by industry,"

"True, but they're all in the Tenderloin–"

"Or by geographics."

"And they're all SROs."

"What does that stand for?"

"Single Room Occupancy. A bath down the hall, that type of thing."

"Okay, so they're all a very specific type of hotel. It makes a certain kind of sense. People from all walks of life cruise the Tenderloin for drugs or prostitution. After scoring, they probably need a flophouse to partake. I don't understand what's so strange about there being an association of these places."

138

"Okay, so far, I agree. Nothing all that unusual. But I rather like the idea of SROs, even with their bad reputation. A lot of people down on their luck are given a place to live. There's something noble about that. But then I noticed that each had come under new management within the last five years. Every last one of them had new ownership."

Constant came out from under the desk and sat beside Andy again, staring Andy down as if that might get him another dog cookie. Andy glanced at him and smiled, staring back for the moment.

Doug knew what Constant was thinking: *Andy, you're my bestest friend in the whole wide world.*

"All of them?" asked Doug.

"Every one that was on the list you gave me."

"Why would investors have a sudden interest in these SROs in the Tenderloin? They can't be that lucrative?"

"Good question. Doesn't make a lot of sense, does it? Though all of them cater to the drug and prostitution trades, a lot of families live there too."

"I thought you said they were single room occupancy."

"I did. But that's all that most of these families can afford. A whole family in one room with one bed. It's sad in a way."

"So the clientele is either prostitutes, junkies, or people one step removed from poverty."

"That's about the size of it."

"I take it you have more for me than that?"

"Of course. Twenty-five hotels all purchased within an eighteen-block area within the last five years seemed more than a coincidence to me."

Andy fetched another biscuit from his pocket and encircled it with his palm so that Constant had to gnaw gently between forefinger and thumb to retrieve it, like working the marrow from a bone.

"There's twenty-five of them?"

"Didn't you even look at the list you gave me?"

"No, I guess not."

"Yes, twenty-five. So I did some digging – actually a lot of digging. It's very convoluted the way these corporations are set up. I didn't complete my research, but I have already traced back the majority of these to one company."

"You're kidding?"

"No, sir."

"Do you know what this company might be up to?"

"Well, from the look of their D&B, I'd say they are out there looking for venture capital. They're running at a loss and their balance sheet is upside down. They can't sustain themselves much longer without an influx of cash."

"But if their P&L is running in the red, who would invest?"

"Sounds to me like they were hoping you would."

"But the parent corporation didn't approach me. They presented themselves as an association. They actually wanted to help me overcome the historical proposal for the Tenderloin."

Doug was leery of broaching the nonexistent meeting at City Hall with Andy again, but it slipped out of his mouth before he could think about it. Luckily, Andy sailed right past it with his next comment.

"And that was a piece of cake, just like I said. So, I suspect, we are still missing a piece of the puzzle."

"Pieces, pieces, and more pieces. Maybe this will all amount to nothing. Maybe they'll never come back. We didn't end our last meeting on such a good note." It dawned on Doug that the association had first showed up the same day as Charlie's original contact.

"I think they'll be back," Andy said. "I don't know what they want, but I get the feeling that we're going to find out." Andy handed a piece of paper to Doug as he stood. "Here's the name of the parent corporation. I'm sure that all the others lead to this one, and I'm going to concentrate my efforts on this company only. Unless…"

"No, that would be fine."

"Anything else?" he asked, moving toward the door with Constant following, sniffing his hand, hoping for more.

"Not today."

"Okay then." Andy patted Constant on the head as he stood by the door. "Something good could probably be done with all those SROs. For the families living there, I mean." And then he was gone, closing the door behind him.

"Stop begging," Doug told the dog once they were alone again in the room. Constant responded to the command by backing up from the door as if caught stealing, and he went back to his bed under the desk. Doug patted him along the side of his ribcage as he went past.

Placing the paper Andy gave him into his in-box, he noticed the empty box that Angel had delivered to him still sitting in the exact center of his desk. He doubted it carried any significance, but it was an interesting puzzle. Maybe the emptiness had a meaning in and of itself. Maybe the box held the sound of one hand clapping. Or maybe "Mama" just forgot to put the intended trinket inside. If so, what might that object be?

Opening a drawer to place his assistant's list within, he came across his bottle of Seroquel. He hadn't taken his medication since before the Quantum Flux concert. Yet, he felt better than he had in a long time. He had more energy, more stamina, a lightness of being. He was even experiencing wet dreams, something he had never done before. He felt that if asked to he could change the world.

Thinking of Angel, the smoothness of her skin, the apparent softness of her flesh, he pulled her business card from his pocket. Imagining himself holding her face between his hands, staring into dark brown almond-shaped eyes, took his breath away. He reached toward the phone receiver and called, hoping she would be available tonight to search for a place for Loose. *No,* he thought, *I don't want to start up on my meds again. Not now; maybe never again.*

18

"Did you say this was probably going to be the best place?" Doug was trying hard not to touch anything in this seedy hovel. He kept one hand on his walking stick, the other in his pocket. Together with Angel, they followed the night clerk down a narrow hall who in turn followed a nappy-headed child riding a small tricycle without rubber on its wheels. The child, peddling fast but moving slowly, was not leading the way, but was more in the way.

The clerk turned and opened a door to the left. Doug was the last to enter the room, Constant at his side. His eyes tried to focus around the shadows created from the bare bulb above, the drastic contrast. There was hardly enough space for the three of them to stand.

The place smelled of urine and bleach, probably from the bathroom right next door, but it was hard to tell with so many offensive aromas converging.

"Well," said Angel, "this is the hotel where most of the financially recovering families are placed by the agencies." After a pause she added, "At least it's furnished."

"Yeah, and I guess it's better than the last two places. But still, I wouldn't sit on anything until it's been fumigated." He pulled his left hand from his pocket and picked up a wooden chair that was lying on its side. Constant sniffed a battered wooden orange crate, side slats busted, in front of the doorless closet to the immediate left: a bed, the chair, a night stand, nothing more. A cracker box. A light switch on the wall was lacking its cover, and there was one power outlet on the wall at the other end of the bed. Years of painting over peeled paint had created a wall texture of sorts in dimly olive green, semi-gloss patterns; dark stains as if the edges where the walls met the ceiling were the armpits of the room. The trim of baseboards and window were painted the same color giving no highlights. The glass was too dirty to see what view might be out the window.

"Is this as good as it gets?" he asked the clerk with a sweep of his hand, "right next to the toilet?" She nodded and mumbled something. She must have been in her early twenties, but the world had already beaten her down. To Doug's way of thinking it was her own damn fault. Doug glanced at her ragged jeans then up to the horsehair mop sticking out at strange angles, her face all sharp edges, no meat sustaining her. The shirt from her shoulders hung like a sheet from a horizontal pole. Doug wondered how she could have no self-respect, figuring that she deserved her lot in life. She was responsible for where she was. She could help herself if she wanted to. For reasons of her own, she had given up.

"Well I get the feeling we won't find any better," Angel said.

Doug cringed, but agreed. "Look at that mattress. That's disgusting." He poked it with his walking stick. Constant sniffed it and looked at Doug as if in agreement, then went to the window and attempted unsuccessfully to look out.

"We could scrub the place down from floor to ceiling." Angel stuck her head into the shallow closet, so thin the hangers even stuck out.

"And get a new mattress."

Constant was getting restless. He jumped up to Doug as if he wanted to dance. Doug caught his front paws but shooed him down. "Not now," he said.

Heaving footsteps down the hall preceded the appearance of a short wide troll of a man huffing his way into the doorway. He wore no jacket, but from his open collar hung a woven necktie, buttons of his shirt stretched to bursting. "You twit! Can't you even follow the simplest orders? Your job is to stay at the front desk. Is that so damn difficult? What the fuck you doing up here?"

Constant took a defensive stance with the hair along his backbone standing on end. The left side of his upper lip snarled up soundlessly. It was immediately obvious that he didn't like this man, not one little bit, which was unusual for Constant who almost always took a shine to people.

Angel immediately stepped into his face, "What she's doing up here is doing your job while you," she waved his breath away with one hand and poked him in the chest with the other, "were obviously too busy in some back room sucking up to a bottle."

"Sassy little lady, aren't you? Who the hell are you to be telling me my job?" The man tried to step back, but the hall was so narrow and he was so fat that he quickly ran into the opposite wall.

Doug was shocked at Angel's reaction. He knew that she was a strong woman, very self-confident, but he'd never pictured her getting this aggressive.

"A little slow aren't you? Didn't you hear me say she was showing us the room?" Angel pointed to Doug standing by the window. "That man over there wants to rent it."

The troll looked Doug's tailored suit up and down and then laughed loud and long, coughing and grinding up phlegm.

"You got a real live one here, mister, tough and with a sense of humor too." Spittle bubbles formed at one corner of his mouth. Angel backed up, apparently to avoid any stray pieces that might fly her way. "A real hotsy-totsy. You want the room? That's ten bucks an hour for the two of you, or twenty-five for the night." Doug was appalled when the man winked at him.

As the young clerk squeezed by Angel and cut through the doorway, the man's fat stubby hand slapped her on the buttocks. "Get back down there and stay there," he said. "That's what I pay you for."

Doug put a hand on Angel's upper arm before she went at the troll again. He stepped around her, placing himself and his walking stick squarely between the two.

"I'm more interested in a monthly rate," said Doug.

"I really doubt you'll qualify for any subsidy." The Troll laughed, checking out Doug's suit one more time. He turned and walked down the hall.

The little girl who had been riding the tricycle stuck her head around the doorframe and smiled.

"What's that?" Doug asked the man while patting the nappy head of the child. He followed down the hall, but Constant pushed his way in front of him, always wanting to lead the way. He heard Angel talking to the little girl.

"All our renters here get some of their rent paid for by the government. Most of them are either on their way down to living on the street, or on their way back up." After opening the door and descending the stairs he said, "The Government thinks they can help. I don't care one way or another as long as I get my rent."

"Which is how much? You haven't answered me yet." Constant ran ahead of all of them and waited at the door to the first floor.

"Four hundred a month."

They walked into a concrete office that had a steel desk and a filing cabinet with a miniature TV resting on top. Constant took his place by Angel's side so naturally, as if she were family, that Doug was surprised.

"How 'bout we say three hundred?" countered Doug.

"The price is controlled by legislation. All the single residencies have the same price."

"What do you mean they control pricing?"

"Because of the subsidies."

Doug hated rent control. He knew that the majority of people living in San Francisco were renters and that any legislation would heavily lean toward the side of the renters. Berkeley was the worst in the Bay Area, but San Francisco was a close second. Yet, once you had to take subsidies into consideration, rent control made more sense.

Besides, this time Doug was a renter rather than a landlord.

The man sat at his orange metal desk, opened the filing cabinet next to it, and handed Doug a preprinted contract. It was a standard agreement, so there was no sense in having Andy review it, and it was only four hundred dollars month to month for God's sake.

As he was signing the papers, Doug got Jasmine on her cell phone. It was after hours, and even if she worked for only a few minutes, he would have to pay her two hours of overtime, but still he told her to purchase a new twin mattress and box spring and send a cleaning crew over ASAP to fix the place up. He was hoping to move Loose in tomorrow.

* * *

"The gall of that man. It makes me angry just having to do business with him," Angel said.

149

Doug offered her a patient expression, "He's only the night manager, Angel." Angel gave him a sidelong glance with raised eyebrow as they walked down the sidewalk, Constant between them, smiling if he could.

"Some of the family call me Lina; some Auntie Ev; but this is the first I've heard Angel."

"You don't like it?"

"Sounds a touch pretentious, don't you think?"

Doug shrugged.

"I'll let you call me that as long as you always introduce me by my full name, okay?"

Doug nodded. He was elated. It felt like a nickname, a pet name that inferred a closer relationship than actually existed between them.

"I'm surprised you didn't come to my defense."

"Huh?"

"He was implying that I'm a prostitute."

"Yeah, well, come to think of it, I suppose he was."

"There's no two ways about it."

"Don't take it so personally."

Angel sneered. "He didn't call *you* a whore."

"Who knows what goes through that slimy mind of his. For all we know, he thought you were a paying customer and I was a gigolo."

"Sure, right." She moved ahead a couple steps taking Constant with her. "And how about that clerk? Did you see the way he treated her, like an object? She should have punched him." She spun to face the direction she was headed. Over her shoulder, she asked, "You wouldn't treat your employees like that, would you?"

Thinking about Jasmine and his review of her project list, Doug had to fight the urge to come to his own defense. He didn't want to be grouped with the bastard of a manager. He figured he was different. He had high standards for his employees and he was strict about those standards, but he definitely didn't go for or defend sexual harassment.

"I'm sure," she said, "you treat all your employees like human beings first and employees second."

Doug wondered why he felt so little empathy for the clerk. He simply didn't believe people were helpless. He figured that if people didn't learn from their own mistakes and better their lives accordingly, then, to hell with them. Yet, this didn't jive with his helping Loose. He wasn't doing it just to impress Angel, although that would be a pleasant side effect. And he didn't believe he was just doing it to make himself feel like a caring human being. That wasn't his style. Nor was he doing it for his niece, though it had started out that way. He sincerely cared about Loose. He shared his niece's desire to help him. He cared about how his niece felt too. He knew the boy didn't like him, because of what he had first said about his father, but maybe this would help to smooth things over.

He decided then and there to start over with his review of Jasmine's work, trying to consider her a human being first and an employee second. He wondered if Jasmine feared him more than respected him. Did he shoot from the hip when it came to termination? Did he have no tolerance for human error?

Looking at his feet, walking a step behind Angel and Constant, a wind hit him in the face so hard it pushed him to a standstill. When he looked up at Angel, her hair was hanging straight toward her shoulders, as if the wind passed her by without touching her. Constant turned and whimpered at him. Ahead, the blacktop of the street along the sidewalk waved like the surf before the breakers, long and powerful. The buildings and sidewalk were rumbling, the road a wave of asphalt, soon to crack and crumble. The wind blew by, followed by a silence so strong he held his nose with his fingers trying to clear his ears with internal pressure. Constant came running back to him in fear. Angel was turning unnaturally slowly. The wave of the road hit Doug, and he wobbled and fell to his knees, wrapping his arms around Constant as he did so. He staggered and fell to his side without hitting his head, taking Constant all the way to the ground with him. As Doug rolled, the sounds returned with a pop, and Angel was leaning over him asking him what had happened.

Doug sat up and looked around. Everything was quite normal again, even traffic on the street. No buildings had crumbled. It was obvious to him that Angel had felt nothing while his dog had seen the same things he had. He was dying to exclaim what had happened, daring her to deny it, but he knew that she hadn't noticed. He didn't want to appear crazy especially since they'd only known each other a short time. She just wouldn't understand. Hell, he didn't even understand what had just happened.

"Did your leg give out?" she asked, perhaps referring to his motorcycle injury.

"I just got dizzy and fell."

"Are you okay? Did you hurt yourself?"

"No, I'm fine. Constant broke my fall."

"It's amazing how intuitive he is. To turn back at the right time and run to your aid."

Doug got to one knee, rubbed Constant's head, and said, "Yeah, he's a good dog." Then he stood on wobbly legs. Angel held one of his elbows to help balance him.

"Well, I think that's enough for tonight," she said. "We've done what we set out to do. You need to go home and get some rest."

"Yeah, rest sounds good. You want to come along tomorrow when I show it to Loose?"

"I'm busy in the morning, but I'd like to be there."

"Good, 'cause I like having you along."

"Thanks." She smiled, which sent a thrill through him.

19

"What do you mean you're not going?" Terra asked Loose. "What are you going to do then?"

"I can live here," he said making a sweep of the van. "This is the closest thing I have to a home. This is where all my stuff is." He seemed on the verge of tears.

"We'll help you move your stuff," said her uncle, missing the point. This was Loose's last connection to his past.

"We're talking about your own apartment, Loose. Do you know how much I'd love to have my own apartment. It's not like you'll be alone. I'll come and visit all the time. Who do you know our age that has his own car and an apartment?"

"Have you seen it?"

"Well, no, but–"

"I know the one. It's a dive. They're all in the Tenderloin. Remember? My dad and I used to live in one before we ran out of money completely."

"If Alphonse was here, I think he'd disagree. He has nothing over his head and anything is better than nothing."

"He's been staying here with me. He likes it here. I'm not giving up my van."

"I've got an idea," said Evangelina. "How about Doug and I keep your van for you until you get your driver's license? How does that sound?"

"I could keep it in the parking garage next to my place," Uncle Doug said.

"You live in the same building Terra does, don't you?"

Uncle Doug nodded. The four of them were sitting on the bed inside the van. Terra felt the comfort there, a cozy warm feeling. Her Tokidoki knapsack sat on the floor by her feet. She was wrapped in a wool quilt that was probably made by Loose's mother. Uncle Doug was placing the photo he had borrowed to identify Loose's father into the frame behind the original.

"So when I visit you," he said to Terra, "I could see my van?"

"Anytime you want," answered her uncle.

Terra caught Uncle Doug smiling to Evangelina, silently thanking her for her suggestion about keeping the van. He held his walking stick in front of him. It was almost too tall for the inside of the van. Constant had crawled up onto Loose's lap, a touch big for a lap dog but Loose didn't seem to mind. In fact, he seemed to enjoy the comfort, his arms wrapped around the dog's chest. Evangelina was sliding her hand down Constant's head to his neck.

"Terra," Loose pleaded, "please don't make me do this. This is all I got left of my entire life. Everything else has been taken away from me."

"I think it's important, Loose. I wouldn't ask you if I didn't think it was. You can always move back into your van if it doesn't work out."

"I don't understand any of this, but I trust you, Terra." He pointed at Doug. "Maybe not him, but you I do."

Evangelina patted Loose on the shoulder.

"You too," Loose said to Evangelina.

Terra was going to cry if they didn't get this show on the road.

"But I don't have any money. How will I live?"

"I told you: Uncle Doug's taken care of all that."

"Yeah? What's in it for him?"

"He just wants to help."

"Yeah right. You really believe that? Just look at him. It's written all over him: He's never taken care of anyone but numero uno."

Uncle Doug, who had already been offended by Loose refusing his generosity, was just about to burst out in anger when Evangelina interrupted by changing the subject back to the van. "One of us can drive the van over there and since we are going to use a parking garage, maybe we can find one real close to the apartment so that you can visit it whenever you want."

They finally headed off to the new apartment, Evangelina driving the van with Loose and Constant, and Terra driving her uncle's car with him riding shotgun. Uncle Doug finally had started to relax while she drove, which helped her stay calm and make fewer mistakes. Terra could tell that driving was going to be one of her main enjoyments in life, the freedom of it, the power.

Once in the apartment, Loose tried to relax in a brand new lounge chair at the end of the bed upon which Terra sat, while Evangelina and Uncle Doug inspected the quality of the cleaning job his crew had done. Though old, the room looked thoroughly scrubbed to Terra. The crew had even taken it upon themselves to scrub the bathroom next door. The desk in the corner, which Terra recognized as one from a cubicle at her uncle's office, had a lamp placed on top and a phone that would be connected for service tomorrow according to Uncle Doug. There were two identical chairs, one pushed under the desk, the other on the side placed against the wall. Constant lay on the floor by the door, panting. They had found an indoor parking lot only a half block away and had brought up a load of Loose's stuff.

Still being early in the afternoon when they finished, and the weather being that strange San Francisco sunshine for this late in the season, Evangelina said, "I just love roller coasters. How about you?" She seemed to be asking no one in particular so everyone nodded together. "How about we take the rest of the day off and go to Great America?"

"Aren't they already closed for the season?" Terra asked while pulling her legs out from under her and hanging them over the edge of the bed.

"They've decided to stay open until the hard rains come."

"That sounds great," said Loose, almost immediately coming out of his funk.

"We've already got the kids' homework for the half day they missed," said Uncle Doug.

"Let's do it," said Terra, launching herself from the bed. Constant got with the program and jumped his front paws onto her chest, barking once. "Hey, do we have time for me to dye Loose's hair? I bought some blue dye for him."

"You want to dye his hair blue?" her uncle asked.

"It's only temporary. He can wash it out tonight if he doesn't like it. He already agreed. It's a great social statement. Strangers even come up and talk to you to ask you about it.'"

"I don't see that we're in any hurry here," Uncle Doug said, looking at Evangelina, who nodded. "But that bathroom just got cleaned, so don't make a mess."

"What about you, Uncle Doug?"

"What *about* me?"

"Why don't you dye your hair, too?"

"What?"

"That sounds like a great idea," added Evangelina. "You can do Loose's while I do Doug's."

"Come on, Angel. Don't encourage her," Uncle Doug said in that serious tone of his.

Terra giggled, thinking that this would be even better for him than the painting therapy 101. "You'll love it, all the attention you'll get." She also noticed the name her uncle used for Evangelina. She'd never heard him use it before, and Evangelina certainly didn't call herself by that name.

"This will be fun," Evangelina said. "And we definitely won't lose you in the crowd."

Uncle Doug turned toward Loose and asked, "Are you really going to do this?"

"Yeah, I think I am."

"Well, if you can do it, I guess I can, too. Let's go."

Terra grabbed the dye and a small jar of Vaseline out of her purse while Evangelina gathered two towels from the closet. Uncle Doug shook his head as if he couldn't believe what was about to take place, probably thinking he was nuts for agreeing. He gathered the two chairs from the desk and they all entered the bathroom leaving the door wide open.

After the boys had laughingly dampened their hair in the shower with shirts off and placed themselves on the chairs in front of the mirror with the towels draped over their shoulders, the girls donned the thin plastic gloves that were included with the dye, outlined the boys' hairlines with Vaseline, and massaged the dye all the way to the scalp. Once their heads were completely covered, they let the dye stand for a half hour. Loose's hair turned a dark blue that brightened and glowed in the sunlight from the window but turned almost black when he stepped out into the hall. Uncle Doug's hadn't taken as well and had turned a light turquoise, except in certain light, where it seemed evergreen. Evangelina had taken photos with her phone during the entire process and now that they had ended she held the phone at arm's length to take one of all four of them.

Looking questioningly at Terra's uncle, Loose seemed to make a decision of some kind, as if Uncle Doug's willingness to dye his hair with Loose made him more accessible somehow. Pointing, Loose said, "All he needs are some Christmas tree ornaments." Everyone laughed, except Uncle Doug, who just looked confused.

"A string of flashing lights might be more appropriate," said Uncle Doug trying to join in the jocularity but still remaining stiff, probably uncomfortable as the butt of a joke. But Constant jumped up to him, and her uncle grasped his front paws. Together they danced in a circle, and Uncle Doug began to laugh.

They rode down the peninsula in the BMW, dropping Constant off at home on the way. The sky cleared, and the sun shone brighter. The temperature rose to a whopping sixty-five degrees. Terra listened to the murmur of the two adults talking in the front as she and Loose sat silently in the back.

When her uncle asked Evangelina about her mother, she answered, "Not now," shaking her head and then trying to nod toward Loose in the back.

"Oh, right," he said.

Terra figured that Evangelina's mother was sick, maybe even seriously, but if so, Evangelina sure seemed to be handling it well. Loose definitely didn't need to hear any details of someone else dying. Today was a day to escape death, to rise above it, to celebrate living. This day was for raising his spirit above his own pain, and Terra was determined to help all she could.

They parked what seemed like miles from the front entrance and had to walk forever to get there. Once they did, though, Uncle Doug upgraded all their daily passes to season passes for next year because it only cost an extra ten bucks per ticket.

"By next year," Uncle Doug said, "You'll have your license and be able to drive the two of you down here without us, any time you want."

Terra smiled at this. "Wow, that's right. I haven't even thought of all the places I'll be able to go. So much easier than BART or the buses."

"We could do road trips and stuff," said Loose. "We could use the van."

They got their photograph taken on the way in, girls in the middle, blue haired troll dolls on the ends. It wouldn't be ready until later, so they'd have to pick it up on the way out.

Though it was probably the second oldest ride, they went to the Demon first because Uncle Doug remembered it as one of the newest when he first went to Great America. Terra was so surprised when he sat in the front row and screamed, "Yeeeee-haw," with his arms stuck straight up in a V every time they went around a corner or turned upside down through a loop, laughing like he was about to burst. He was crazy and jazzed like Terra had never seen him. Evangelina wasn't quite as loud, but she raised her arms and laughed right along. Loose was as excited as her uncle.

Uncle Doug kept peering over his shoulder at Loose, smiling and screaming.

"Let's do it again," said Uncle Doug almost immediately after getting off the ride. The others looked around and saw that, probably because the ride was getting old, the line was short. Uncle Doug grabbed Loose by the arm and went to the back row this time. Loose seemed hesitant at first and kept watching Uncle Doug. Soon, though, he was imitating what Terra's uncle was doing, raising his arms and screaming. The two of them kept nudging each other and laughing.

After riding the Demon for the third time, Loose asked, "Can we go on the Drop Tower next?" He lifted himself up on the balls of his feet and back down to his heels over and over.

"What's the Drop Tower?" asked Evangelina.

"It's where they take you up in a cage about twenty stories and then just drop you."

"If I'm not mistaken," Uncle Doug said, "That used to be called The Edge."

Though Terra wanted to go on the FireFall because she had never ridden that one, it was much more important to do whatever Loose wanted. "Yeah, that sounds great. Let's do it!" she said.

"We should get lunch soon, too," Uncle Doug said. "I'm starving."

"Probably not a good idea right before we do the Drop Tower, Doug," said Evangelina.

162

"Besides, Uncle Doug, I don't think I've ever seen an adult enjoy a roller coaster as much as you did that last one."

"Hell, lil lady, I been a roller coaster rider from way back when," he said in his version of a southern drawl. "Come on, Loose, let's go."

Together the two of them ran ahead, first one in the lead, then the other.

Clear skies did not mean there was no wind. With the wind came a chill as they stood in line. Movement helped, so each in their turn walked in place, some back and forth, some in circles, to keep warm. Because of this, the line expanded and contracted, a snake swallowing multiple rats.

A clown walked by pushing a cart with hot dogs. His face paint gave him the only smile he had. He wasn't even trying to get customers to buy; he just walked on ringing a bell periodically without even looking around.

They got into the cage together, four people to a ride, sat and pulled the safety bars over their heads. Loose followed Uncle Doug on, obviously trying to stay close to him. The cage rode jerking like an old elevator up to the twenty-second floor, then moved forward over pure empty space.

"It's like dropping off the edge of the world," squealed Loose.

"Yeah, without a parachute," said Uncle Doug.

When Terra looked down, her stomach leaped before the cage even dropped, and her body tingled from head to toe. Then the world fell out from under them

Later the food court was reasonably empty, owing to it being mid-afternoon. They chowed down on burgers and dogs with lots of fries, chasing all that with shakes or cola. The gulls came to beg, and the sparrows swooped low and then flew off chasing each other. The swallows hopped and chirped. An old man was picking up tossed paper items with a mechanical "arm" which had three pincers to grasp with when the handle was squeezed. In the opposite direction from where they sat, the wind blew a mist from a fountain there. Terra and Loose decided to toss pennies into the fountain as the adults finished eating. Terra could still hear their conversation from the short distance.

"Being the age I am and never being married or having children makes me wonder if I ever will. Is this my destiny?" Evangelina asked.

"I've never married either, you know," replied her uncle.

Terra had missed the first part of the conversation. She wondered how they got to such a serious subject in this fun place.

"So what's wrong with us? I was always taught that family comes first, yet, I have none of my own."

"How come?" he asked.

"No children?"

"Yeah. Why not?"

164

"Well..." Evangelina looked uncomfortable for a moment. "To tell the truth, I never even dated until I was twenty-five. Boys were always interested in only one thing. There was this one guy, though. His mother was friends with Mama, and they introduced us. It got pretty serious. I mean, I was thinking of marriage and having kids and all that. But it turned out he was still married to a woman in the Philippines. I found out because his wife showed up with a baby he didn't even know he had. I was devastated."

"What a creep."

"Yes, he was." Evangelina took the last sip through her straw and toyed with the empty cup. "I was taught that children are the result of the love between two people. I just never got close to anyone else." She paused. "Maybe I have some trust issues."

Uncle Doug nodded and then changed the subject. "My parents divorced when I was only seven. My sister was eleven. She lived with my mother while I lived with my father. I never had much family. I didn't have any cousins, and I never met my grandparents. I don't even know anything about them."

"We Filipinos are known for the size of our families. I have more cousins than I can keep track of, and even my nieces are having children now."

"The only child I have is my business. And of course, since my sister died I feel quite responsible for Bug."

"Bug?" Evangelina asked.

Listening, Terra cringed.

"It's a nickname for Terra, for cuddly bug. She doesn't want me to call her that in public, so mum's the word."

"That's cute. Anyway, I don't believe business is a good substitute for family. For one thing, a father is always a father, and a son always a son, but an employee can be replaced."

"But doesn't that make the relationship even more special? A son you have to accept no matter what you get, but you choose an employee from a large group of people. That makes the one you choose more special than the rest."

"I don't know. I think you work harder at a relationship when you know it's permanent."

Terra agreed. She had always wanted a younger brother. And didn't all those who had lost their mothers wish for their mothers back? She didn't want to get into this line of thought right now. The day was too nice, and they were having too much fun – even Uncle Doug. So she skipped over to Loose, took him by the hand, smiled, and walked back to the adults.

"Let's go to Logger's Run," said Terra.

"I think we should save the water rides 'til the end, so that once we get wet we can run for the car and turn on the heater," stated Uncle Doug. Terra pictured each of them with a hot cup of cocoa.

"Sure," said Loose. "Let's hit some more roller coasters first."

Eventually, they made their way toward Logger's Run. Screams and laughter came from beyond the wall on their left, and a wave splashed over the concrete soaking all but Evangelina who was furthest to the right. Loose cringed. Uncle Doug laughed. Terra squealed, and Evangelina burst into unstoppable laughter, deep and low from her diaphragm. Terra joined in first at a much higher timbre, giving Evangelina a sloppy hug. Loose took a couple of steps beyond where the rest had stopped and then began to chuckle.

"Well," said Uncle Doug, "we might as well just go home since we're already wet."

Terra could tell he was kidding. "Come on, Uncle Doug. Getting wet isn't the goal of taking the water ride. It's more like the payment for a good time."

"I like getting wet," said Loose. "Reminds me of camping by the lake. Those are good memories." But his face saddened.

Evangelina responded quickly. "Well, I haven't gotten wet yet, so I'm feeling a little left out."

Terra snapped her wrist, splashing Evangelina in the face. "We'll just have to work hard to turn the tube your way when we come to a turn."

"Or we could try to tip it over," said Loose, a touch overenthusiastic.

"Look," said Terra, pointing.

"What?" asked Uncle Doug.

"Don't look now," said Evangelina, "but your hair is dripping."

Both Uncle Doug's and Loose's hair dye was running down their necks and onto their foreheads. Evangelina wiped some of the dye from Uncle Doug's forehead to show him.

"I'm kind of enjoying having a blue head."

Evangelina reached for his hand. "I like it too. Now take me on that ride."

Terra was pleased with how playful her uncle was being. This was the person her painting lessons were supposed to bring out. This person had been there all along, waiting to come to life, maybe waiting for someone like Evangelina—whom he called Angel. The nickname seemed appropriate somehow, his own personal Angel, a rescue angel, if there was such a thing.

Loose came up from behind Terra and looped his arm through hers. They skipped together to the line for the ride. This was the second time today she had skipped. It felt right, she felt like skipping. She was happy and carefree. This day seemed to be doing every one of them a world of good.

After the water ride, the breeze had died down and Uncle Doug said, "Let's do the Demon one more time." The temperature was a warm San Francisco seventy.

"But everyone's wet," said Evangelina, though she herself still hadn't a drop on her.

"Aw, come on, man. It'll go real quick and it's right on the way out, man" he whined in a poor imitation of a teenager, maybe one from his own time. He was tugging on Evangelina's sleeve, getting all wiggly, shuffling in place like he was about to wet his pants.

"Boy, what some people won't do to get their way," said Terra, laughing as they headed for the last rollercoaster of the day.

Uncle Doug walked up to Loose and placed his arm across his shoulders. He whispered into Loose's ear so softly that Terra could not hear what he said. They shrugged at each other and then grinned conspiratorially. Suddenly Loose and her uncle ran ahead, racing each other, two blue heads bobbing in and out of the crowd.

Terra's heart lifted even further at seeing the two of them getting along so well, especially after such a rocky beginning. "You guys go on and we'll meet you at the front gate." They waved back at her to confirm that they had heard, two boys caught up in a good time.

20

As the Demon came into view, Doug and Loose slowed to
a power walk. The crowd around them was thinning out in the
late afternoon. Doug looked over his shoulder and said, "I guess
we left the girls behind."

"Yep," agreed Loose.

"Just you and me."

Loose looked up at him. "Uh-huh."

"The Boys!" Doug announced.

Loose nodded.

Doug tossed his hands to the sky and twirled in a circle,
shaking his hands in the air. "Now, let's see; what trouble can we
get into. You like riding in the front?"

"Of course. It's our destiny."

As they approached the end of the line, Doug grabbed
Loose's arm and brought them to a stop. Before them were three
girls clustered together who must have been the same age as
Loose. Doug leaned in close and whispered to Loose. "You like
girls?"

Loose gave him an insulted, almost angry look. Doug had
not seen Loose react to him this way since they had been at
Loose's van and the boy had questioned his motivation for paying

for the new apartment. The moment was awkward but Doug quickly recovered, punching Loose in the arm and chuckling.

"Stupid question, huh?"

Loose smiled and nodded, the catastrophe avoided. They took their place in line behind the girls. Doug nudged Loose's shoulder with his elbow trying to coerce the boy into saying something to the girls. Loose shoved him back with both hands, but with a huge grin on his face. Doug laughed.

One of the girls glanced at them, then at their blue hair. They began to giggle.

"Bet you I can scream louder than you," Doug challenged his partner.

"No way," Loose responded, looking incredulous, puffing up his machismo. The three girls looked at them again, listening.

Now they were at the head of the line, only the girls before them, waiting for the next coaster to arrive.

Doug asked them, "You plan on riding in the front?"

All three girls looked at each other and then shook their heads in unison.

"Naw," one said. "We like the back." And they all began an enthusiastic nod in agreement.

"This is Loose." He tossed his head the boy's direction. "I'm Doug."

There was a moment's pause before one of them said, "Hi," and then hurried off.

Doug watched them as they hustled to the rear, play-fighting for who would have to sit alone in the second to last row. So, Doug and Loose got their wish; shoving each other and laughing, they entered the front seat, first Loose and then Doug.

"You don't have to be introducing me to girls," Loose said shyly but obviously not offended.

"I wasn't doing anything. Just being friendly."

The car jerked forward as it engaged.

"I'm telling Evangelina," Loose said jokingly.

"Come now; those girls are a little young for me." Doug laughed as the rollercoaster shook its way forward up the ramp. They both held their arms in the air. Though they were still damp from the prior ride, the mist up through the tunnel made the skin on their arms and faces tingle.

And then they were at the top, looking over the edge, hanging until the rest of the train could reach the cusp. The waiting was filled with the anticipation of the rush to come. As the car released and accelerated each looked at the other and screamed. At the bottom of the first curve Doug whooped; Loose smiled and then they screamed again as they went upside down through a loop, twisting to the right. Doug always had the fear that his raised hands would hit the structure, but they never did.

Doug glanced at Loose's blue hair, vibrant in the wind, translucent from the late sunlight. He almost appeared doll-like, or cartoonish, animated.

"Weeeeeee," Loose squealed.

"Yippee," Doug hollered back.

As they banked again to the right Doug nudged Loose hard with his shoulder. When the car turned left, Loose shoved back. This then became part of the game, leaning into each other adding to the centrifugal force. Doug smiled and felt like they were two teenage cohorts, a closeness of two young boys skipping school together. The feeling remained even after the ride had ended.

Loose got off first from the other side from which they entered. He immediately took a stance, holding his hands, palms up, which Doug slapped as he stepped off the ride.

"That was fantastic," said Loose.

"You're one hell of a partner." Doug felt like tossing his hair but resisted and placed his arm around the boy's shoulder instead.

"Is that what I am?"

"You bet."

"In crime?" Loose seemed pleased.

"Why not." They walked down the ramp swaying together. Loose slowly wrapped an arm around Doug's waist. Doug remembered a walk he'd seen when he was young on reruns of an old TV show called "The Monkees," about a British Pop band. First they would step in unison, way to the left, and then they'd step far to the right, having to bring the right foot over their fellows' far-stretched left leg. Then again with the left stepping over the right leg. Loose learned quickly, and soon the two were jostling crab-like down the walkway, chuckling and stumbling.

"Do we have to go…back?" Loose asked suddenly as if out of nowhere.

Doug slowed them to a straight walk. Loose released his hold on Doug who brought his arm off the boy's shoulder. Loose stared at his shoes as he shuffled along. Doug watched the boy. He knew what he meant. Loose had nothing to go back to. Doug flashed back to the time, after his parents' divorce, when his sister had decided to stay full time with their mother. He, still moving between his parents' households, had felt abandoned. His sister had been, during the time of the divorce, the one consistency in his life. That was the first time he had felt truly alone. But this feeling could be nothing like what Loose was now feeling, nowhere close.

To Doug, no words came to mind to easily console the boy. He placed a hand on Loose's shoulder bringing them to a standstill. They looked into each other's eyes.

Loose fell against him, clutching him, burying his face in Doug's chest. Doug felt uncomfortable at first, then he raised his hand to the back of Loose's head, petting him, holding him close.

"I want to stay here," whimpered Loose in his arms.

"I know you do," said Doug. And then from deep in his soul he added, "Me too."

The two of them clung to each other as the sun slowly set. Doug held fast until the boy stopped shaking. He leaned back and lifted the boy's face by the chin.

"I'm here, Loose," was all he could say. "I'm here."

Loose tucked himself into Doug's arms again, giving a long hard hug and then released him. He snuffled as he wiped his nose with the back of his hand.

"Better?" Doug asked, knowing in his heart that nothing would make it all right.

Loose nodded.

"The girls are probably wondering what's keeping us. We should get going."

Loose shrugged his shoulders. "Okay."

Doug took a step forward, poised like a runner at a track meet. "Last one there is a rotten egg," he shouted and took off.

21

After spending about twenty minutes at Loose's new apartment, getting him comfortable in his new surroundings, the three of them left him to his new life, which still included homework.

Evangelina watched from the passenger seat as Doug pulled his car up to the curb in front of his place and looked over his shoulder at Terra in the back seat.

Terra shrugged and asked, "What? You're not coming in?"

"I thought the two of us," he said, glancing at Evangelina beside him, "might go get something to eat."

Evangelina looked back at him in mock surprise, but didn't say a word, wondering what he might have in mind.

"Okay, then," Terra said. She opened the door, but hesitated. "Uncle Doug?"

"Yeah."

"Thanks. Both of you. For everything."

"It was a good day, wasn't it?" said Evangelina, turning all the way around to look Terra in the eyes.

"It most certainly was."

"Bug?" said Doug. Evangelina noticed that Terra didn't cringe at the use of her nickname. Before Terra could respond, he continued by saying, "Could you feed and give Constant a walk?"

"My pleasure." She climbed out of the door, then leaned back in to grab her knapsack off of the seat. "'Night."

Evangelina sat with her hands in her lap staring out at the street. A motorcycle passed loudly, revving its engine right by Doug's door. She looked at Doug.

"The girl is dying," she said.

"Who?"

"The high school girl in the ICU. The one I told you about. The one in the motorcycle accident."

"Oh. I guess she doesn't stand much of a chance."

"No, she doesn't; too much broken inside." She kept her eyes on Doug. "There are so many people hanging around, family, friends from her school, all in shock. They just can't believe it." She turned her head and watched the motorcycle merge into traffic. "That must be almost the worst thing in the world, having a child die so young, and so violently too, so much pain."

"Yeah. The only thing you could wish for is that she never gains consciousness enough to feel it."

Evangelina started to think of Mama and decided to change the subject. Why had she brought this up anyhow? It was so hard to keep her mind from returning to her mother. Everything reminded her. The only way to avoid it was to just do the next thing. "So what's this all about?"

Doug put the car in gear but didn't take off yet. "Huh?"

"Dinner."

He stared at her. "You think I have some ulterior motive?"

She raised her eyebrows. She had a habit of making quick judgments of people, even through small talk, and then having a hard time letting go of those opinions even when they proved wrong. Doug was a successful businessman, and everyone knew that powerful people were most likely corrupt. How else could they have gotten so successful? They manipulated everyone to their own benefit. Still, she found it difficult to categorize Doug. Her instincts told her what he must be capable of, yet she wanted to believe that he was helping Loose from his heart, that he was a good person. Could he be helping Loose just to get to her?

Doug said, "Actually, I do. There's something I want to ask you over dinner."

She crossed her arms and waited.

"Okay, okay, okay. I want to do this over dinner. I'm going to ask you to be my girlfriend. Not now, but during dinner. When I ask, then you can respond."

She was dumbstruck momentarily and then she laughed. It was difficult to take him seriously, with his blue hair glowing in the light from the setting sun. "You're silly." It was strange that he would tell her what he was going to ask her and then pretend that he hadn't asked her yet. Doug was still in a playful mood from the day's activities. That he would even want to ask her this question instead of just letting it happen seemed very juvenile, very high-school-ish. Maybe he was going to ask her to "go steady." Maybe give her an ID bracelet with his name on it.

She laughed again. "All right, let's have dinner. But I'll make us something at my place." As he pulled the car from the curb, she gave him directions there.

How would she answer his question? She couldn't decide. It was making her nervous thinking about it.

After placing some rice in the cooker, she went to the refrigerator and removed a bowl of leftovers covered with some clear cling wrap. Doug was watching over her shoulder.

"What's that?" he asked.

"Short rib adobo."

"Looks good. Filipino?"

"It's a recipe I learned from Mama, but hers always tastes better than mine."

She looked at him, noticing the blue streaks running down the sides of his face. While the adobo heated on the stove, she went to the bathroom, got a washcloth, and ran it under the faucet. She got Doug to sit in one of the kitchen chairs and then wiped his face and the back of his neck, the white cloth turning blue. His eyes seemed to glow. Maybe the blue of his hair set off the blue of his eyes. A deep beautiful blue. Though she had been in America since she was a little girl, she found herself surrounded by Filipinos, family and their friends. They all had brown eyes. Of course she had seen blue ones before, but never this close. Even so, Doug's seemed to be special. She found herself staring while holding the towel aloft. He was watching her with amusement. She turned away feeling self-conscious.

When the rice was done, she gathered plates, placed flatware on the counter, and said, "Help yourself." She waited for him to fill his plate before taking hers. She scooped out some of the sauce and poured it over his rice first and then her own.

He watched her as she used her fork and knife to scrape the meat from the bones. It made her wonder what he would do. Most people just used their fingers to eat the ribs. She watched as Doug finally decided to try imitating her by using his fork, but the ribs in the sauce just slipped out from under the pressure. Evangelina stifled a laugh, and then continued preparing her meat while glancing up at him.

Doug shrugged in defeat. He chomped down on a rib, getting sauce over his fingers and face. He smiled like a guilty child, sucked the fingers clean on his right hand, and used his fork to follow with some rice.

Once she removed the meat and stacked the bones in a neat pile on the edge of her plate, Evangelina took her first bite of the meal. The meat was tender and flaky, and the rice was moist. She had been worried because she was serving leftovers, but everything was good. Even the potatoes and beans were still firm, not sloppy and overcooked.

"This is wonderful. I've never had this sauce before. What do you call it again?"

"Short rib adobo. The word is Tagalog. That's the native language of the Philippines."

"It sounds a little like Spanish."

Evangelina was always a touch insulted by the comparison, even though it was true. It did sound like Spanish pronounced in the sing-song way of Chinese. Maybe it was a cultural thing, not wanting to be compared to the Spanish, nor to the Chinese for that matter. Yes, Filipinos are Asian and proud of it, but they aren't Chinese.

"Do you always eat with a knife and fork?" he asked.

"Yes, even chicken."

"Chicken?"

"Yes, chicken." She held her fingers aloft and wriggled them in the air showing Doug how clean they were. He looked at his own covered in thick sauce and he exaggerated a frown and raised one eyebrow. She smiled.

Doug was being silly. Evangelina liked that about him. It was a surprise. Who would have thought a man in his position would have such a sense of humor. Because it was unexpected, it became even more endearing, like a devious grin on a child. She laughed just thinking about it.

"What?" he asked.

"Nothing."

"Come on."

Smiling and peeking at him from the corner of her eye, she said, "You."

"Me?"

"You're silly."

"I am?"

"You are."

"I never thought of myself as silly."

"Really?"

"Goofy, maybe. I always liked Goofy," Doug said.

"As in Mickey Mouse?"

"Yeah." He licked his fingers and ate some more rice.

Evangelina took a few bites herself before she said, "Pluto's my favorite. I used to have a t-shirt with his picture. I wonder what happened to it."

"Did you ever notice that Pluto is the only one that's an animal?"

"They're all animals."

"But Pluto acts like an animal. He's Mickey's pet. And he doesn't talk. He barks."

"I guess that's true. I never thought about it before. Are you sure that all the rest of the Disney animals talk?"

"Pretty sure. That's why he was always my favorite."

"Yours too?"

"Yep."

It was such a silly thing to have in common, but nonetheless Evangelina found it enticing. It made her mind wander. They finished the meal in silence. He helped her clear the table and then he rinsed while she placed the dishes in the dishwasher. As he handed her a plate he held on to it and leaned over and tried to kiss her on the lips. She pulled away without moving her feet. When he released the plate, she swayed forward and gave him a quick peck, then bent hurriedly to put the last of the dirty dishes into the dishwasher.

She knew that the moment had arrived, and she tried to ignore it. But it was too awkward to ignore. She put dish soap in the washer and closed the door, setting the dials. She stood there before him waiting. She forced herself not to think of what she was about to say, dreading this moment. She didn't want to hurt him.

Doug fumbled with the cabinet under the sink and threw their paper towels away, first dropping them on the floor and finally getting them into the trash basket. He dried his hands nervously on a dishrag and stared at her. He tried to smile, but his face kept sliding into seriousness. She'd never seen him this clumsy, though she'd noticed him get self-conscious like this the first time she'd met him in his office. She figured he'd be smooth with women and it made her wonder if this was a unique experience for him. She wanted to believe it, that somehow *she* made him this way. That she was different somehow from all the others – and she was sure there had been plenty of others.

Doug took her hand in his and bent one knee in a parody of kneeling. He smiled when he said, "Angel, will you be my girlfriend." It looked as if he was proud of himself for simply asking the question, yet his hands were shaking with the seriousness of the situation.

Evangelina held her breath for about ten seconds and then released. "You're a lot different than I expected." That seemed like a dumb thing to say, but it just slipped out. She hadn't wanted

183

to like him. She had actually fought against it. But he had endeared himself to her in so many ways.

"Different? Is that good or bad?"

"Oh, it's a good different. I really like you." And she could feel him cringe as if waiting for her to say, "But not that way." She *did* like him that way, though. "I don't want to hurt you."

"I sort of hate to admit it, but I've changed since I met you. I've changed because of you. Not because I wanted to impress you, but because you made me feel like I could be a better person."

Doug wasn't making this any easier. He was ignoring the implications of where this was leading. He was forging ahead.

She talked before he could say anything else. "It's complicated right now. I don't have the time for a relationship." It wouldn't be fair to him. She wouldn't be able to give him the attention he deserved. "Mama needs me now more than ever." She pulled her hand free and moved to the table. Doug followed and sat beside her.

"I don't plan on making it harder for you. I should actually be there to help, to make it easier on you."

Doug just wasn't getting it; she could tell. It wasn't that he wouldn't be good for her; it was that she needed to give all she had to her mama. She had nothing left to give him. It just wouldn't be fair. He deserved more than that. She wouldn't be able to stand that. It would make her feel as if she were failing him. She just couldn't do it. She found herself shaking her head, staring at the table.

What came out of her mouth wasn't quite on point, but it wasn't gibberish either. It was connected even if she didn't quite know how. She was still trying to make him understand. "I was her baby," she said, "the youngest. I was special. She always told me that. From the moments I first remember, it was Mama and me. All the other kids by then had moved out, so Mama and I lived alone, together, the two of us, first in the Philippines, and then here in America. We were family. We were what I grew up with. And now she's leaving."

"I was the youngest of my family too," Doug said.

At first Evangelina had trouble coming out of her reverie and understanding what Doug had just said. Then she realized it was another thing the two of them had in common, both being the baby of the family.

"Is your mother alive?"

"No. My only sibling died too, my sister. She took her own life. She was Bug's mom."

"I'm sorry." There was a pregnant pause and finally Evangelina struggled to fill it. "Terra must miss her badly."

"Yes, I think somehow she blames herself."

"How?"

"It was pretty bad. My sister blamed her with her last words."

"You're kidding."

"No, that's the truth. Terrible, but true."

"That *is* terrible. Who could do that to her own child?" Although Evangelina was quite interested in the change of subject, she was a touch overly enthusiastic in the change itself. She was unrealistically hoping for it not to return to the relationship between them. But Doug didn't seem to notice.

"My sister was a very vindictive person. Though, without trying to defend her, I like to remember that she was drugged out at the time. Her internal system was shutting down. She was dying." He wiggled in his seat, looking uncomfortable talking about it.

"What about your father?"

Doug looked up at her when he said, "We're distant. We don't talk much. When we do, it's about money."

"Oh. I take it you weren't born into money."

"Didn't I mention that already?"

She shook her head.

"I thought I did. Anyway, no, we didn't have any money. My dad built the house I originally grew up in, before my parents divorced. And he wasn't all that great a builder. It was more of a cabin really, two bedrooms, outhouse with a hand pump outside. I didn't even learn the trade from him, though maybe a little from his mistakes. He could never hold a job for very long, always looking for some get-rich-quick scheme. He drove me crazy. He's still looking. I kind of avoid having conversations with him."

"That's too bad. I think family is very important." The silence after that sentence was quite poignant. They had already talked about family and its importance earlier this afternoon.

Doug shifted uncomfortably again. "I'm beginning to feel that way with Bug, as though she were my last chance."

"It did feel like one big family today, didn't it?"

"Yes it did. Loose sure seems like a nice kid."

"I think the day did him a world of good."

"Yep. I like him. I noticed that Bug seems to act like a big sister around him. Something she's never been. Probably good for her too." Evangelina caught herself before she made a comparison of her and Doug being like the parents. That might mean that there was a relationship between them, or the potential of one. But then she noticed she was too late. Doug had already picked up on the inference.

"Listen," said Doug, jumping right back into the topic, "You don't have to make up your mind about us tonight. Give yourself a few days. Think about it. Then give me your answer."

She thought she had already given him an answer, but he obviously didn't like it, so he was ignoring it. She let that slide. She liked Doug; she liked him a lot.

"Well, it's time I should be heading home. Constant's probably wondering what has become of me."

Evangelina thought it cute that he worried about what his dog was thinking. She loved Constant's personality, but she doubted that he could think the kind of thoughts Doug claimed he possessed.

"Okay." She got up from the table and walked him to the door. It seemed like an abrupt end to the evening, an inappropriate end to the long day, but she wasn't sure what else she should say.

Doug opened the door and stood there for a moment, waiting.

Evangelina leaned forward to give him another peck on the lips, but before she knew it, she was putting some weight into it. It was a closed-mouthed kiss, but it lasted a lot longer than she intended. She stayed there enjoying it until he placed his hands on her shoulders and pressed his body against hers. She opened her eyes and saw him staring into hers.

She rested a hand on his chest and gently pushed him away and out the door, closing it behind him without another word. She pivoted on one foot and returned to the kitchen, worried at first about the mixed signals she was giving him. Then she paused in mid-step, a smile slowly spreading across her face.

22

The next morning Doug, while washing the blue dye from his hair, smiled into the stream of water and let it pulse between his teeth. The pressure felt good on his gums. The stinging mist made his lips tingle. He thought about all the different colors he might dye his hair in the future, and decided that next time, he'd choose bright yellow. He was surprised at himself for even thinking of doing so again, but at least for now, it seemed like a good idea. Hadn't it added to the splendor of the day yesterday? It had been the big icebreaker.

He turned up the water temperature as hot as his skin could stand, turned away from the showerhead so the water was running down his back, and touched the tiles in front of his feet with the palms of his hands fifty times, legs kept straight, water warming his kidneys. His leg muscles stretched to a glorious ache, and his back muscles loosened.

After a breakfast of steak and eggs for himself and dry food for Constant, Doug was ready for his day at work. On the steps to the sidewalk outside, he found Loose, appearing nervous and on the verge of crying. Doug sat down beside him without saying a word as Constant ran down the alleyway for his morning constitutional.

Loose didn't look up from his feet. "Terra already left for school. I thought I could get here early enough, but I guess not."

Loose apparently had showered this morning too, the blue no longer in his hair. He looked up from beneath his thin brow at Doug.

"What's up?" asked Doug.

"Homework."

"Having trouble?"

"Math. I shouldn't be having trouble. If I want to be a programmer, this should be my best subject."

"Algebra?" Doug was always good at math.

"Geometry."

"I don't think you need geometry for programming. Though learning to be as thorough as you need to be with a proof is important. But the math itself isn't." Doug got up from the stoop.

Constant was headed their way with a tail wagging. Loose ruffled the mutt and then stood up as well. Constant, waiting for more attention, rubbed against Loose's leg, and then walk around in a circle like a very large cat.

The foot traffic was just building. A young couple with a child of roughly three or four in tow walked past leisurely, as if on a Sunday stroll. The little girl, dressed in a pink cotton dress and patent leather shoes, pulled her hand free from her mother and stopped to stare at Loose. She smiled and Loose returned it. Then the mother called to her and the tiny girl skipped ahead to join her parents, her hands pressed within a fluffy white muff.

Loose watched as they crossed the intersection. He looked up at Doug.

"Well, if we're going to get you to school on time, we better get to work," Doug suggested.

Loose stared up at him, bewildered. "You gonna help?"

"Math is one of my specialties. Come on."

They entered the lobby with Constant following somewhat reluctantly. He was ready for his morning walk and was disconcerted by this break in his routine. Yet he was more than happy to play indoors with Loose. He moved up so that his head would catch Loose's hand as it swayed back and forth.

"You live here?" Loose asked, looking around at the empty lobby.

"Just me and −Terra and her father," Doug caught himself before he used Terra's nickname.

"You all live together?"

"Different apartments."

"Looks like it's abandoned."

"It's a redevelopment that my company is working on. I always like to live in my newest projects. Gives me an opportunity to watch the work as it progresses."

"I been by a few times to see Terra. Never seen any workers. Never been inside though."

"We'll be completing an office building first and then come back to finish this up. What do you think?"

"Looks like an old hotel."

"It does have its charm." Doug looked at Loose as they waited for the elevator door to open. The boy did not seem impressed. But once they were in Doug's place, Loose wandered around in astonishment, touching everything.

"Let's set up on the dining table," Doug said, motioning with his hand toward the heavy dark wood table in the corner of the main room that served as an alcove, an iron chandelier above with fake candles, the bulbs shaped like flames.

"So, you're interested in programming." Doug said it more like a statement than a question, but Loose nodded to confirm it.

"Gaming," he said. "I even have a college picked out in Orlando, but it's probably way too expensive for me. It's private. The website says it's for-profit—whatever that means."

"Well, we'll just have to make sure that your grades are good enough to get you a scholarship. Show me where you're stuck and we'll see what we can do."

Loose looked at Doug with distrust. Doug ignored the expression and motioned for him to pull his books from his knapsack and place his work on the table. Doug rested his walking stick across the arms of the chair at end of the table and rested his suit jacket over the back of it. The chairs were massive, and it took two hands to lift them or scoot them away from the table.

Once they were seated side-by-side, Loose said, "I just can't seem to memorize all these formulas. Even if I could, I never know which one to use."

"Let me take a look." Doug studied the section in the textbook and then turned to the page with the problems. He glanced at the worksheet. Loose had completed the first two, but eight more remained. Before they worked on the actual problems Doug decided to attack this from an intellectual perspective. "All these formulas are really the same, you know."

"What do you mean?"

"You understand algebra, right?"

"Yeah, I'm real good at that. I already took Algebra I."

"Good. Now which of these formulas do you always remember?"

Loose reached for the book and pointed at sin2 + cos2 =1. "That one's easy. We use that one a lot in class."

"You probably know the definition of a tangent, tan = sin/cos, right?"

"Sure."

"Well, if you take both sides of the first equation and multiply it by cos2, what do you get?"

"That would be sin2 over cos2, which is tan2, plus cos2 over cos2, which is 1, equals cos2." And he wrote it down at Doug's urging, tan2 + 1 = cos2. Doug pointed at the same trigonometric function that was dsplayed in the book. Loose was amazed. "Cool."

"You see, all these functions that you use in geometry are interrelated. I always say that all equations with an equal sign are 1 = 1. The questions is always, one what?"

"Huh?"

"Never mind." Doug had the urge to ruffle Loose's hair but remembered how much he had hated that being done to him when he was young, so he stopped himself in time.

Constant got bored with sitting and watching the two and wandered off to the kitchen to see if there was any food left in his bowl. Doug heard him nudge the empty bowl across the wooden floor licking the bottom of it.

Doug helped Loose through the next two problems before he said, "You seem to be doing just fine with these."

"Yeah, I feel I'm getting the hang of it. This is easier than I thought."

"Sometimes when I get stuck, the frustration seems to shut me down. It always seems to help if I just take a break from that problem and move on to the next, to keep the momentum going. Then I can return to the problem that was giving me trouble later. I think my mind is just looking for an excuse to quit."

"Well yeah, sometimes homework is a real pain in the..." Loose didn't finish his sentence. He stared down at the table with a guilty expression. "Oops," he said and Doug laughed, wanting once again to ruffle his hair. Loose smiled back, but then his expression seemed to darken. "My dad used to get upset with me about homework. Procrastination, he said, was my downfall. Those were his words. He said that by the time I got to it, what little time was left put too much pressure on me."

Doug thought about how things built up. He had long ago learned to do things when he first thought about them, otherwise he would turn around and there would be too many things to get done in too little time.

"Your dad was a smart man."

"Yeah, I guess so."

Doug knew where this was leading and didn't want Loose to break down; he didn't know if he knew how to deal with it if he did. Loose's father had just died and any reminder of his father seemed to be only a shadow cast over his life. Other people's emotional responses had always been too much for Doug, making him feel uncomfortable or inadequate. At times it even made him resentful. How dare they put him in such an awkward position? But this time he only wanted to help, and knew that maybe this time, his presence alone was enough. He remembered Loose not wanting to leave Great America yesterday. He wondered how long it would be before Loose would break down, before he really let the pain come out. But it was probably better that the pain came out slowly, a little bit at a time, no more than the boy could handle. He rested his hand on Loose's shoulder and stood up from the table.

He squeezed as he said, "So from now on, we'll just have to take his advice and stay ahead of the game, huh?"

Loose nodded his head without looking up. Doug squeezed again and then patted the shoulder two times before letting go.

"Anytime you need help with your homework," said Doug, "You just give me a call." Doug pulled a business card from his pocket and laid it on the table, which felt too impersonal somehow. This wasn't like a business deal. This was much more than that. "That there is my cell number," he pointed. "Call me any time; even if you just want to talk." Loose sniffled but again did not look up and only nodded. "You work on the rest of those problems. I got some work to do, bills to pay." Loose nodded again and sat up at little straighter in the dark oak chair.

Doug went across the room and turned on the computer on his desk. First he sent an e-mail to Jasmine notifying her that he would be a touch late to the office. Then he opened his Quicken program and entered a few bills.

He glanced at Loose slouched over the massive table busily scratching away.

And he thought about Angel and what the opportunity last night seemed to hold, smiling to himself over his audacity at asking her to be his girlfriend. It seemed so juvenile. Yet it felt so right. He had never proposed that someone be his girl. Sure, he had had girls all his life, but somehow this felt different. He wanted her by his side, not in his bed. Well, in his bed too, but not *just* in his bed. He imagined her there in all the facets of his life. Sharing all he had to share and being a part of her life too and wondering what that might entail.

He continued to watch Loose as he thought about what children he and Angel might have together. It was a strange thought that appeared as if out of nowhere. He followed the train easily to the point where he could envision himself with an infant child, rolling on the floor giggling as Angel looked on, joining in the laughter. He wondered if work would feel different if he knew he was working to make their lives together better and planning the future of their child. What would it be like to pass on not only his genes but a legacy of sorts, an empire, a world that Angel and he would create to keep their child safe and happy.

Amazingly, this vision came naturally to him. As if it were his goal all along – a wife and child.

His head rested on his hand while Loose worked diligently.

The problem was that Angel said she didn't want to be his girlfriend. But that was because she as yet didn't realize what good he could do for her. He needed to prove how he might help her through these troubled times, how he could be an asset rather than a liability. Someone who could help and comfort her. For what seemed like the first time in his life, he wondered how he might be of service to another and this felt good.

Doug laughed aloud, and Loose looked up from his math. Doug nodded and Loose went back to work, smiling. Very shortly thereafter, Loose dropped his pencil loudly on the table and stretched. He stood, raising his hands above his head, arching his back.

"Done already?"

"Yep."

"And without even having to ask for any more help."

"Seems like it got easier overnight. Simpler today."

"Yeah, well, like I was saying, sometimes our brains just get overloaded and need a break." Doug printed out three checks and stuffed them into envelopes as Loose sat next to Constant and scratched under the dog's chin and throat. Doug watched and thought about how a boy needed a dog, a constant companion, a buddy. But Loose's apartment was no place to raise a dog. This made Doug wonder how long it would be before the authorities came to claim Loose and pack him off in the guise of taking care of him. If they did, could he do anything about it? Obviously, it was just a matter of time before the Department of Human Services found out about Loose. Could Doug get in trouble for helping Loose, for putting him in an apartment? Was he doing something illegal? Getting up from his desk and turning off his computer, Doug said, "Time you got to school."

"If I hurry, I'll be only a few minutes late. Maybe Mrs. Rasky won't mark me tardy. Get too many tardies and they drop your grade. Three tardies and they drop your grade like from an A to an A-."

"You have a lot of them?"

"None. My dad always made sure I got there early."

"Good for him."

Loose appeared forlorn once again. Doug helped him pack up his things. Constant waited impatiently knowing something was up, something was about to happen.

"Listen," said Doug, taking Loose by the shoulders, "you work hard today at school."

Loose nodded, staring into his eyes.

"Your dad would want it that way."

Loose nodded again, tears welling in his eyes. Unexpectedly Loose grasped Doug in a shaky but firm embrace.

At first Doug didn't know what to do, but he knew not to move. Loose needed him there. It felt good to Doug as he wrapped one arm around the boy's shoulders, the other gripping the back of his head. "You make him proud now," Doug said, and he could feel Loose nodding, grinding his face into Doug's chest.

The two of them gathered their things without another word and followed Constant out the door, both uplifted in their own way, and ready to tackle another day.

23

Later, at the office, Doug placed the picture of the four of them from when they had entered the park the day before in a drawer. He still found his blue hair fascinating.

He pulled the file containing Jasmine's project list and placed it on his desk before him. He thought about the manager at the apartment building yesterday and how he had treated his employee, about how badly this had affected Angel. He had no intention of ever appearing that way to her. He would not be able to stand her look of disgust. He wondered if his hard-line management style could be viewed the same way, but he had decided on the spot that he wasn't going to take any chances. He didn't want to be anything like that man.

And sexual harassment? Hell, he'd never stoop so low. He rarely fraternized with employees other than Andy. He stayed away from that scene. He kept the relationships simply business because it was less complicated that way. He even went so far as to have only cityscapes and landscapes on the walls throughout the building so that they could never be misconstrued as provocative. He wanted a nice clean working environment.

Did he treat his employees as human beings first and employees second? Doug had never even thought about it. Was it possible to empathize with them and still make the tough decisions? He expected the best from his employees. He didn't want mediocrity infecting his business. If they worked hard and their production was enough above average, he basically left them alone. Then he was a hands-off manager. But if the production slackened because of lack of effort, he wasn't willing to hold their hands. It was easier just to replace them. Sure, his management team worked hard with the people toward the bottom of the performance scale. Doug believed that by raising the level at the bottom, some would inevitably rise to the top. Of course, there was always the person that worked twice as hard and still couldn't make the grade. Those had always been the hardest for Doug to fire. Wasn't that empathy?

There was a knock on his door and Doug buzzed Jasmine into the inner sanctum. She came in quietly and sat down on her side of the desk, hands folded on her lap holding pen and notepad, her posture perfect.

"I'd like to talk to you about your project list," said Doug, tapping the folder in front of him.

Jasmine lifted her gaze from her lap and smiled at him. "Absolutely, Mister Sirius, but before you do, I'd like to thank you for the glowing review." She pushed her rump a touch further back on her seat. "To tell you the truth, I wasn't expecting it. I wasn't even sure if I'd still have a job. Since this was my first review directly from you, I wasn't sure what to think."

Doug closed his mouth. He knew he had not yet talked to her about her performance. Yet she acted as if he had.

"You liked it, huh?"

"Yes, I already signed it and sent it to HR. I hadn't realized you would want to talk about it too."

Doug gained his composure quickly. "I just wanted to know if you had any questions."

"No, sir, not at this time. As I work my way through my new goals I may have some, though."

"Well, anytime you have a question I'm right here. Now if that's all, don't let me hold you up."

"Thank you again, sir."

Jasmine got up and walked to the door.

"By the way," Doug asked, "How long have you been with the company?"

She hesitated at the oddity of the question, but Doug really didn't know how long she had been there. "Three years now, but less than one reporting to you." She waited for a moment, and when Doug said nothing more, she left.

He opened the folder and glanced at his comments in the margins of her list. He was astounded to find that all his comments were as "glowing" as she had said they were. He'd even written, "I couldn't have done better myself" in one instance. As far as he knew, he'd never said that about anyone else's production. But there it sat before him in his own handwriting! Could this really be happening?

All the strange happenings in the recent past came crashing in on him. Here was proof in his own handwriting that no one was messing with him. There was no great conspiracy.

He was going crazy.

He called Jasmine on his intercom.

"Yes."

"Refresh my memory. When did I give you that review?"

"You handed it to me personally the day after I gave you my progress report, just like you promised."

"Thanks."

"Your ten o'clock appointment has just arrived."

Doug had to untangle his thoughts from the project report on his desk and its implications. The men from the Tenderloin's merchant association were here. "How many this time?"

"The same three, sir."

"Take them to the conference room and offer them coffee or something to drink. I'll be there momentarily."

He had started his day on a high note having had such a wonderful day yesterday. He hadn't even washed the dye out of his hair until this morning, and while he was doing so, he thought he might just want to try that again some day.

Since he had met Angel, his life had begun to change. His attitude was still changing. He was grateful for the opportunity, the time he got to spend with her. Until recently he hadn't really thought that there was something missing from his life. Bug knew the truth, though. She had mentioned it to him often, but he had brushed off her comments as romantic adolescence. The excitement he had felt recently was new for him. He'd never felt better in his life.

Yet, somehow he seemed to be going nuts. The proof sat in the folder in front him. He opened the top drawer of his desk, staring at the prescription bottle there. He hadn't been taking his medication lately. Could both the happiness and the hallucinations be the result of a manic episode? He didn't feel as if he were manic. Yet, euphoria and paranoia were common during mania, and he was experiencing both. Still, he couldn't remember ever hallucinating before. What were these earthquakes he was experiencing?

Doug stood slowly and stretched.

And if it was mania making him feel euphoric...?

He closed the drawer.

"Come on, Buddy," he said to Constant, who crawled out from under the desk. "Let's get this meeting over with."

In the conference room, Constant immediately recognized the three men across the table and wouldn't go to his bed in the corner, instead sitting alert beside Doug's chair. He looked up at Doug and then back at the men as if to say, *I got you covered buddy. Just give me the signal.* Doug rested his hand on his dog's head and rubbed his left ear between his fingers to soothe him and tell him that he understood.

"You gentlemen made the appointment, so it's your show," Doug said as he waved his hand and leaned back in his chair as if to listen casually, even though his nerves were tweaked. He didn't like anything about these people, and he certainly didn't trust them. He didn't even like being in the same room with them, but this was business and he wouldn't let his personal opinion get in the way. He refused to be rude in return, as they had been at their last meeting.

"First of all, Mister Sirius, we came to congratulate you on getting approval for your office building," said the fat man who sat between the other two the same as before. "We see it as the first step toward the improvement of the Tenderloin."

Doug nodded.

"We are also aware that you have purchased the old Grand Hotel on O'Farrell and are planning on turning it into condos. In fact, if we're not mistaken, you already live there yourself."

"And your point is?"

"We would like the opportunity to convince you that you'd be better off keeping it as a hotel rather than making it private residences." The fat man snorted some of the words.

"And how might this be of benefit to the members of your merchants' association?"

"Well now, the cleaning up of the neighborhood—"

"— doesn't depend on whether my building is a condo or hotel," Doug said, finishing the sentence for him. "Let's cut to the chase, gentlemen, and just maybe if you explain some things to me, I might be willing to help. First off, there *is* no association. You're a conglomerate of cheap hotels that cater to hookers and junkies and the homeless. I understand that if my place were a hotel we wouldn't be in competition, different clientele and all. But how could another high-end hotel help your business? That's my question, gentlemen." Doug inflected a touch of sarcasm into the last word.

"Ah, you've been doing some research. Good. Then maybe you already know about the subsidy for the homeless," said the fat man.

Doug remembered just yesterday that the manager at Loose's apartment had mentioned it, though Loose wouldn't qualify because it was technically Doug's apartment. He nodded and said, "A little."

"Understand that our hotels are forced to offer the subsidies based on comps in the district. With the new Hilton and if your building were to stay a hotel, we could probably more than double what we're charging."

Doug leaned forward and pointed at the fat man. "I think I understand. If you are allowed to raise the rent at your hotels, which up until now has been controlled by comps, most of your tenants won't be able to afford their share of the rent. They'll be pushed out onto the streets and probably end up in some other district."

"That's the plan."

This was basically what had happened in the Fillmore during Doug's prior project, but he hadn't purposely done so. It had just been a repercussion of some of the zoning laws he'd helped change.

"And what happens to those people then?"

206

"Though the people in the Bay Area have been sympathetic with the plight of the homeless since so many became so back during the earthquake of 1906, the City itself would like the problem to be swept under the rug, shall we say. Hunter's Point is enough on the outskirts to not be an eyesore. I'm sure they will make fair efforts to move the homeless there. The Tenderloin is in the heart of the City, bordering the Civic Center and the Financial District. The tourism shopping at Union Square stumbles into it."

"Hunter's Point was built on landfill."

"So was the Marina."

"But the Marina isn't toxic."

"I've never heard that the toxic level out by Candlestick Park is any threat to human beings, and frankly, I don't give a damn."

"So I surmised," Doug softly spoke. "I've seen your balance sheet on D&B. You've run out of investment capital. I gather you hope this change will increase property value so that your company can attract more investors."

"Or we might be acquired. Maybe you and your companies might be interested."

Doug thought of Loose and Alphonse. He considered what Angel might do in a similar situation. He wasn't even sure what he was going to say as the words left his lips. "You can take your proposition and your company and shove them where the sun don't shine. I happen to think human life is more valuable than the almighty dollar, especially regarding the profit of scum like you. I'll tell you what I am going to do. I'm going to do everything within my power to stop you. I don't like you, and I sure as shit don't like what you are doing." Though his words were biting, Doug kept his tone level. He stood to leave.

The three men looked at each other and then burst out laughing.

The fat man said, "You're a little late to be stopping us. And look whose calling the kettle black. We're peas in a pod, Mister Sirius. I don't know what makes you think different." The fat man stood before the other two and leaned over the table holding his weight on his knuckles. "Try to stop us. Give it your best shot. In the meantime, we've got other investors interested. You were only a backup plan."

Constant stood and growled loudly. Doug opened the door to leave. He was angry and he didn't like the feeling of losing control. He thought the man was pure bluster. He was hoping they needed him to keep the place where he lived as a hotel. But he wasn't sure. He turned and said, "We'll see how far you get." He let Constant out the door. "And by the way, it's not called Candlestick anymore." When he left, he closed the door behind him and then asked Jasmine to escort the men all the way out of the building.

"They really pissed me off," Doug later said to Andy. "I seriously almost lost it."

"You were considering violence against corrupt people? God forbid." Andy was sitting on the couch paging through the book on the coffee table titled, *Attorneys and other Reptiles*, a book he had given Doug.

Doug sat across the coffee table from Andy in a chair the same color and design as the couch, art deco yellow. "I feel powerless to stop them. Any ideas?"

"What about the historical proposal. You could reinstate it and personally spearhead it up in Sacramento."

"Yeah, right. And what would that do to our project?"

"It definitely wouldn't benefit the company, but there are always other projects we could do. Like I said before, the proposal might be good for the people who live in the neighborhood."

"We're too far along now to turn back. Damn! I wish there was some way to crush them. You should have heard them laugh at me when I said I'd stop them."

Andy turned another page of the book without looking up.

"They even implied that I'm a vulture just like they are."

Andy seemed to be ignoring him.

"Don't tell me you agree with them."

"I plead the fifth."

"Oh, come on."

"Doug, it's not like you have ever been overly concerned about the effect your projects have on others."

Doug thought about Andy's tendency to want to save the whales and hug trees. But Doug wasn't made that way. At times like these, though, it felt as though Andy was trying to be his conscience. "I don't wake up in the morning thinking about who I can fuck today to get ahead, either."

"I didn't say you did. All I said was that you don't spend a whole lot of time thinking about the impact of what you do. You take no responsibility for others. I don't blame you, in a way. You don't go out of your way to hurt anybody, but you don't go out of your way to help anyone, either. I understand. You asked and I gave you my opinion. If you don't like it, find someone who gives you the answer you're looking for."

Doug thought about that. People were responsible for their own lives. That was one of his main truisms. Yet he also believed in teamwork. He preached that the team was more important than the individual. They had to work together to get the job done. But a group was only as strong as its weakest individual. Each one's personal goals must also be met if the team was to succeed. Doug knew this. He used other's goals for motivation. But did he really care one way or the other whether or not these people met their personal goals beyond how it affected the team?

"Okay, I'm sorry. I get it. But I don't make excuses for it. It's the way I am. I believe what I believe. That's the way it is. I do what I do to get things done."

"Still friends?" Andy said half-jokingly.

"Sure, I guess."

24

Seated in the Franciscan Crab House at Fisherman's Wharf with the late-morning sunlight angling over Angel's shoulders, Doug enjoyed the view of her as he placed another spoonful of crab chowder in his mouth. The two of them were eating an early lunch on the second tier. The windows faced Alcatraz, but the view across the table was much more enticing. He couldn't help smiling like a loon.

"What?" Angel asked.

"Nothing." The sunlight radiated through her hair, casting shadows into the hollows of her face. "Just enjoying the moment. I feel wonderful. You look so beautiful today."

"Does that mean that I didn't yesterday?"

A moment passed before he realized she was kidding. "Well, now that you mention it..."

Angel reached across the table and socked him in the arm. "Watch out! You're playing with a woman's vanity. You wouldn't want to experience 'Evangelina's Wrath' quite so early in our relationship."

"Heaven forbid."

She finished the last of her oysters in lobster sauce, smiling as she swallowed, raising her chin ever so slightly, cocking her head at three quarters profile. Her eyes were staring at him from the corners.

"Keep it up," Doug said, "and pretty soon you'll have a drooling idiot on your hands. You make it very difficult for me to keep my composure. I'm a man of the world, I'll have you know."

"Really?"

"Yes, really. I should be debonair, somewhat aloof, forcing you to struggle for my attention."

"Really?"

"Can't you just feel the draw of my masculinity?"

Angel coughed twice and rolled her eyes to the ceiling. "I think you have this little scenario backwards. Who will be vying for whose attention?" She turned to face the window, as if ignoring him.

The waiter appeared with their entrees asking if Evangelina would like more wine. She declined, but Doug asked for another diet cola.

"My youngest sister called me this morning."

"How much younger is she than you?"

"Oh no, I'm the youngest in the family, remember? She just happens to be the closest to my age."

"Okay then, how much older is she than you?"

Evangelina paused to take a bite. After she swallowed she said, "Twelve years."

"Wow. And you have two more sisters?"

"And three brothers, two of whom are dead. But anyhow, she called me from jail."

"Jail?"

"For embezzlement. She was asking for twenty-five thousand as a down payment to the bail bondsman. I refused."

"You're just going to let her sit in jail?"

"Everyone knows my sister has a money problem. She's borrowed money from everyone in the family. I have no idea where all the money goes, but she's always in trouble. It doesn't surprise me. Maybe this will teach her a lesson, snap her out of it."

"You're doing the right thing. I've always believed that people should live with their own consequences. We shouldn't do for others what they should be doing for themselves. What's the old saying? If you carry your child for fear of them falling, they'll never learn to walk."

"She makes me so angry," Angel said, wiggling in her seat. Doug got the sense that she was a very private person, and he considered it a compliment that she was sharing this with him. "Not just because of her behavior regarding money. She tried to make me feel guilty for not helping her. She brought up times she had helped me, but I never asked for her help. I never needed it. I pull my own weight. She's done some minor things for me over the years, but I've done much more for her."

Tears welled in Angel's eyes. "I lent her a ton of money to get a new car and it turned out to be a lie. She didn't need a new car. Her husband told me so. I still don't know what she did with that money."

"I don't know why it is," Doug mused, "but people always want to make you the bad guy when you don't do them a favor, as if it isn't a favor but an obligation. I guess maybe they need to blame somebody for their own predicament."

"I just don't know how to feel. I'm angry at her for making me feel this way."

"Anger seems to be our default emotion. We choose it over being hurt. It's okay to be hurt. Empathy in and of itself is enough." Doug wondered where that thought came from. Did he actually practice it?

For a moment, neither of them said anything. Then Doug said, "That was a wonderful time at Great America."

"I really enjoyed myself. I didn't know you could be so playful, so childlike. You know, Mama took me there shortly after my father died. Papa always loved roller coasters, so we pretended he was with us and we were sending his spirit to heaven. Filipinos believe the spirit lingers on Earth for three days after death. It's up to the survivors to set the spirit free, so that's what we did. We laughed and giggled to show Papa that we were okay, that he could leave peacefully, that he didn't have to worry about us."

"That's wonderful."

"Yes it was. We lived in the Fillmore at the time—"

"Really, where? I used to live in the Fillmore."

"On Beideman Street."

"What a coincidence. I'm surprised we never met before."

"What do you mean?"

"Do you remember how they used to move those old Victorians around on flatbeds in the middle of the night."

214

"You mean like trucks?"

"Yeah, big flatbeds."

"Is that how they did that?"

"They'd jack them up onto wooden platforms during the day. At night I'd stay up late to watch. It would take forever to get them onto the truck. Then they had to pull them out straight to avoid hitting the adjacent buildings. Gods, it was amazing to watch those three-story buildings move down the street. You could imagine one of them toppling over."

The memory of it brought back so many feelings for Doug, the excitement, the achievement. Rarely had Doug experienced something so majestic as those buildings rolling down the street in the dark. He caught himself staring out the window at Alcatraz, though in his mind's eye, he was picturing the old Victorians being trucked down the city streets.

He looked over at Angel, and saw her head down, staring at her plate, her hands in her lap.

"What's wrong?" he asked.

"I just remember waking up every morning to find another home gone."

Doug was astonished. In his excitement, he hadn't noticed her reaction to his memory. How could their reactions to the same thing be so totally different?

"It was very sad to watch," she added.

Doug had thought it had been glorious, a telltale sign of man's achievements, a foreshadowing of better things to come.

"That was the community I grew up in," she said so softly Doug almost missed it. "I watched it get destroyed. Piece by piece, it was slowly dismantled. There was nothing we could do."

"But it was replaced by that beautiful complex." Even to him, this sounded weak in the wake of her sadness.

"Beautiful? That monstrosity?" she asked, gently placing her napkin from her lap to the table beside her unfinished meal. Her hand shook ever so slightly. She immediately withdrew it back beneath the table. Doug was astounded at the turn of events, the emotional charge her simple movement conveyed.

Doug felt his blood pressure raise at this attack on his "first child." Before he could think about what he was doing, he took a stand. "I'm the guy who built that complex on Beideman."

"Don't even joke about that." Angel's hands were shaking violently as she raised them to fiddle with her flatware on the table, knuckles white, as if she were about to use them as weapons.

"What's wrong?" Doug reached across his own plate to try to take her hand, but she refused. "What's the matter?" He reached again toward her hand, but the table suddenly seemed to put a long distance between them.

"How could you? Tell me you didn't."

"What are you talking about? It's beautiful. I'm proud of it. It was my very first development. Why don't you like it? What's not to like?"

"That...development...forced Mama from her home. You took our home away."

216

"But I—"

"Tell me you're kidding, Doug."

He then realized the hole he had dug for himself. If only he had not told her. But he couldn't take back what he'd already said. He could find nothing to say, no way out of this situation.

She looked at him but could not keep her eyes on his, as though it hurt her to do so. "How could you be so cruel? Don't you think of anything but money? I can't believe that was really you." She was imploring him to take it back, to deny that it had actually been him.

All he could do was move forward. "But it improved the whole district. Everything got upgraded after that." He couldn't stop himself from defending his actions, though he already knew that she didn't want to hear it.

Angel stood and wrapped herself in her coat. "And you made it unaffordable for those who lived there, thank you very much," she said sharply. "You ruined our home, Doug Sirius."

With that, she turned and left.

"But I..." Doug said, not able to save himself. He watched his Angel flying away. She walked down the stairs to the street. He wanted to pursue her, but he knew there was nothing he could say.

Against the clatter of dishware and what seemed like intentionally hushed voices, words again came to mind from the Hendrix tune "Angel."

Fly on my sweet angel

Fly on to the sky

Fly on my sweet angel

Forever I will be by your side

Unbidden, tears came to his eyes, which he quickly wiped away with his napkin. He looked around the restaurant. The others around had not taken notice of Angel's leaving. Doug wondered at how life kept moving on around him. How could something in his past, something he had been so proud of for so long, suddenly have such a terrible effect on his life? It was as if in a moment the past had changed. But that wasn't true, was it? Only his perspective had changed. Just minutes ago, his world had been so good; it had recently been getting so much better. But the universe itself was laughing at him, showing him that no matter how hard he tried, he would lose in the end. He thought about his words to Angel just last night about how he wanted to be an asset in her time of need. Now the truth came out. He was worthless. More than worthless, he was the enemy, the destroyer.

He looked at the white of the fake marble tabletop then waved angrily to the waiter for the bill. The anger came naturally. It was him against the world, and he was bound and determined to prove the world wrong. If the universe wanted a battle, he'd give it one. Hadn't that been what he'd done all his life, fighting against the odds? His shoulders involuntarily slumped with the thought, but his anger didn't subside.

25

"I don't care what it takes. I want that demolition to happen first thing tomorrow morning," Doug demanded from Jack. He was in a fighting mood.

"Okay, okay, simmer down. I'll get it done." Jack probably knew from Doug's tone of voice that this was non-negotiable. He didn't even offer his own opinion, as he usually did.

After Jack signed off, Doug held the receiver in his hand standing behind his desk at the office. He breathed with determination. As Doug placed the phone down, the room shook and swayed, knocking him to his chair, which tipped over sideways to the floor. When Doug opened his eyes, Constant crawled over and licked his face. The only sound he heard was Constant's shallow breathing. He sat up and scooted his butt over to the wall and leaned against it.

The room still swayed, but the earthquake was over. It had been the biggest earthquake Doug had ever felt. A wind sounded against the wall of glass to his right, a gale howling. When the swaying ceased, Doug crawled on hands and knees back to the desk with Constant alongside him. As he pressed the intercom, the wind died abruptly.

"Yes, Mister Sirius?" Jasmine answered.

"Are you okay? Is there any damage out there on the floor?"

"Damage, sir?"

Doug got to his feet. Constant sat leaning against his left leg, looking around the room.

"From the earthquake, dammit!"

There was a pause, then timidly Jasmine said, "I'm sorry, Mister Sirius. I don't understand."

"Are you telling me you didn't just feel a gigantic earthquake out there?"

Another pause. "No, sir."

Doug slammed his hand on the off button of the intercom. "What the hell is going on around here? You felt that, didn't you?" he said to his dog, who only looked up at him. "Well? Say something." Yet, he knew full well that his dog had felt it by the way he was acting. But why hadn't Jasmine? Nothing but the chair was knocked over, and he had knocked that over himself while falling.. More things should have moved during a quake so strong.

This wasn't the first time this had happened – and each time the quakes had gotten stronger.

Doug picked up the chair and sat down. Constant stayed beside him. On his desk sat the empty box from Angel's mama. After what he'd done to her life, why had she sent him the empty box? Doug rolled the chair closer to the phone and called Angel's number again, but once more there was no answer. This was the bad part of caller ID. Angel knew it was he who was calling and would not answer by mistake. She was angry, and he wondered if she was ever going to forgive him. Not that he felt that he had done anything to be forgiven for. What had happened was a side effect. Still, Doug had finally found a woman who could keep up with him intellectually, who was emotionally stable, only to lose her before the relationship even started.

He wasn't about to give up so easily. He decided to swing by the soup kitchen on his way home. With Constant beside him, Doug stood on the sidewalk peering in, but Angel wasn't there. Maybe this wasn't one of her evenings to volunteer. When he was leaving, he saw Alphonse walking toward him down the street, glasses askew, and hair tufted in a circle around the crown of his head.

"Beautiful fall day, isn't it?" Alphonse said as he shook Doug's hand.

"I suppose," said Doug, disengaged.

Constant sniffed the old man's hand.

"Reminds me of when I was a young whipper-snapper before my father passed away. He used to gather all the leaves in a pile and us young ones would jump from a ladder into the heart of it. Good memories." Alphonse's southern accent was seeping into his voice. "He was a good man. Used to wrestle with us kids when he got home from work. We'd hang from his curled arms or ride him like a horse. Wonderful man. Died when I was in the sixth grade. Yet my memories of him are like they happened yesterday. Speaking of fathers, how's Loose been?"

Doug's father was still alive, yet his memories weren't as clear, and certainly not as favorable. No crawling around on all fours with his children, no leaf piles that Doug could recall. Nothing.

"Haven't you seen him around today?" asked Doug.

"Noooo. Went by his van, but it wasn't there anymore."

"We got an apartment for him. The van's in a parking garage next door." Doug gave him the name of the place and address. "I was sort of hoping you would keep an eye on him."

"Oh, I plan on it. And thanks for the address. But how'd he afford a place of his own?" Alphonse sat down on the curb and waved for Doug to join him. Constant snuck under one of his arms and set his butt on the concrete, front paws resting right on the edge.

"Well," Doug sputtered, not really wanting to take credit for Loose's apartment, not in the mood to toot his own horn, not in the mood to talk at all.

"You didn't." One hand resting over Constant's sloping shoulder, Alphonse dragged the other through his wispy hair. He smiled a crooked smile and looked up through his askew glasses. "You did, didn't you?"

"Well, yeah." After considering the effect of the filthy concrete on his suit and then throwing caution to the winds, Doug placed himself carefully on the curb close to Alphonse, Constant on the opposite side. "I helped him with his math this morning before school. He's a bright kid."

Alphonse seemed to be sizing Doug up and down, maybe changing his evaluation of him. "Loose *is* a good kid. Yes, and

222

bright too. Doesn't deserve what he got: both parents. Now that's a shame. Boy needs a family. I guess that's you and me now."

Doug thought about Alphonse as the wise grandfather and himself the father, with Bug the sister. It was a commitment he knew he would fulfill. Maybe he couldn't replace Loose's father – and come to think of it, he really didn't want to – but he could be a fatherly figure. Hadn't he already felt that way toward Bug? Hunt wasn't quite the ideal fatherly figure so hadn't the role fallen to him? And even though Doug would be busy during the workdays, while Loose was out on the streets, Alphonse could cover for him.

Doug said, "We'll make a great tag team."

Alphonse smiled broadly. "Sounds like a deal to me." He paused to consider, stroking the dog's head. "Not all of us street people are what we appear to be. We're not just worthless dregs."

Doug looked at the tattered old man and remembered how children had surrounded him, and how he'd taken the time to teach them, to tell them stories. "I never said they were."

"Hush, now," Alphonse interrupted. "Listen, I grew up on the outskirts of Atlanta. Every year there, the big event was the county fair. And us young ones would sneak in for free by picking up a branch and following alongside the animals being herded in, switching the beasts with a stick. It was a grand time, the annual fair." Alphonse laughed, which set him to a coughing fit. When he recovered he patted Constant on the head and then resumed talking.

223

"There was this crotchety old man who always had the largest watermelons. Always won first prize.

"One year, my brother and I got it into our heads that we would steal the largest watermelon from his patch directly before the fair. Now, every child knew that this man was mean, maybe even a witch or warlock or what have you. But that just made it all the more enticing to my brother and me. We couldn't resist, you see. The temptation was too great. We were just boys, you know, country boys with spirit, full of spit and vinegar, longing for adventure. And there had always been talk between all the children around, daring each other to take a watermelon from under this devil's nose. Many claimed they did, but none had come back with the prize.

"Like the proverbial haunted house in every small town, gossip alone about this place could send shivers down our spines. There were stories upon stories about the wickedness of this old man, alone and stewing and conjuring spells on those who dared cross his path. And each story would build upon the next or arguments would ensue about what was true and what was a lie. The shotgun that leaned against the rail of his porch, how many had it killed, that sort of thing. Stories that took on a life of their own and traveled with the wind from one end of the county to the other."

Alphonse's voice became eerily soft. His words slowed as he said, "So we jumped the fence in the darkness of night, all the lights in the house being off. We squatted in the stillness as we shuffled from melon to melon searching for the best we could find. I used the length of my arm for comparison and, though each was quite large, we came upon one that was surely a monster among the rest. We broke the vine from the end and rolled it a touch from side to side back and forth to loosen it from the dent it had created in the dirt.

"Just as we'd each grabbed an end, a creaking came from the porch of the cabin, and a light came on from a wooden post at one end of the garden where a bare bulb had been strung. From the light we could see the old man in undershirt and bib-alls where the shoulder straps still hung from his waist. He grabbed his shotgun from the rail and we not only saw but heard him snap the chamber open and hastily cram two shells into place. My brother took off and made it over the fence before the gun was loaded. I was frozen in a squat looking between the shotgun and my brother, unable to follow him as he ran down the street, never looking back. Like a jackrabbit, he jerked a crazy path down the road, trying desperately to outmaneuver any bullet that might come.

"But me, I squatted low, thinking that the man might believe he had chased the only rascal out. But I was wrong. I heard him on the porch; he shuffled about trying to get a better view of the garden. 'I know you're there. I can smell you like vermin,' he said. 'Get out of there 'fore I blast you out.' I could tell from the insufficient light that he was still searching, his head moving from side to side. I held no thought of how I would accomplish the feat; I was simply determined to take the melon as proof. So I scuttled and grunted, the melon in my arms, resting the weight of it on my bent knees, scooped secure against my chest, and hefted its weight to a crouch, my back groaning from the strain. I waddled and stumbled to the fence where I stopped, not knowing how, for the life of me, I was going to climb over. I could barely take another step from the struggle of just getting that huge melon as far as I'd gotten it. I placed the watermelon down with a thump, thinking I might be able to roll it under the fence. But as I straightened up, while still standing over that monster of a melon, an explosion burst from the porch behind me and I was knocked to my knees and onto my face. The melon beneath me cracked and shattered as I fell into it. My buttocks felt as if they had been torn from my backside. My hands grabbed my burning flesh, the rump of my trousers wide open. Warm moisture covered my hands from my wounded rear as my bladder let loose to dampen my front. I struggled to free my knees from the ruptured melon. They were buried in glop and my bloody hands had to dig their way into it to release my knees with a loud sucking sound. The burning in my rump kept getting worse. Slipping my way to the fence and over, I could hear the old man cackling from the porch as if he were having the time of his life."

Though Doug hadn't been interested when the story had started, he now waited in anticipation of the end, but Alphonse paused so long Doug wondered if this was all he was going to say.

"And?" he finally asked.

"Though at the time I thought I was going to die, the old geezer had shot me with rock salt. I carry the scar to this day." Alphonse pulled on the waist of his trousers, as if he might stand up any second to show Doug the proof of it.

"Well, my Daddy died the next year, and me being the eldest of five boys, I set off to the north, to Indianapolis, then on to Detroit. And though I routinely sent money back to my family, I didn't return to the hills of that Atlanta region until I was a man in my early twenties."

Doug noticed then what he had missed during the telling of the story: Alphonse had slipped into an even deeper southern drawl.

Constant obviously liked the old man, staying beside him during the entire telling of this story, never once seeming to get distracted from the sound of his voice, the combing from his hand.

"So I put in a visit to the old man, and though he was as crusty as ever, there was a weakness to his face, some humanity that I had not remembered. He was just a man, not a demon, not a monster, just a lonely old man. So I followed him into that cabin of his and told him the why of my visit: to apologize for the destructive behavior of my youth. I was ready for an outburst, a recrimination, or his disdain, but you know what he did?"

Doug shook his head.

Alphonse laughed and didn't continue until he stopped coughing.

"He laughed hard and long as I sat there dumbfounded. He said to me as we sat at his table in the lamplight, 'So you were that scurvy little devil, were you? You got guts there, Boy. That was the only year I didn't win the grand prize. I remember you. Your adventure added to the stories told about me. Good of you to return so I might shake the hand of the only rug rat that got so far.'

"And that's what he did: he shook my hand. But I was perplexed and told him so, which made him laugh again, deep and hardy. He said, 'Why do you think I grow them melons? Not for the prize, mind you. Not for the thrill of it, least not for me. The kids need the challenge of trying to steal 'em. It gives them the thrill. What's an old fart like me got to do, anyways? Everyone I knows is gone and buried.'

"And to this day I'll never forget his words, so shocking were they. Neither will I ever outlive the thrill of the night my brother and I climbed that fence." Alphonse chuckled, then sputtered and coughed, entertaining himself, reliving his story. He looked younger and more alive than he had at the beginning of his tale. Then his face fell a touch as he stated, "Yet I'm the last to remember; being the oldest. One shouldn't live to see the death of all one's younger siblings. But I have. So here I am."

He slapped his thigh with his hand and smiled a crooked smile that matched the angle of his cockeyed glasses.

"You see," he said, "we're not monsters, us vagrants. We're not ogres from some forgotten mythology that have emerged to prey on decent folk. Each and every one is a living breathing human being. Really! Every street person has his own wondrous story. You just have to take the time to listen."

Doug chewed on that for a moment. He thought of the man before him, and the story he had told. He thought of Loose and his sad, sad story. Even Bug had hers. And he felt ashamed of himself in a way he couldn't explain. He couldn't quite get his mind around it; it was out of focus. But he knew, in a general way, that he just hadn't taken the time, hadn't taken the long journey back, to listen to all the stories.

"Are you going inside, 'cause I need some dinner?" asked Alphonse.

"No, I need to be getting home, but I'll see you tomorrow, right?'"

Alphonse got up and waved as he walked into the soup kitchen, wobbling like a top on its last few spins, and his response drifted away with him. "Tomorrow, and the day after that, and the day after that, and the day..." His smile seemed to hang, lingering in Doug's mind like a Cheshire cat's in a cartoon.

Doug thought of the story on his way home, the way the monster had changed so quickly at the end. And he thought of his own story, his first project on Beideman Street, and how he had changed so rapidly into a monster. It was almost as if, in both cases, the past had mysteriously changed.

At the site the next morning, the demolition team was ready to take the old building down. Doug was excited and so was

Constant. Doug had just finished a conversation with Jack when he spotted an old friend from his college days who was dressed for success. Mark had been an art major back then, and if Doug wasn't mistaken, used to drive an old Volkswagen van very similar to Loose's, though his had been spray painted in a collage of color.

"Doug? Doug Sirius, is that you?" Mark asked with his hand outstretched.

"Mark..." and for the life of him, Doug could not remember his last name. He knew he had worked in the sculpture department, bronze casting if his memory served, during college. Mark had been a punk rocker too, maybe the only one Doug had ever known personally. He had come to the area from New Mexico and had carried a blaring boom box wherever he went. "How are you doing?"

"Long time no eye contact," Mark said, shaking hands hard on the words "long" and "eye." Then he let go and placed his hands on his hips spreading his suit coat open across his flat chest and stomach. Mark was over six feet tall and lean like a swimmer. Around his neck hung a camera. "What's happening?"

Doug wasn't sure if Mark wanted an update of his life, or if he was simply curious about the demolition, but Doug assumed the latter for convenience's sake.

"I'm putting up a new office building."

Mark took a few photos then said, "Tearing down the old and up with the new. You're a developer then?"

"Yes. And you?" asked Doug.

"Own a gallery in SOMA. I try to give new local artists a chance to be viewed. Small place but it's got a name for itself, Optico Solace. Heard of it?"

They exchange business cards. Doug noticed that Mark's last name was Spurling.

"I'm not up on my art galleries at the moment."

"Never did like art much, did you?"

"It's good for filling wall space." Doug thought of Bug and her little therapy sessions. "Lately I have taken up painting though, at my niece's insistence. She seems to think it will get me in touch with myself."

"I've always thought art should be for the people, more to be express than to be admired. It's a celebration of the life one lives. Everyone should participate. It's not to be locked up in gold cages. The art itself is almost a byproduct. It's the doing that counts." Mark scratched his head and laughed. "In other words I agree with your niece. Everyone needs to learn to express themselves. The more they try to express what they feel, the more they have to get in touch with their feelings."

Doug stared at Mark as if he were speaking Greek. Emotions seemed to Doug to be something in his way, something to be controlled at all costs. They were embarrassing at best, confusing most of the time, and disastrous if not kept in check. He was reminded how playful he had become at Great America, and he wondered if maybe he had been missing something. Maybe painting was having an effect on him.

Mark said, "Maybe I could come over and see what you've been painting. I'd be interested."

"Yeah, well, my brother in-law is the real painter. I'd like you to see his stuff."

"Maybe you haven't been hearing what I'm saying. A painter is someone who paints. His work doesn't have to be hung in a gallery, or a museum. A writer is someone who writes. He doesn't have to be published. If you paint, you're a painter, and I would be interested in seeing the results of your efforts."

Mark took a few more photos. "I used to be an anarchist. Down with everything, especially the established. Now I don't know. There's value in the old things." He took one more picture of the building. "But I like new things too. I'm not one of these people who glorify the past. But I no longer want to tear it down. I feel the past and the future can coexist."

Again, this sounded like Greek to Doug, only this time he didn't have a response.

"Why would you build an office building in the middle of the Tenderloin? Who would want to work here?" asked Mark.

"The way I look at it, the Tenderloin is due for a major uplift."

Jack had moved away from the men in red hardhats. Jack wore a hardhat too but his was school bus yellow.

"Looks like it's time for detonation," said Doug.

Doug and Mark, together with Jack, walked from the fence on the lot and gathered on the sidewalk across the street to stay clear of the dust. Andy arrived and joined them there. Constant was agitated and whimpered, trying to get Doug's attention. He seemed scared, yet he kept circling as if he wanted to run to the building.

Doug grabbed his collar to restrain him. "What's with you, boy? You don't want to go in there. It's dangerous."

"I think that dog is trying to tell you something." Mark said, laughing. "Maybe you should postpone bringing down the building until you find out what he wants."

"A little late for that." Jack said.

All but one of the men with red hardhats had moved off the property and out to the street. The last man remaining lifted a plunger and struck it down hard and then took off as the explosions began in the lower regions of the building.

"Lift off," said Mark as if they were sending the building to the moon. He took shots rapidly with his camera.

The building collapsed in a cloud of concrete dust.

Constant struggled in Doug's grasp and howled.

Later at his office Doug received the bad news from Andy. It seemed two police officers had arrived in the lobby demanding to see Doug.

"They identified a body they found earlier this afternoon," said Andy.

Doug stood up getting ready to go meet with the police. "A body? What does this have to do with me?"

"A homeless man was found while clearing the debris."

"Are we talking about the demolition this morning?" Doug sat back down. Constant stared at him from the floor.

"There's no reason to get alarmed. I'm quite sure the responsibility rests solely on the subcontractor. They're the ones who applied for the permit. They're the experts. I gave the police their name."

Doug's senses tingled. "Andy, our project just killed a man. I'm glad it wasn't one of our men, but still...A homeless guy, you say?"

"Homeless and old from what I gather. A man by the name of Duncan. Probably just sleeping one off somewhere in the building."

"Duncan? Duncan what?"

"Does it matter?" Andy asked as he looked through his notes. "Duncan was the last name. First name was Alphonse."

Constant turned at the name. He stood and whimpered and rested his head in Doug's lap.

Doug placed his hand on Constant's head, absentmindedly stroking it. "You've got to be fucking kidding me."

When Doug had first met Alphonse, he had walked him to the building. The old man had told him that he lived there, that others were living there too. But that wasn't true any longer. The past had changed, and Doug had put up the fence when he first bought the place. Alphonse himself had said so. What the fuck was going on?

"Don't tell me you know him."

"Yeah, I knew him. And he wasn't in there sleeping it off. Just finding a place to sleep is all." Hadn't Alphonse suggested that there was a way in? "But the place was boarded shut. There was a goddamn fence around it. We even had guards, didn't we?"

"I mentioned all that to the police."

Doug got up and began pacing the room. How had Alphonse gotten around all the security? He couldn't picture the old man scrambling over the fence. Maybe there had been a way under. He doubted the patrol could watch all sides of the building all night long. But, goddammit, this shouldn't have happened. He liked the old guy; he needed him. Who would help him take care of Loose, now? Who would watch over the other homeless kids? Who else cared enough to help them learn?

"How did you know him?" asked Andy.

"A friend of a friend, so to speak. There's this homeless kid, a friend of Bug's whose father died, name of Loose. I was sort of helping him out."

Andy raised a brow.

"What?" asked Doug.

"Just doesn't sound like you, helping the homeless."

"I was doing it for my niece." But that wasn't the truth anymore, was it? Somehow he had become involved.

"By the tone of your voice, I'd say there was more to it than that."

"The old coot told me just the other day how hard it was at his age to wake up in the morning. You'd think all the noise would have woken him. He probably didn't even know what hit him." Doug sat again and put his head in his hands. Ultimately, he was responsible. It was his project. His hands began to shake. He pressed them harder against his face. "If I hadn't moved the schedule up to this morning from the afternoon, he'd probably still be alive." He'd killed a man. That's the way he looked at it. He had been responsible for taking the life of this – an innocent and good man. Gods, what was wrong with him. Didn't he give a damn about anyone but himself and his stupid projects?

"Sure. And if you were a woman, you'd probably be in fashion instead of construction."

"What?" Doug had lost the string of the conversation.

"Don't beat yourself up. You could think of a million ways things might have been different. But it's not your fault. Things just happen. You can't go back and change the past."

"Maybe not, but I sure as hell can atone for my sins. If he had to die, I want it to be a lesson learned for me."

"On that note, I'll leave you with your thoughts."

But Doug didn't like his own thoughts.

What would Bug think? Could she ever forgive him? He didn't think there was a chance in hell. He was never going to be able to forgive himself.

And Angel? As if she wasn't mad enough for what he had done to her mama's neighborhood. He could just kiss that relationship goodbye.

His life was tumbling out of control and there was nothing he could do to save himself. He had never felt like this before, so totally helpless. But hadn't he brought this on himself? Everyone took second place to his own selfish desires, his need to succeed. Nothing and no one else had ever mattered. He was the scum of the Earth.

And now all he could do was feel sorry for himself and the damage   he'd   done.

26

The next day at the office while Doug was moving his computer mouse from one window to another, an IM session popped up. Doug didn't even know he had Instant Messenger installed on his computer because his IT department adamantly advised against it in the workplace, seeing it and Skype as opening a port to hackers.

"Good Morning, Doug," came the words across the screen within the window of IM.

Doug immediately guessed whose words these were. "Hello, Charlie. I'm not in the mood for chatting today," he typed, and moved to click on the X in the upper right hand corner of the IM window.

"I thought you would be in a good mood today. You were slated to bring down the building yesterday afternoon to begin your new project. I take it that went on schedule?" The words seemed to be mocking his changing of the schedule.

Doug had stayed in his penthouse last night. He had wanted to tell Bug about Alphonse, but he didn't know how. He knew he needed to face her, but he had hid from her instead.

"A man died yesterday," Doug reluctantly typed.

"Lots of men died yesterday. I take it we are talking about someone in particular."

"A very special old man."

"A friend of yours?"

"I'd like to think so."

There was an extended pause before the next words appeared on the screen.

"Old people die, Doug. That's just what happens."

"How would you know? You're just a figment of my imagination. You don't even exist."

"I know more about old people than you would think." The words paused as if Charlie were deciding whether or not to tell him something. "I already know about Alphonse and how he died."

"You do?"

"It was an accident."

"Yes, but an avoidable one. He was crushed beneath the building we took down. We caused the building to fall on him."

"But nobody knew he was in there."

"He was just trying to keep warm, looking for shelter." Doug thought again about his decision to move the schedule forward, about how Alphonse might still be alive if he had just left the demolition in the afternoon. He'd only moved it forward because he was angry that Angel had walked out on him at the restaurant. All sorts of thoughts reverberated around his mind. They barraged him with all the insignificant things he might have done differently. If only he could change the past.

But of course the past *had* been changing, hadn't it? He was fully aware of this, even if no one else was. Was there some way to control the changes?

"He was a homeless man," Doug typed, "a good man. He didn't deserve to die. If only I hadn't pushed so hard."

"You think you are to blame?"

"Not so much to blame as not acting when I was in a position to make a difference." Doug stopped typing to pet Constant, who had come out from under the desk to console him. He remembered the dog's agitation before the building collapsed. Had Constant known something? Maybe even his dog knew better than he did.

Doug didn't know how to soothe his own soul. He wanted so desperately for things to be different. He said aloud, "If I could go back in time..."

Charlie must have heard him. "You can't change the past," she wrote.

"You and I," Doug said, instead of using the keyboard, "we've had this conversation before. You seemed surprised when I told you I noticed the past had changed. You weren't surprised about the changes; you were surprised that I noticed."

The words slowly appeared this time, one letter at a time. "You need to accept the things you cannot change. Just because you can notice the passage of time, doesn't mean you can control it." Again, the words seemed to be mocking him, challenging him.

Doug stood up and began to pace. Constant's head moved each time Doug passed.

"There's got to be something I can do," he said.

"It's never too late to do the next right thing."

"And what's that supposed to mean?"

"That's up for you to decide. I like Andy's idea of reinstating the Historical Society's proposition to make the Tenderloin a historical landmark."

Doug thought about how this woman knew things, about Alphonse dying, about Andy's suggestion. Had he told her about Andy's suggestion in an earlier conversation?

"And what good will that do Alphonse?"

"Might it be what Alphonse would have wanted? Maybe you could just do it in his memory."

"No, I think the next right thing to do is to tell Bug – right now."

With that, Doug crashed his computer by hitting the power button without shutting down. As his computer speakers crunched, his cell phone rang.

"Hello?"

"Doug? Hunt. Listen. I found it," said Hunt.

"Found it?" asked Doug. "Found what?"

"The IP address."

"I'm sorry, Hunt. I'm at a loss. What address are you talking about?"

Doug sat down. Constant rested his head on his lap. Doug reached around and patted the dog's chest.

"The address of those strange communications you're getting. They originate from the hospital over on Geary. I have a friend over there in IT who's going to get back to me with the exact department."

That was the same hospital where Loose's father had died.

"Yeah, well, I'm not sure that it matters anymore."

"What do you mean, it doesn't matter?"

"Look, do you mind if I stop by later this afternoon?"

"Since when do you have to ask?"

"I need to talk to Bug."

"Bug? I've never heard you call her by her nickname before. In fact, I find it a little strange that you want to talk to her. Are you feeling okay? Are you trying to change your ways, or something?"

Doug was having trouble with this conversation. He always called his niece by her nickname, sometimes even in public, to her chagrin. Hunt was making it seem like they never talked at all. He looked up at the painting that he and Bug had done together, only to find that it had been replaced with a print similar to the rest of the artwork in the building. He thought of asking Jasmine about it, but why bother? She'd only look at him dumbfounded, stating that she had never seen such a painting. He'd almost begun to expect the changes to the past. The latest seemed to be that he no longer had the relationship with his niece that he remembered.

"Isn't Terra about to get her driver's license?" Doug asked, probing.

"Funny you should mention it. I hired an instructor at the beginning of the month. Shouldn't be long now." Hunt paused momentarily. "I look forward to you stopping by. I'm just finishing a new painting for the gallery. I think even you might like it."

"Gallery?" Doug fingered the card in his pocket that he had got from Mark yesterday. He had been meaning to give it to Hunt. "What gallery?"

"What's with you? You must be busy because you sure don't have your mind on this conversation. I'll talk to you when you get here." Hunt hung up without a goodbye.

Walking to the door, Doug turned off the lights. The room dimmed because it was overcast outside and the blinds were closed. In a daze, he glanced around the room, feeling as if he were forgetting something. Constant heeled by his side.

"You want to go see Bug?" Doug asked. Constant cocked his head to the side and Doug scratched him behind his left ear. "You don't really know what I'm talking about, do you? Probably think I'm nuts. Welllllll, that makes two of us."

On his walk home between Soma and the Tenderloin, he took his time going along the Bay by the Embarcadero. Bug wouldn't be home for quite some time. He had lunch at Fog City while Constant lay tied to a parking meter, but he brought him the leftovers. Something he rarely did, trying to keep him on a strict diet of dry food.

He circled around to his project along the way and stood across the street watching as the workers with cranes and forklifts loaded debris onto trucks. In the past, this sort of site would have brought a smile to his face. Not today, though.

Maybe not ever again.

27

Terra couldn't believe her ears. Yesterday she had heard that the dear old man had died. But today Loose was telling her that it was all the fault of a construction company by the name of Sirius. She knew her uncle was a moneygrubber, but this? How could he be so negligent? And just when she thought about her uncle, who should come walking down the street but the devil himself. She wanted to run up and kick him in the shins. Anger turned to tears.

"Hello B–"

"How could you?" she interrupted him.

"I take it you've received the news." Uncle Doug's words sounded so cold to her.

"Don't you care about what you've done?"

"It was an accident," Uncle Doug whispered. "It wasn't my fa–"

"Don't give me that." Terra was toe to toe with him, but she was crying. "D–Don't even try that bullshit." She looked for a reaction to her profanity and found none. "You people never take responsibility for your actions. All you ever think about is money. I suppose the building just accidentally fell on him."

Loose began to slip away. Not even knowing her uncle, he seemed embarrassed to watch this. But on his face was a look of condemnation. He was her only support, and she was not about to let him leave her here alone. Terra took a step back, grabbed his arm, and held on tight.

Her uncle softly spoke. "No one knew he was in there." The rush of the late afternoon traffic almost covered his words.

"Bet you looked real hard. Were you there when it happened? Were you on a tight schedule?" Behind Loose, Constant was hiding.

"I'm sorry."

"Sorry? You think being sorry is going to bring him back. Sorry doesn't mean squat. This old man was worth twenty people like you!" She'd never felt so much like hitting someone before.

"What do you want me to do?"

"How about you go jump from a bridge. Save all the people you're going to crush in the future. Just do us all a favor."

Terra turned with her hand in Loose's, and ran right into her father standing close behind her. She took a step back and rubbed her nose on her sleeve, using her hand to wipe away tears. She stared defiantly into his eyes.

"Don't you think you're being a little harsh here?" her father said.

Terra spoke through her clamped jaw. "Yesterday he killed someone very special."

"He's family."

"And for that I am ashamed."

Her father placed his hands on her shoulders. "I'm sure there's more to the story."

246

Terra shook his hands away. She distributed her weight evenly on both feet, letting go of Loose's hand, and clenching hers into fists.

"Your uncle has helped us in lots of ways. He introduced me to Mark at the Optico gallery. It meant a lot to you that I could stop being a nine-to-five guy, right?" "So that makes it all right to turn a blind eye?"

Her father turned to face Uncle Doug. "No, but it does earn him the right for us to give him the benefit of doubt. Doug, let's hear your side of the story."

Uncle Doug looked down. "I don't have a side. She's right. Ultimately I'm responsible for the man's death. I didn't actually kill him, but I didn't go out of my way to save him either. It just never occurred to me."

"Didn't occur to you?" Terra squealed. "You dropped a building on him. Didn't you even bother to check if someone was inside?"

"We *did* check. The place was fenced off, there were warning signs everywhere. The building was boarded up. I had hired guards there twenty-four hours a day. We had no idea he was sleeping in there, how he got by the guard, or how he got in the building."

"Who was he?" asked her father.

"A harmless old man," answered Uncle Doug.

"A *wonderful* man," added Loose. This was the first time he'd spoken since her uncle's arrival. "His stories were so...I don't know...entertaining. He taught us lots of things. I guess he didn't give up on us like everyone else does."

"I'd sell my soul to change what happened, but I can't," said Uncle Doug. "There's nothing I can do to bring him back."

The finality of that statement struck Terra as the end of the conversation. So she took Loose and entered the building, leaving Constant waiting by the door. Her tears began to flow again. She didn't want to share them with her uncle.

28

Doug made arrangements at the hospital for Alphonse's cremation and to pick up the man's ashes later in the week. He had plans for the ashes. Afterward, he meandered through the lobby in a daze, walking stick in hand. As it turned out, Angel was there, probably to visit her mother.

"Angel," he said tentatively. She ignored him, obviously still angry. "Evangelina?"

Angel stared at him as if she was thinking of something else.

Now that he had her attention, Doug didn't know what to say.

"How's your..." he almost said mama and then caught himself because it sounded too intimate "...mother?"

Angel walked up to him and said softly, "I'm sorry. Do I know you?"

From the tone of her voice, he could tell that she wasn't angry with him. She also wasn't just pretending not to know him. She really didn't remember him. The changes in the past had taken care of that. Feeling a creeping sense of defeat, Doug introduced himself and she did the same while shaking hands. The entire thing was awkward.

Then her phone emitted a ringtone he'd never heard before.

"Hello, this is Evangelina...yes...oh no...oh my God." Angel disconnected, and Doug saw that tears were already coming to her eyes. To Doug she said, "I'm sorry; I've got to go."

She turned to leave and Doug kept pace with her. "What's wrong? What's happened?"

"It's Mama." She pushed the Up button for the elevator. "She died, but they have resuscitated her."

Doug wondered what "resuscitated" meant in this context. They probably used those electrical paddles that he saw doctors use on TV dramas. He wanted to comfort Angel, but he was a complete stranger to her now. She even seemed oblivious to his accompanying her. She pulled her phone from her purse and gave it a voice command.

"Agnes' Cell."

There was a pause while the phone dialed. Doug was surprised that it was working in the elevator.

"Agnes...it's me. They just resuscitated Mama.... No, I don't know what that means.... Agnes, calm down.... Yes, you might want to be here. They've put her on the ventilator again.... I'll see you soon."

Angel placed her phone back in her purse as the elevator doors opened. She hurried down the corridor. Doug rushed to keep pace, using his staff in long strides. Angel slammed her fist onto the large circular steel button on the wall that opened the doors to the ICU. Inside, Doug could see the nurse's station in the middle surrounded by the rooms for the patients. Curtains were drawn on many of them. One had a cluster of staff outside its door.

Angel approached them. Doug stood at a distance by the counter in the center of the room. It was so quiet here. After a prolonged conversation where the words "Power of Attorney" had been whispered more than once, Angel entered her mother's room. Doug waited patiently outside.

Later, other family members arrived, and Doug was struck with how many there were and how quickly they'd gotten here. Doug was the only white man there. Like many cultures, it seemed that Filipinos preferred their own kind in marriage. One of the men approached him.

"Are you a friend?" Doug's quizzical look must have made the man add, "Of the woman in this room."

"N-no, no I'm not," replied Doug.

"A woman was brought in a couple days ago... a motorcycle accident. Are you here for her?"

"No."

"That's probably good. From what I hear she has more broken bones in her body than she does whole ones." The man brushed his hair back with his hand. "She probably doesn't have long to live."

Doug walked toward the ICU lounge, limping, thinking about the agony his own motorcycle accident had caused. The memory of it returned in a flash, the crunching of his right thigh.

He cringed. He came out of the thought clutching his staff in both hands, breathing heavily, the sound erratic. When he opened his eyes, he found a nurse staring at him.

"Are you okay?" she asked holding out a box of tissue. She must have thought this was grief.

"I'll be fine in a minute, thanks." Doug pulled a tissue from the box and proceeded to blow his nose. "The girl in the motorcycle accident, does she have family visiting?"

"Family and friends. Seems like half her high school has come by to visit. Do you know her?"

The nurse seemed so calm. People were dying all around her and she kept her composure the entire time. Doug wasn't so sure this was such a good trait, becoming numb to death. Yet, this nurse appeared compassionate to the survivors. Wasn't that all one could do, help the survivors grieve. There was nothing one could do for the dead. That much he knew.

Inside the private room, he saw Angel's family gathered around the bed. Angel was on the far side holding her mama's hand. One woman began to wail, begging her mama not to leave. All of the family needed to touch the body, the head, an arm, or a foot. Some kind of contact, a connection. Everyone was crying, some loudly, some silently, but all were mourning their loss.

Doug felt like an intruder. This was a very private moment, and he didn't belong here. Though his heart reached out to her, Angel no longer remembered who he was. The past had changed. The memories he carried of them together were his alone.

He left the ICU dragging his walking staff behind him like the tail of a dog who'd done wrong.

29

Though Doug feared what other changes might be in store for him, he figured it couldn't get much worse. He mourned the loss of Angel. He missed his relationship with his niece. He'd heard that Loose was still living in his van, though now, because of Doug, he was probably living all alone. All of this had happened because he chose to move up the time of the demolition of his building.

He and Constant took their morning walk. The streets were still wet from the previous night's rain. The sun had already risen from the Oakland hills.

Time seemed at a standstill.

He had nothing left to do.

Only weeks before, he'd had a full life. Now it seemed so empty. Nothing of value remained. He still had his job, still had his projects, but that didn't matter anymore. He'd had just a small taste of something sweeter, and now the old tasted sour. If only he'd remained ignorant of what his life could be, of what he was missing.

Doug and Constant entered the apartment complex he called home. The lobby was spotless, so he assumed the men from his company had come by to clean it up.

Constant wandered away from Doug, who lazily passed the staircase and came to the old front desk. He placed his walking stick on the counter and then lifted himself, with a quick twist, to sit on it. He planned on leaving the lobby pretty much as it had always been, though obviously with a different function. Maybe he'd place a security guard here once he finished the rest of the floors for occupancy. He figured that people from his project, people who would work at the new office complex, would need places to live. He'd move out as they moved in.

For a while, he was lost in thought about all the work that needed to be done on the place. He almost wished this project were over. Then he could be moving. He wasn't sure if he was comfortable living right next to Hunt and Bug anymore, a reminder of what he'd had.

Then he remembered something Charlie had once said to him: it was never too late to do the next right thing. So he lifted his butt from the counter and hopped down, favoring his good left leg for a landing. He grabbed his stick, whistled for his dog, and went to the elevator. They rode up to the second top floor and he rang the bell. Hunt's smiling face answered.

Constant pranced inside immediately.

"Doug, glad you stopped by. I'm just getting ready to send my newest painting to the gallery and I wanted you to see it. I didn't have a chance to show it to you the other day, and you never seem to have the time to get to Optico. This one is really special."

"You're home from work already?" Doug asked, as he entered the apartment.

"Work? You mean like a day job? I quit that a long time ago. It's been ages. But you know that already. Are you okay?"

"Just a touch out of sorts. You have a show at Optico Solace?" As far as Doug knew, he had never had the opportunity to give Hunt Mark's card.

"On permanent display ever since that first show. Again, *you know that already.*"

Hunt led the way into his art studio. On an easel in the middle of the room was a 4' x 4' canvas. It was a painting of Bug. The face was in ¾ profile. The entire piece was softened with a white wash, except for the pupil of the right eye and the circle entering her ear, which were painted pink. The hair was streaked with washed pinks, greens, and whites. There was a large blue circle around the left eye. The face was so big the mouth wasn't even on the canvas.

Doug gaped at it unable to move.

"I call it, Bug Eyes," Hunt said.

"It's... the most beautiful thing I've ever seen," Doug whispered reverently, as though he didn't want to disturb the sight with the sound of his voice. The piece went beyond being a representation of his niece. It held her seriousness, sure, but also conveyed her playfulness.

"Thank you," said Hunt. "I'm glad you like it. I hope the critics are as kind."

"Is she around?" he asked.

"No, she took off right after school with some friends. There's an anime convention over at the Moscone Center for the entire weekend. She wanted to take off from school today, but sometimes I have to put my foot down and be a responsible parent. That sucks, but she didn't seem too upset about it."

Doug was deeply disappointed. He had wanted to ask Bug to go to Great America with him, hoping it would be like the last time. In his heart, though, he knew that even if Bug had been home, she would not have wanted to go with him. Not only was he on her shit list, but it seemed to him now that they had *never* had a close relationship. The changes in the past had taken care of that.

Doug flicked a thumb toward the canvas. "How much are you selling your paintings for these days?"

"They keep going up, but they're averaging about ten grand."

"That's a lot of money."

"I can do about two or three a month. A hell of a lot better than my day job used to be. I'm even putting away some for Terra's college education."

"I'd be interested in this one."

"Great. I mean, Mark would still want to show this in the gallery, but I'll have him place a sold sign on it and you can discuss the price with him."

Constant sat by Doug's left foot. Wondering what changes might have occurred in the relationship between his dog and his niece, Doug said, "Could you watch Constant this afternoon?"

"Sorry, but like I said, I have to take this down to the gallery. I'm meeting the framer there. He's the guy who does all the work for SFMOMA. I like his input for all my frames."

"Okay then. Don't forget to put the sold sign on it. Have Mark give me a call."

Up in his own apartment, Doug paced. He straightened pictures on the walls. He vacuumed the Oriental rug in the main room. He even wiped off the kitchen counters with Lysol towelettes. Minimal comfort came from the repetition of the mundane. But it did seem to relieve, somewhat, his mind from racing in that eternal loop of what-if.

There was nothing he could do about the past and no way to predict the future. Only in the present could he act. So he put on his coat and grabbed his walking stick and said aloud, "I gotta get out of here."

Constant got excited at the prospect of going for another walk. He too was bored of Doug's pacing around. His expression made it abundantly clear.

"You stay," Doug said holding his hand up like a traffic cop.

Constant sat, tilting his head, probably thinking, *This guy is nuts. Now is not the time to be alone.* His tail uncurled, trailing behind him limp on the floor.

But Doug had no choice. Dogs weren't allowed at Great America and that was where he was headed. He needed help to get out of the state he was in and the other day at Great America was one of the happiest days of his life.

"You be a good dog," Doug said, patting Constant on both sides of his snout.

He found a parking spot close to the entrance on this particularly dreary day. The park had already announced its intention to close for the year following the weekend.

A lone pigeon flew overhead and then landed by a flock that was digging through some trash at the curb. *Rats with wings*, thought Doug. Better on the ground than in the sky, he supposed.

He dragged his feet a few steps and then tried to skip, but it only made him feel foolish. Who was he trying to kid? This day was doom and gloom, but he kept moving forward anyhow. In search of a direction for his life to take. A new direction. Maybe something of his old life could be salvaged from the ruins.

At the gate, he realized he didn't have the pass he had purchased on his last visit. But then again, there *was* no last visit; the past had taken it away. He bought a new pass and upgraded it for a yearly pass for next season, believing he'd come back regularly in an attempt to relive memories of that lost day.

A bone-numbing wind came in from the north. Doug turned up his collar and stuck his hands in his coat pockets. He felt destitute.

He wandered almost aimlessly, yet found himself on a bench by the Demon, the first roller coaster he had ever been on at this park. The sky drizzled a fine mist that reminded Doug of

259

the first ramp of the Demon, going up to the sky through a tunnel of mist, making one's arm hairs stand on end in a warm summer breeze. No one was on the roller coaster. The rumble of the empty cars sounded like distant thunder.

The sun hid so well that it was impossible to discern. There was dense cloud cover from horizon to horizon.

No people walked by his park bench. This area was deserted.

In his pocket, his cell phone vibrated once, meaning he had just received an e-mail. Probably his office looking for him. He hadn't called in all day and wasn't planning to do so. Still, he pulled out his phone and glanced at the screen, dismissing the e-mail. He looked through his contacts for Angel's number, though he knew it by heart. It was not under A or E. It no longer existed in his life.

Though Doug hadn't known it at the time, his niece had been right, his life had been lacking. He thought about painting with Bug, her driving lessons, Loose's apartment, Angel by his side. Things had been changing for the better.

He remembered the conversation he and Angel had had over lunch during their visit here. They'd talked about how they'd never gotten married or had children, and Doug confessed that his "only child" was his business. On that day, he felt that things were about to change. Now, though, all he had was his job once again. Only this time it seemed so empty.

And what was he supposed to do with his project? There was no way he could simply continue, not after the death of a wonderful man. Doug's self-will had brought devastation, and he couldn't bear to risk that again.

He thought about his communication with Charlie. She, whoever she was, had somehow reached out to him. But why had she tried to reach him? She had wanted to warn him, had wanted him to change his ways. Why?

She had said that it was never too late to do the next right thing. That was the message, as simple as that. But how does one know what's right?

And just then, like divine inspiration, he knew what the right thing was. He intuitively knew what to do.

30

On the way to the office that same day, Doug picked up Constant and the urn with Alphonse's ashes, placing the urn in the center of his desk. That was when he first noticed that the empty box from Angel's mother was gone, another thing swept into his – and only his – memory. He wondered what it meant. He had liked the empty box, the symbolism of it, and now it was gone. An emptiness had disappeared or, more likely, never existed. Now that was a crazy thought.

From his desk drawer, he got a biscuit for Constant. Doug noticed the bottle of Seroquel there, but ignored it. Constant sat patiently as Doug balanced the cookie on the dog's snout, reprising their trick.

Doug opened the blinders on all of the windows along the wall. It was like a new day. The sun was struggling to get through the overcast. The Friday afternoon was going to be all right.

Yeah, right. Doug felt like he was about to morph into a werewolf, the muscles stretching, the joints popping. Everything elongated and twisted.

Maybe he should rearrange his files. Maybe not.

He wanted to sit.

He wanted to pace.

He wanted to throw his chair out the window.

Anything was better than this.

He straightened the three pictures on his walls meticulously.

Taking the clutter from his desk, including the papers in his inbox, Doug tossed them in the garbage. He kicked the trashcan, sat on the edge of his chair, picked up the phone, and dialed Jack's extension.

"Yo, Boss," Jack answered.

"We need to talk."

"So talk."

"We need to shut the project down."

"The police have pretty much done that already."

"I'm not talking about a delay."

"Okay, you got me. What are we talking about?"

"Shutting it down permanently."

"You're kidding, right?"

Doug rested the receiver on the desk and pushed the speaker button. He came out of his chair, stood with one set of knuckles on the desk, the other hand on his hip.

"No, I'm not."

"What are you going to do with an empty lot?" asked Jack.

Doug had no idea what he would do with it. "That's none of your concern. Just shut it down."

"We haven't even finished clearing it."

"Well, clean it up and call it a day."

"Boss, listen—"

"I don't have the patience for this. Just do what I tell you."

Doug hung up and dialed Jasmine's extension.

"Get Andy in here ASAP."

Doug walked over and plopped down on the leather couch leaving the chair vacant for Andy. Constant walked between his legs, placing his head on his lap. Doug scratched behind his left ear with his right hand and stroked his cheek with the other. Constant smiled a dog's smile, wagging his tail and probably thinking happy dog-thoughts. Doug squeezed the animal's chest between his thighs.

A soft tapping came from the door. Doug opened it and then resumed his position on the yellow couch. Constant watched Andy walk past to the chair and then returned to Doug for more attention.

"Jack tells me you're disbanding the project," said Andy.

"Yep."

"So what's the plan?"

Ignoring the question, Doug asked, "Do we have any subcontractors for this job?"

"A few: Drywall, painting–"

"Notify them we're pulling the plug."

"Are you going to tell me what's going on?"

"I want us to do whatever it takes to reinstate the Historical proposal and get it approved in Sacramento. That is, as of now, our highest priority."

"Does this have anything to do with those twenty-five SROs?"

"That fake association? No, but I wouldn't mind if they got their just deserts in the process. We want to protect the old architecture in the Tenderloin. We're going to improve the area without tearing anything else down. I want to improve it for the people who already live there as well as new tenants."

"And what about our lot?"

"I think we need to get involved with the community before we decide what is most needed there. First, let's make the entire area an historical site, then we'll worry about what we have to contribute."

"You want to talk about it?"

"What?"

"Whatever it is that caused this change. Does this have something to do with that old man dying? You knew him, right?"

"Not as well as I could have. And yes, I suppose he is part of the reason. I just feel so disconnected. I need to get more involved with all this." Doug made a sweeping gesture with his arm. "All the life around me. It's almost like I'm not even here, like I could disappear and no one would even notice." He glanced over at the urn on his desk, remembering the empty box that had been there. "That homeless old man had more of a life than I do. He used to teach all the homeless kids around the neighborhood, used to tell them stories too."

Andy cleared his throat and said, "Doug, I don't think there is anything wrong with wanting to give back to the community."

"But..."

"But, I don't see what harm finishing the project would do."

"Maybe the question isn't what harm it will do, but what's best for the people who live there. Maybe we could do something really useful."

"Okay, Doug, count me in. I'll start working on getting the area protected as an historical site. You start getting involved with this community you're talking about. We don't want this taking so long that we go out of business. What good could we do then?"

Doug knew they wouldn't go out of business. Each of his corporations had enough other work to survive. Of course, the lot itself was a liability at this point. Sure, it was an asset, but an asset that was just tying up cash at the moment. And in his business, cash was king.

Then it occurred to him that he had told Charlie about the historical proposition and that she had liked the idea of his reinstating it. It pleased Doug to think that she would appreciate what he was doing. At the same time, though, he wondered if he would ever hear from the woman again. He missed her nagging at him, her ridicule. Her advice, though sounding crazy at the time, was starting to make more and more sense.

Andy left Doug's office. Doug stayed on the couch, leaning back and putting his feet up. Constant came very close and sniffed his face.

Doug looked around his office and noticed how impersonal it was. His home was the same way, with nothing to distinguish it from anybody else's. Like a picture cut from a magazine. Like a display in a furniture store with fake books and a cardboard computer monitor.

How could one work so hard only to find, too late, that one's attention was on all the wrong things?

31

Months passed. It took time but Doug eventually knew everyone at the soup kitchen. Hell, he'd been coming every night. Yet, he couldn't help noticing that no one had taken Alphonse's place with the children. The back of the room where he had seen the children gathered seemed empty now. No one taught the homeless children anymore. Did they even go to school?

One evening, just before Christmas, he walked into the place and several regulars waved to him. An old man named Jack walked up and bent to pet Constant.

"Evening D-D-Doug," he said with his usual stutter.

Jack had lost his wife after he had become sober, but he had more than enough time to make his amends to her. He had something like twenty-eight years of sobriety. He came here every night, went to AA meetings every day, though he was now in his late seventies. He'd said that he wouldn't miss this for the world. This was his life.

"Hello, Jack," Doug said, clapping him gently on his back.

"We're having a couple of alcothons for the holidays. Have you signed up? We can always use the help"

Alcothons were quite popular for AA members. The holidays were such a trying time for alcoholics. It was a lonely time for many without families. Even those who did have families found it hard to participate in the family gatherings with all the drinking that usually took place. It was a season for relapse. So, the members of AA gathered in their own celebration, a twenty-four hour affair, with meetings beginning every hour on the hour.

"Haven't signed up yet, but I will."

"There's a s-s-sign up lis-st in the b-b-back," Jack said, pointing. "There'll be a s-s-speaker at twelve-thirty and live music f-f-following that. Are you and C-C-Constant g-g-going to d-d-do your m-m-magic d-d-dance for us?"

The first time Doug and Constant had done their signature jig in the middle of the dining hall, everyone referred to it as his "magic dance," asking periodically for a repeat performance.

"Sure, Jack, sure, but only if you put on your dancing shoes and join us."

"Okay, then. I g-g-guess we'll b-b-be d-d-dancing."

Though others knew who Angel was, none had seen her in a long time. Throughout the fall and spring, they talked of her as if she were a sorority mother gone missing. Rumor was convoluted: she'd gotten married and moved away from the Bay Area; there was a family disaster and she had to go back to the Philippines; she'd been hit by a truck and gone to heaven. In the minds of the homeless, it seemed that only something monumental could keep her from her flock. Yet, no matter what the rumor, everyone seemed to think that she would miraculously return some day. So Doug hunkered down and waited.

Business at the office was dwindling, probably because he wasn't paying much attention. His development company would be in trouble soon if he didn't do something. But his heart just wasn't in it. He didn't want to do any more damage. Sure, his organization had plenty of remodeling and repair work, but the development company wasn't doing anything, and development was a big part of all his other companies' workload. Remodeling simply reinforced what people already had whereas new projects would change the neighborhood. His first project in the Fillmore had taken away Angel's Mama's home. How many other lives had he devastated during that project? He wanted to help people, not hurt them. It angered and pained him that he could not come up with a project for the Tenderloin that would be a benefit for all those who lived there, so he avoided thinking directly about it. While Andy worked on getting the Tenderloin declared an historical landmark, the office employee count dropped, especially the architects and engineers that he didn't need for remodels. Development had been the icing on the cake, a vehicle to the next financial level.

A couple of months after the holidays, Doug came to the office, and walked through the main area. Jasmine kept her head down as he passed, pretending to be busy. Constant heeled by his left side the whole way through. Foreboding was thick in the air, like a waiting room at a hospital ICU. Doug sequestered himself behind his private door to gain distance from the scene. Immediately his cell phone began to ring.

010-101-0101 appeared on the screen. At first, Doug was too amazed to answer. It had been months since he had seen that number. Even though in a strange way, he missed his conversations with Charlie, he hesitated, wondering what she might berate him about now. Obviously he was an open target for "I told you so," and his wounds were open wide.

"Hello, Charlie," he said when he finally answered.

"Hello, Doug," she said in her soft sing-song voice. He noticed that she hadn't butchered his name as she once did. Her voice sounded solemn.

"It's good to hear from you," Doug said.

"Really?"

"Yes."

"You miss me?"

He paused to think about it and was surprised with the answer. "Very much."

Only silence returned to him over the phone. In the distant background, he heard a perturbing beep, repeating itself like the heartbeat on a monitor.

"So, why have you called?"

"To say goodbye, Doug. It's time to say goodbye."

Beep...beep...beep.

"I won't hear from you again?" He found himself suddenly sadder.

"No, Doug, you won't."

Beep...beep...beep.

"So that's it, huh? You hound me to death and then you just leave me like this." He chuckled nervously, another hollow sound. He wanted to argue with her, somehow convince her to stay. Resting his phone on his shoulder he spread his arms wide. Constant came and lay his head on Doug's thigh, looking up at him through a sympathetic gray brow. Doug sighed, placed a hand on his dog's head, and said very softly, "So I failed, didn't I?"

Beep...beep...beep.

"No, Doug, you didn't fail. You did the best you could with what you were given."

Beep...beep...beep.

Gods, that sound was irritating. "My company is dwindling, my personal life is permanently in the toilet," he thought of Angel and the look on her face as she left him, "I have no family life anymore," an image of Bug appeared in his mind, "but I did good, huh?"

"Yes, Doug, you did good."

Beep...beep...beep.

"But everything sucks. Nothing is right. Everything is wrong and there's nothing I can do about it."

"You're on the right...path now. I have confidence in you. Even without my help, you're going to stay on the right path."

Beep...beep...beep.

"Well I don't have any confidence in me. I can't make a decision to save my ass."

"Maybe that's a good place to start, with a little self-doubt. You're not used to that, are you? But when the time is right, you'll do the next right thing. I believe in you. Trust me."

"Do I have a choice?"

"You always have a choice, Doug. That's what makes the world go round."

The beeping changed to one long, sustained sound. This slowly faded into the distance, replaced by white noise.

Immediately the buzzer of his door sounded. Doug placed his phone on his hip and got up to answer. It was Andy, with a smile on his face. He entered, and before Doug closed the door, he glanced outside at the solitude there; so many of the pods were empty.

"Ah, I'm glad you're here," said Andy, grabbing a cushioned chair around the coffee table. Constant sat alongside Andy who fiddled with one ear.

Doug settled down on the couch. "What's up?"

"I'm off to Sacramento. There's meeting after meeting I need to attend. Lots to do." Andy leaned forward, placing his elbows on his knees. "Why don't you come along?"

"Well..."

"Come on. There's nothing to do here. Everyone here is in maintenance mode. Unless you've come up with something new."

Andy said this last thing with a bit of sarcasm, and Doug raised an eyebrow. "Nothing comes to mind."

"I didn't think so. So, what do you say? The companies will do fine without you for a few days."

"No, I think you can handle it."

"I wasn't implying I couldn't. I just thought you'd like to come along. Get out of this place. Maybe something new will help you think more clearly."

"I'm fine."

Andy scratched again at Constant's ear. "I don't think so."

"Nonetheless, I think I'll stay here."

"Well, suit yourself," he said, standing to leave. "You can't say I didn't try."

32

Doug had decided to get involved at Saint Anthony's thinking he could maybe make a difference. He'd started by making coffee and emptying the butt can by the door. Over time, he moved up to dishwasher. Once he'd perfected this chore, he was asked to serve food because he was becoming adept at conversing with the clientele. Now, he showed up early and helped prepare in the kitchen in addition to serving.

"Are you telling me," Doug asked Marcia while the two of them served spaghetti with a side salad one evening, "that the majority of the kids don't go to school?"

"If the parents aren't absentee from being too drugged out, then they're too embarrassed about the shoddy clothes their children have to wear." Marcia was a mousy woman in her early thirties. Her hair was straight, but she curled it around her face. She was buoyant and dressed like an Abercrombie and Fitch model.

"Maybe there should be a school especially for them. Where quality of clothes doesn't matter. Where the education is steered toward what they need to know not only to survive on the streets, but how to get off them," said Doug.

"One of the biggest problems for people on the street is the misconception that these people deserve to be here. Alcoholics and addicts didn't grow up thinking, 'Hey, when I grow up I want to be a drunk or a junkie.' It just doesn't work that way," stated Marcia emphatically.

"Well something must have happened to let themselves fall this far," Doug said keeping his voice down so as not to offend.

"See? Even the way you say that makes it sound like they had a choice."

"You can't tell me it's society's fault."

"I'm not saying that. But people who have cancer didn't do anything to get cancer," Marcia said.

"Hello? How about smokers who get cancer?"

"Smokers tempt fate. That's true. And some of the homeless chose not to conform to society, not realizing where that might lead, or if they did, they didn't care. There are homeless that, given the choice, would choose to stay on the streets. But that's not the majority."

"Okay, so what does this have to do with educating the children?"

"First of all, let's ignore the perception that the people on the street are subhuman, though many people believe that. Society doesn't think it needs to help people who have it within themselves to get off the street if only they'd get a job. But it's not that easy. Would you hire these people to work for you?"

"Probably not. But if we could educate the children, at least they wouldn't be destined to stay here."

"That's true. But like you said earlier, they need a special education. They're not going to learn it in their public schools and they're certainly not going to learn from a parent who is stuck here. The government is not going to fork over more funds. They already pay enough to keep these people alive."

"So you believe it has to come from the private sector?"

"Listen, I work here 'cause it's the one time during the week I can get out of myself and care about somebody else. It gets me off my pity pot, stops me from building my own problems out of proportion, and makes me feel good about myself. Alcoholics Anonymous figured it out a long time ago. It's one alcoholic helping another. I'm saying that you can't throw money at this problem. If everyone who cared just volunteered one weekend a month, they'd be better off for it. Don't do it for the people here. Do it for yourself. These people do not want your pity. They have enough of that."

"Are you suggesting something like Big Brothers or Big Sisters?"

"Sure, why not. If each person just became a friend of one of these people...you don't have to change the world. There's no magic required, no fancy plans, just one person at a time. Pick one, and make him your friend. Treat him like a friend, and he'll respond sometimes in kind, not always, but sometimes. It's why Alcoholics Anonymous has sponsors."

Doug thought of Alphonse's story, the one about the watermelon patch. If Alphonse had not gone back to apologize to the man, Alphonse would never have heard the watermelon man's story. That story had changed Alphonse's life.

Doug went to get another pan of spaghetti, taking the foil off and resuming serving.

"It sounds too simple," he said. He thought about taking the time to listen to other people's stories. He wanted to do that because of what Alphonse had said. He wanted to hear all the stories. If he could do that, wouldn't that be the right thing to do? Could he be a friend, just be there, someone to talk to. He remembered how it had made him feel, when he had been helping Loose with his math homework, how just being there for him had felt right. And wasn't he here because it made him feel better to do so? Wasn't it the right thing to do? Here, he didn't feel so helpless. Here, he was actually doing something to help others, even if it was something small like serving them food.

"Conceptually it does. But it takes people to get involved, people to commit themselves. That's a lot harder than it seems."

"Yeah, I suppose so. But like you said, if people did it for their own benefit, they'd be more motivated."

"In AA, an alcoholic helps another alcoholic to keep himself sober. Coming here keeps me sane."

"I like the sound of that. I never much liked that do-goody bullshit." Doug realized that listening to all these people's stories might make him a better person, maybe help him feel more connected to the life around him. He needed to do it for himself, if not for them.

Marcia nodded in agreement. Doug wondered if Marcia had a drinking problem and this was her way of staying sober. Not that it mattered. She said it kept her sane, and he believed her. He did feel good about himself every time he worked here. Even talking to her right now got him out of his own problems for a while.

Doug looked up to see Constant at the door greeting people as they entered. People loved his dog and everyone knew Constant by name. He was like a companion they could trust. And Constant basked in the attention and affection. He was like a young pup while he was here.

When it was time to go, Doug grabbed a pamphlet discussing AA's twelve steps, and a meeting schedule from a table by the door. To him this new concept intrigued him, one drunk helping another. Once outside the door, Constant stopped, his attention on a group of young hoodlums at the corner across the street. His curled tail wagged. Doug took a second look.

There was Loose looking tough and streetwise. Doug's mood dropped immediately. Doug barely recognized the kid. In the light from one street lamp this boy appeared darker and more angular, older and meaner. It hadn't been that long since his father had died, yet significant changes had taken place. The gang was passing a joint around and shouting obscenities at anyone who walked near. The heavy traffic crept by, windows closed, and doors locked. A police station was only a block away, yet no cop was in sight. A bum was selling newspapers that were essentially free. Next to him was a dog on a leash with a cat strapped to its back. And on top of the cat was a rat. The three of them seemed to get along just fine, though they were scraggly and weather worn. A man in a suit stopped to take a picture and dropped some coin into the bum's cup on his way to some gala on Market.

Doug remembered the look Loose had given him the last time he'd seen him. He remembered the stupid comment he had made when he had first heard that Loose's father was missing. In this new reality these were the only two times they had met. How could Doug form a relationship with this boy from that? With Alphonse gone, Doug imagined, there was no one to look after the boy. After losing both parents, it would be hard enough trying to convince him that the world was a wonderful place full of opportunity. He'd been dealt a cruel hand. And here he was, carving out a place for himself.

Doug thought of the photograph of Loose's family vacation on a lake. Doug could remember it though he doubted that now, with so many changes, he had ever been to Loose's van. Did Loose live there alone now, or did some of these boys live with him? Given his options, where might this boy end up? What was his destiny? Doug doubted Loose was thinking any longer of becoming a gaming programmer.

Doug wanted to approach him, wanted to help. But they had nothing in common, nothing to say to each other.

Constant waited for Doug to cross the street, wanting to say hello to Loose, but Doug turned left down the sidewalk away from the young hoods feeling very sad, almost destitute. At the corner, Doug bought a newspaper and read the obituaries, something he now did daily, looking for any sign of Angel's mama, but there was none. Angel had simply disappeared, busy with her own life, one without him, and with enough problems of her own. So much time had gone by. He had originally volunteered to keep an eye out for Angel, but then he had become involved. Now he was a regular and everybody knew him by name. Still, she had never shown up.

All the young children he knew from the kitchen were destined to relive their parents' lives. If only there was one small sign of hope. Even a gift of an empty box was better than nothing, but even that box had disappeared. Everything was gone.

Doug limped down the lonely street, his walking stick swinging loosely. Constant stayed beside him, but even he hung his head in despair.

33

The workday was over and the evening settled in when the news came. There was a knock at his office door. Jasmine turned to get up to open the door, but Doug beat her to it, even though he had the longer distance to travel. Andy entered carrying a bottle of champagne. The track lights for the artwork were low and the fluorescent lights were off. With the blinds open, the city shone in the distance, an array of sparkles in the night. Doug was learning to dread the night, the long hours of lying in bed. Even though work offered few challenges, he spent his evenings working late. Jasmine had been helping him keep his days structured. He kept endless lists of small jobs his businesses had contracted because he had trouble focusing. Sirius Development was dwindling but he didn't know what to do to revive it. Though all his other companies were doing fine, here he had had to lay off about a third of his workforce.

Yet here was Andy and his champagne, which could only mean one thing. This news was the thing Doug had been waiting for, the thing that still brought passion to his heart.

"You're kidding, right?" he asked with a smile on his face. Andy sat down next to Jasmine and popped the cork on the bottle. Champagne bubbled over the neck and his hand.

"Nope. It's time to celebrate."

"You did it?" asked Doug, building enthusiasm.

"Absolutely. We did it."

Doug felt a little as though they were going to be celebrating the closing of the barn doors after the horses had gotten out, but he shook off the feeling and tried to get into the moment. He had waited so long for this.

He passed Andy three glasses from the shelf behind his desk that held snifters and wine glasses. He had bought them simply to put on display, a romantic, masculine gesture. He kept no alcohol in his office. There was a small fridge off to the side, but it was filled with water and soda.

Andy filled the glasses handing one first to Jasmine, then to Doug. Doug stared at Andy, silently waiting for the official announcement.

After what seemed like an interminable amount of time, Jasmine asked, "What are we celebrating?" She took a sip from her glass and wrinkled her nose from the bubbles.

"The State," Andy held his glass high, "has declared the Tenderloin an historical site."

Doug raised his glass to Andy's and Jasmine did the same. The tinkling of glass was loud in the calm quiet of the room. Constant watched; he seemed to know that something important was happening.

"Congratulations," said Doug. This was it. Finally they had done something that would make a difference.

"Too bad the others aren't here to celebrate with us," Jasmine said, referring to the rest of the employees.

Doug looked at Jasmine and tried to remember that he'd once intended to fire her. Not only could he no longer imagine himself giving her a bad review, he actually thought he remembered making those glowing comments in the margins. It was as if this new memory were taking the place of the old.

He focused back on the present.

Doug thought about how many people he'd had to lay off. "I'm not so sure that they'd agree that it was something to celebrate, considering...."

"I think," said Andy, "they're waiting for the project to start up again. Have you decided what you want to do with our lot there?"

"I haven't even decided if there will *be* a project."

"Well, what are you going to do, just sell an empty lot? We'll lose our shirt on the deal. The bank is already breathing down our necks."

Doug set his glass down untouched. Suddenly, he wasn't in the mood. "I know, I know. I need to make a decision." He twirled the glass, his eyes shifting to the urn of Alphonse's ashes. "It just feels that no matter what we do, it won't be enough."

"Enough for what?" asked Jasmine.

"I usually try to see the ramifications of any project we might do...but my mind is just all confused." Doug leaned back in his chair. He had never thought about the entire effect his efforts might have on others, the ones who originally lived there. The thought was daunting, overwhelming. Constant lay down on the floor outside of the dog bed. "There are consequences to our actions. Things will happen to the neighborhood." He leaned forward again and twirled the glass. "I'm not sure I'm ready for that responsibility. I'm not sure I ever will be."

"Doug, it wasn't your fault." Andy pointed at the urn in the middle of the desk. "Accidents happen."

Doug thought about when he had had the fence placed around the property of his building when he had first purchased it. He was surprised that he remembered it that way. The fence wasn't the result of Alphonse telling him about the vagrants living there. He had done it from the get-go. That's the way he now remembered it. The other memory seemed like a false one.

Once again he wondered how Alphonse had made his way into the building. There had been security around it 24/7. He couldn't imagine the old man scaling the fence. There must have been a hole.

"Yeah, well, maybe if we just sit still, no more accidents will happen."

"You can't just stick your head in the sand. Too many people here are dependent on you." Andy drained his wine. "There are consequences to your inaction too, you know. We've already lost a third of our work force. Those people are out of a job." It sounded to Doug as though Andy was repeating his own words back to him. Yet, they sounded hollow somehow. Though his conglomerate was doing fine, it wasn't growing. Without new developments, it was stagnant, the momentum deflated. Overall, the companies were still earning lots of money. But soon Sirius Development might be out of business. Only the contracting businesses would remain.

"Yeah, I know. I know I'm being silly. My head feels like it's stuffed with cotton, or concrete, or something. Give me a few more days and I'll pull out of it. I was hoping this news would help."

"You know, in my opinion, for what it's worth, you've done a good thing here. This historical protection is good for the neighborhood, and it's good for the city."

"Thanks." Doug lifted his glass, held it aloft in a toast, and then took a sip.

"We're in the development business, but that doesn't mean there isn't lots of work in the Tenderloin fixing up all those old buildings," said Jasmine. She wiggled in her chair. "Look at what they did to City Hall."

"That's right," said Andy. "They even retrofitted it to bring it up to code for earthquakes. They spent a fortune on that place. And after this project, nothing says our next one has to be in the Tenderloin. There's still tons of stuff that can be done here in SOMA."

"Yeah, but everything here is so expensive now. The next big boom will be in the Tenderloin, and that's where we need to be to stay ahead of the curve." Doug wondered if that was still true with the Historical protection. It would be costly to remodel the old buildings, but it could be done. Doug started getting excited about the prospect.

Of course, they had blown up their building. They couldn't remodel it. They could have just fixed it up. It had actually been quite a nice old building. It could have worked. If only…

After Jasmine and Andy had gone home for the evening, Doug was turning off the track lights when he stopped and glanced back at the urn on his desk. It seemed to be waiting for him to do something. Walking stick in one hand, urn in the other, he left the building with Constant heeling on his left. The two of them walked side by side across town to the empty lot that not all that long ago had been a critical part of Doug's future.

At the fence, he showed his badge to the guard there wondering what good a security guard did now. What was he guarding? Doug had simply forgotten to discontinue the service. The guard looked at him questioningly but let him pass.

Near the center of the lot, Doug stopped. After placing his walking stick on the ground, he held the urn before him in praying hands. He glanced over his shoulder only to see the guard watching. Constant meandered around sniffing the ground off in the distance.

"You and I were supposed to be a team," he whispered to the urn, "working together for Loose." He shuffled his feet and looked up at the moon. "I've never been a very good team player. But without you I'm not sure what to do."

Dark clouds swept past and covered the moon so his eyes came back to the urn.

"I have no relationship with the boy and I don't even know how to start one. Bug thinks I'm disgusting; I doubt she would help me."

Constant came back to check in, sniffed Doug's knee, and took off again.

Doug shifted his weight to his good left leg. In his head, he had imagined this scene many times. He had envisioned himself saying so many things, but now, his thoughts were muddled. He was surprised that he hadn't made a list. It seemed that nowadays he made a list for everything.

"I'm sorry," he said at last. "I wish I could change things. I can't bring you back. You used to live here and I even took that away. But I did make sure that no one could tear down any more buildings. I don't know what's important to you, but I did this for you. It seemed like the only thing I could do." Doug wiped away the tears in his eyes with the back of his sleeve and sniffled. "It seemed like the right thing to do. But it's not enough, is it? Yet it's the best I can do."

Constant brushed against Doug's legs as the dog sat down in the dirt next to him. He glared up at Doug as though he understood and was offering his own support, his own condolences. Doug patted his head.

"You miss him too, don't ya boy?"

Doug remembered what Alphonse loved to do most, telling stories to the children.

And a thought came to him.

"I can do better than this," he said, holding the urn up to the sky. There was an unnatural silence in the air. The cars drove by silently. "Why hadn't I thought of it before? We'll put a school right here for the homeless children."

Lightning flashed through the clouds and thunder cracked, breaking the silence. "Maybe we can even have a rehab center for the parents. Or a place where they can learn a trade."

The ground began to shake, and Doug fell to his butt, still holding the urn aloft. Constant licked his face and wagged his tail. Though it must have been another earthquake, Doug was too ecstatic to care. The wind picked up and howled through his ears.

Doug laughed and tussled Constant's hair. The dog crawled under one arm and nuzzled there. Doug squeezed him and then stood up. "We can do this." He opened the urn and scattered the ashes in the wind. "And this will be your home." Doug turned in a circle tossing the ashes this way and that. When he finished, everything calmed down. No more lightning. No more thunder. The ground ceased to shake.

Doug grabbed his walking stick and left the lot. Two blocks toward home, he spotted a shopping cart parked against a building. It was filled with what looked to Doug like garbage. Next to it lay an old woman in a grungy, oversized fur overcoat, torn nylons stuck into shoes with the heels broken off. She was holding an old dented coffee can, which was tipped on its side. A cardboard sign had fallen face down before it. She was snoring and reeked of stale booze.

Doug used a hand signal to get Constant to sit. He entered a liquor store, purchasing a pre-wrapped sandwich and a plastic bottle of orange juice from the man behind the counter. Upon placing his wallet back in his jacket, he noticed he still had the AA brochure and meeting schedule from the other night.

When he got back outside, Doug saw that Constant had moved closer to the bag lady, as though he were looking out for her. Doug decided that "bag lady" was a pejorative term and decided to eliminate it from his vocabulary.

He tried to awaken the woman by shaking her shoulder, but she wouldn't stir. Still leaning over her, he crammed the sandwich and juice behind her so that no one could notice enough to steal them. Then, very gently, he slipped the AA meeting schedule into her pocket. Maybe she'd use it. He tucked her overcoat around her more tightly trying to keep her warm for the night. One never knew what might save someone's life.

Doug, charged by the evening's accomplishments, quickly shuffled three steps down the sidewalk, pointing his walking stick toward the sky. Constant leapt to follow.

34

That night Doug dreamed of Doctor Krause, a burly man with bushy gray eyebrows. Doug remembered the eyebrows more than anything else about the man. Doug was in fourth grade again, a skinny little thing, always small for his age as a child.

After two consultations with Doug, the doctor called a meeting with him and his parents.

"I'm going to prescribe lithium for your son. He's what we call hyperactive, and we need to slow him down a notch."

Doug's father, though holding his tongue, was against the whole idea of psychiatry. He believed there was nothing wrong with his son that good hard work couldn't cure. But even at that age, Doug knew that something was wrong with him. There were too many times when what he remembered drastically differed from everyone else's memory.

"These flights of fancy he has," continued Doctor Krause, "are a form of paranoia. He doesn't want to face reality. I believe they are caused from an overactive mind. This medication I'm prescribing should remedy the situation. He has to take it every day, and you should expect him to have to take it for quite a long time. Some children grow out of it, but those are rare cases. Don't slack on his medication even for a day. This stuff works best when we are consistent."

In a very small voice, Doug asked, "Why am I different, Doc?" He didn't want to take drugs to be normal. Would the drugs make him forget who he was?

But before the doctor could answer his question, Doug woke up from his dream.

He was glad to be awake, because he didn't like those memories, not one little bit. Over the years the prescription had changed as new and better drugs were invented. But somewhere along the way, Doug had forgotten about why he was taking them, what had originally caused his mother's concern to take him to the doctor. He simply took it because more recently he had been diagnosed bipolar.

And now that the memory had returned, he hurried to put it aside. He didn't want to remember his delusions, if that's what they were. So he got out of bed and busied himself getting ready for work. He was excited about announcing the return of the project. He had an idea and he was sure it would work. Of course, there was the question of how to afford it. How could he make money on this new project?

He and Constant took a taxi to the office after their morning walk. Doug had to pay twice the usual fare to take the dog along, and the cabbie still grumbled about it. Constant looked offended and seemed to be about to put up an argument, but he instead sat on the bench seat in his best doggie-behavior pose.

At the office building, waiting for the elevator, Doug glanced at the sign that stated what businesses were on what floors.

It said his businesses were taking up every floor. But that wasn't right. Someone must have screwed up the sign.

When he and Constant got off the elevator, the sound of bustle confronted them. Doug was amazed at how many employees there were, more than he'd ever had at one time. Who were these people? He didn't recognize many. Many of them seemed to be cleaned-up versions of the homeless people he'd met at the Saint Anthony's. Constant even greeted them warmly and a few called the dog by name.

Doug rushed forward through the crowd. Without stopping at her station, Doug said to Jasmine, "Come with me," and used his badge to enter his office with Jasmine in tow. She held the door until Constant followed.

"What is going on?" he asked.

She stood by the door as she replied, "Do you want a complete rundown of today's activities? I have the newest update from Jack I could print out for you." She turned to go back to her desk when Doug stopped her with his next question.

"Who are all these people?" he asked as he sat at his desk with his hands steepled in front of him. Constant followed Jasmine to a chair and sat down on the floor next to her, expecting attention, which she gave by sliding her hands over his ears. His curled tail wagged in appreciation.

"I'm sorry, Mister Sirius," she said, "I don't understand."

"There's a crowd of people out there. What are they doing?"

"Their jobs?" she asked rather than stated, as though he were playing some kind of guessing game with her.

"You're saying they work here?"

"I'm not sure where you're going with this. Yes, as you well know, all those people work here." She sat smiling at him nervously.

"But they look like some homeless people I know," Doug said trying not to sound judgmental.

"They *would be* homeless if it wasn't for The Sirius Program," she stated proudly.

"The Sirius program?"

Jasmine chuckled. "Is this a pop quiz? Okay, I can handle it. The Sirius program is a work relief program. We teach people a trade, and they come work for us. You started it what...years ago. Before I even started working here, sometime after your first construction in the Fillmore. The majority of our employees come through the program."

"I did? I mean, they do? I seem to be a bit foggy this morning."

Doug thought about the previous night, the lightning in the clouds with no rain, the thunder, the earthquake, the scattering of the ashes.

"Was there an earthquake last night?" Doug said, taking the empty urn from his satchel and placing it on the shelves behind his desk.

"Not that I know of."

"No thunder and lightning?"

"I think I would have noticed with how rarely it thunders around here. It didn't even rain last night. Are you okay, sir? Is there something I could get for you?"

"No. Well, yes. I want to meet with Andy ASAP."

Jasmine left, and while Doug waited, he noticed that the painting he'd done with Bug was back up on the wall. Down in the left-hand corner were his initials; in the right were Bug's. This meant that he and his niece had a relationship again. The past had changed to give him back his Bug, and that by itself was worth celebrating. He couldn't wait to see her.

There was a loud knock. Doug walked over and opened the door rather than using the buzzer to unlock it. After Andy had entered the office, Doug left the door wide open. Why did he need it closed anyhow? Maybe he should just leave it open all the time.

Doug's mood had changed dramatically. He was looking forward to hearing about all the changes in the past this new day had brought. He was no longer frightened about facing them.

"What makes you so chipper?" Andy asked.

"Chipper?" he said while crossing the room. "Of course I'm chipper. It's a new day." He glanced once more at the painting to make sure it hadn't changed again before sitting in his chair with a sigh of relief. Andy sat down across from him, handing a treat to Constant, whose bushy gray brows wiggled as he chewed.

"Tell me," Doug said, "didn't we get the Historical proposal approved yesterday?"

"Yes we did."

"Then why aren't we celebrating?"

"Everyone is waiting for the meeting this afternoon."

"Ah, they're waiting for me to announce what the new project is all about." Doug picked up the latest summary from Jack and glanced at it. It didn't make sense to him. The second page showed a floor plan of the main floor of the building they had torn down.

"New building?" Andy leaned forward and placed a palm on the desktop. "What new building? We're in the middle of a remodel. We always do remodels. It's what our slogan stands for, 'Sirius Development to Preserve the Past.'"

"Are you telling me the old building is still standing?"

"Doug, we've been working on it for weeks. We almost have the first floor done. We'll be able to start classes sometime next week while we finish the other floors. The concrete sign for The Alphonse Center goes up today."

"Classes? At The Alphonse Center?"

"For homeless kids. You named the place after that old guy who was always teaching the kids at that kitchen where you do volunteer work. We'll also be moving the rehab program for adults there on the second floor."

"You know Alphonse? Do you know where he is?" Doug's words were pouring out of his mouth faster than his mind could think them. Then his thoughts started rushing as well. He wondered about Loose and if he and Alphonse were working together. "I need to see him." Could it be true? Might the old man have miraculously come back to life?

"Doug, you know as well as I do that Alphonse is dead. That's why you named the center after him."

"So we did kill him." Doug's intertwined fingers unlaced and worried over his palms and the back of his hands. He couldn't understand. If the building hadn't been demolished...

"Don't you remember? We found his body in the building. Apparently he had been living there. But he was an old man. He just went and died. We didn't kill him. I don't know where you'd got such an idea. Old people just die sometimes."

Doug sat back and let his hands fall loosely to his lap. Suddenly he felt exhausted. The conversation was making his heart run rapid.

"Why don't I let you get some work done before our meeting this afternoon?" As Andy rose to leave, Constant stood looking forlorn at losing the opportunity for another treat.

"What meeting?" Doug said, realizing that it couldn't have been to announce the school.

"Quit screwing around," Andy said as he approached the door. "*You* put the meeting agenda in the corporate folder. Maybe you should take a gander at it."

With that comment, he left.

Doug slowly maneuvered his mouse so that his cursor rested on the corporate folder icon. Before he clicked on it, he realized that right there, sitting in the middle of his desk as if just waiting for him, was the empty box Angel had given him from her mother. Letting go of the mouse, he grabbed the box, thankful for its return. Did this mean that Angel once again knew who he was? Might they have a relationship?

But the box wasn't empty any longer. He could hear that there was something inside. Doug opened the box slowly and tipped it upside down. Out came a small card with a flower on the front. It had the look of something that had been read many times. Inside the card were two words: Thank You.

Doug was surprised by how much this affected him. How could two little words mean so much? Why would Angel's mother be thanking him? He didn't know, but it made him feel good nonetheless. Maybe for the first time, it felt as if someone was telling him, "You done good, boy," something he had never heard from either of his parents. He felt like a child receiving his first gold star.

With renewed vigilance, he returned to the corporate folder on his computer and read the agenda for today's meeting. He needed no further inspiration; he intuitively knew what he should do.

35

At the meeting in the conference room, Doug and Andy sat on one side of the table facing the three men who sat the same way as they had at the last meeting, fat man in the middle. Constant sat at attention between Andy and Doug, just waiting for a wrong move. Doug rested his hand on his dog's neck, soothing him, holding him back for the time being. He rarely saw the dog more protective. It was something to admire.

"Well, gentlemen," Doug said, using the term out of habit, "we all know why we're here. I've made a generous offer to buy your assets, assume your loans on the twenty-five SROs, and basically get you out of bankruptcy. Today, that offer runs out. Did you show up here with the signed contract I sent you?"

As the fat man pulled the contract, in triplicate, he said, "I wouldn't call this a generous offer."

Doug slapped both hands on the table and began to rise from his chair while saying, "Then I guess we're done here."

"Hold on," said the fat man with a sweep of his arm, palm extended. "I didn't say we wouldn't accept it." He pushed the three copies across the table to Andy. "At this price, we're taking a big loss."

Taking up the contracts to peruse, Andy said, "You overextended yourselves. It's quite common with new entrepreneurs."

Just for a moment, Doug wondered how he was going to afford this purchase. Might he be setting himself up for failure? He didn't like going into debt. He liked to build slowly from his own profits.

"That's not the problem and you know it," the fat man said to Doug. "You pushed the State Historical Resource Commission to get the resolution passed on the twenty-fifth," he said, referring to yesterday, July 25, 2008. "Since you started working on it last fall with the mayor, our plans fell into the dumper. We couldn't get the demolition for our new building approved. It was a great plan."

Doug tapped his fingers on the table waiting for Andy to tell him it was okay to sign. "And your point is?" he asked of the fat man.

"With our plans for the new building squashed, we couldn't get more financing. It seems like too much of a coincidence."

"How's that?" asked Doug, smiling.

"You didn't by any chance revitalize this commission simply to lay your hands on our properties, now did you?"

"Interesting theory," Doug said, and then turned to Andy. "How are we doing over there?"

"Sure enough, these are the original documents we sent over to them, signed, sealed, and delivered."

Andy slid the papers over to Doug for his signature. Doug signed.

"Tell me," asked the fat man, "what are you going to do with these buildings now that you own them?"

"People live in those hotels. We're going to fix them up and make them livable."

"And how do you make money doing that from a bunch of worthless derelicts?"

Doug grinned and rose from his chair signifying the meeting was over. He opened the door with Constant at his side, wondering to himself how he was going to make money with this purchase.

Andy followed, saying, "The money will be wired to the account designated in the documents by the end of the day. Here is your copy." He tossed one of them across the table and left.

Once out in the main area, Doug waved the copies to a waiting crowd and announced, "We are now the proud owners of 25 SROs in the Tenderloin," to which all the employees cheered. "And our first change will be that we will no longer rent by the hour, or even by the day. The minimum will be a week. Then, after we finish the Alphonse Center, we will draw straws on which hotel we will remodel first. But trust me when I say, we will remodel all of them." There was loud applause and hooting.

Doug leaned over to Andy and whispered, "Can we really afford to do this?"

"You're kidding, right? You're the biggest developer in the city. The Sirius Conglomerate is huge. Don't you attend your weekly senior staff meetings? Don't you go over the cash flow at each meeting?"

Doug thought about the sign he had seen before he entered the elevator this morning. They *did* occupy the entire building.

He softly breathed, "Wow."

Andy cocked an eyebrow. "This whole idea of yours to help homeless people was inspirational, not to say very successful, very profitable. These people would do anything for you, Doug. You saved their lives."

Who would have thought that helping people could be so profitable? Obviously these people were hard workers. Given the chance, they had become successful. And from what Andy had just said, apparently they treated these companies like their home, treated each other like family.

Doug looked around at the smiling faces in the crowd. All these people had stories. Like the man who grew watermelons so that the kids could try to steal them. Doug promised himself he would learn each and every one of them. He'd take the time to listen to their stories.

Jasmine sifted through the crowd carrying what looked like a sparkling cider for Andy and a sparkling water for Doug in clear plastic cups. Obviously, Doug realized, there would be no champagne for this crowd of alcoholics and addicts. Doug thought that even having the appearance of bubbly was probably a mistake, a reminder, a temptation of sorts. But nobody seemed uncomfortable with it.

Jack came up and toasted Doug. Two other employees slapped Doug on the back. An old woman thanked him for believing in them.

Jack pulled Doug aside and said, "There's enough work here to last years. I'm just wondering if there's enough profit in it."

Doug thought Jack might be referring to the loss of revenues from the hotels no longer substituting as one-night crack and whorehouses. From what Doug had gathered from the financial statements, well over half of the income was derived from these activities.

"These hotels have promoted criminal activity. Hopefully by no longer catering to that clientele, the neighborhood streets will be cleaned up a little. We'll just have to help more people get sober. And maybe a new kind of person will move into our neighborhood."

Andy joined them. He listened while he sipped his cider.

"There'll be a lot of fallout," Jack said. "Many of our employees relapse."

Doug looked to Andy for support. "We need to focus on our successes."

Andy waved his finger in front of Jack's face. "They already go through random drug testing once a week. Furthermore, they have all contractually agreed to the garnishment of their rent. Most prefer it that way. They don't want the temptation of extra cash." Andy took another sip of his cider. "All these people can afford to live in better places, once they're sober, once they really start performing. The reason they want so badly to fix up these SROs is that all their friends are there.

"The more people that get sober, the more employees we'll have, the more renters, the faster we'll get all the hotels remodeled. The faster we'll be making a profit. Our profit margins all around will be small, but we'll just have to make up for it in volume."

Jack didn't look pleased but he nodded his understanding. He circulated back into the crowd.

"That guy is just never satisfied," Andy said to Doug when Jack was out of earshot.

"That's what makes him good at what he does. He's never satisfied with the workmanship. Always demanding more."

"Yeah, but I don't think he'll ever quite accept the quality of the work these people provide. He just seems to keep judging them because of their past. But it's because of their past that they want so badly to change their future. The reminder of their past can change their future."

Don't I know it, Doug thought. And what I do today, apparently, can actually change the past.

Doug thought of all the people that would move into this area once it was a safer place to live, wanting to live closer to the financial district. It was a great plan.

Later, Doug was alone in his private office. Even Constant was still out there mingling. In one hand Doug held the box and in the other the thank you note. Charlie had mentioned to him that his decisions not only affected the future but also the past. He was beginning to understand what she meant. But with so much resting on his decisions, he was afraid he might become incapable of making any choice. But those days seemed to be over.

Doug dropped the note back in the box and placed it at the center of his desk. He picked up his Kindle and downloaded the day's news. In the obituaries, he saw that Petra "Charlie" Guzman had passed away the night before. The announcement was only one sentence; a more detailed announcement was pending. However, in that one sentence was something that stunned him: Angel's mother had the nickname of "Charlie."

Could she be the one who had been contacting him? It was too much of a coincidence to not be true.

From her deathbed Charlie had reached out to him. Somehow, as she was dying, she had seen alternate futures and had reached out to him for help. Hadn't Hunt said that the IP address had come from the hospital?

It was incredible.

Thinking of Hunt made him remember the number 010-101-0101 that had displayed when the calls came from Charlie. The phone had said the line was "deceased." Angel's Mama had been in a coma ever since he had first met Angel. Was it possible that Charlie's mind had already died? That her body had remained alive through life support? He remembered the beeping the last time he talked to her. Now even her body was gone. He would miss their conversations.

Who but he would know her story, that she had reached out at the end of her life and changed the world? It was a beautiful story, if only he could tell it. But anyone would think him nuts if he did.

And what might Angel be doing now? Most likely dealing with funeral arrangements. He wanted to be there with her to comfort her, but he was reluctant to call her. What was their relationship like now? He had no way of knowing. If they had any kind of relationship at all, she would probably call him soon. He decided the right thing to do was wait.

The death of Angel's mama meant something more to him now that he knew she was Charlie. So did the little thank you note that was in what had once been an empty box. He would never get to thank Charlie in return, for she had changed his life. Somehow she had made him feel less crazy regarding what was happening to him. And in the midst of that craziness, she had set him on in the right path.

But then again, what if his conversations with her had not actually happened? What if that was simply another manifestation of his madness? Of course if he had only been talking to himself, he would try to convince himself that he wasn't going insane. But he remembered Hunt told him that he had traced the communication back to the hospital. He was positive now.

Doug opened the drawer to put away his Kindle. In there was a bottle of his medication. On impulse he held one pill from the bottle, telling himself that it was a good idea. But he stopped with the pill halfway to his open mouth. What if his awareness of the changing of the past was because he had stopped taking his meds? And what if this awareness could help him control the changes of the past? Hadn't he just proved he could, at least a little? There were so many things he would change, so much good he could do. He drank the last of his sparkling water and tossed the plastic cup and the pill in the trash.

If this was madness, he chose to embrace it.

Placing the pill bottle back in the drawer, he looked up and noticed the sand worm painting again. He wanted to hurry home to see if his relationship with Bug had been returned to him.

As he walked out the door to his office, Constant came to him and stretched directly in his path with an expression that said, *don't mind me, I'm just stretching here.* But Doug knew it to be a ploy for attention, so he stopped and scratched the dog along his back.

"Let's go."

36

Terra opened the door for her uncle and gave him a big hug, then followed this with a hug for Constant. Ruffing up the dog's hair, she whispered excitedly, "Good Dog. You're a good dog, aren't you? Yes you are. That's my dog. Good dog."

"I got a new job," She said to her uncle, feeling proud and wanting to share her excitement with him.

"You didn't like the one you had?"

"I appreciate you helping me get it." She sat down on the couch and closed the book she had been reading, marking the page with a business card. Constant immediately snuggled up next to her. "But it wasn't really me. I could do it all right, but my new job is as a seamstress. That's what I really want to do, design new clothes. I can start with sewing and move my way up to design."

"You've always been good at making your own costumes for those anime conventions."

"Cosplay."

"What?"

"Dressing up like anime characters. That's what it's called: cosplay."

"Oh."

"I just went in and showed them photos of what I had made and they gave me the job."

"I'd like to see the pictures sometime."

"I'll show you when I get them back."

Uncle Doug took off his jacket and hung it up on the coat rack by the door. She noticed that he must have stopped at home to change before coming over. He was wearing jeans, a Quantum Flux t-shirt, and red tennis shoes: an outfit good for painting. He followed her into the art studio and both of them put on blue plastic smocks. His only went down to his knees, yet he never seemed to get any paint on his legs or shoes. At first he seemed hesitant about getting ready, as if he didn't know they were going to paint. Then he buttoned up the snaps on the front of his smock while Terra changed her shoes to ones covered in paint.

The painting on the easel was their most recent effort. It was a range of volcanoes shaped like industrial smoke stacks in greens and browns and ocher, with a touch of purple within the smoke. The volcano in the foreground had a hand around it as though it was a cup of coffee. There was a jagged rip down the side of the volcano, leaking lava.

Uncle Doug studied the painting like he had never seen it before. What was wrong with him today? He must have his mind still on work. But that's what these painting sessions were all about – giving him a way to relax. He needed more art in his life, or at least some hobbies, something other than work.

Terra opened a can of light blue house paint and used a very small brush to highlight the closest edges of the smokestacks where the flames were hottest. She handed the brush to her uncle and grabbed a small putty knife. With it, she painted a thin line drawing of a spaceship shooting laser beams at the crack in the volcano. The lines she created with the edge of the knife were so thin that they were nearly invisible.

"Come on," she said to her uncle. "Step right up." Though Uncle Doug was always uncomfortable with this process, this was when she felt closest to him. He was like a shy boy trying his hardest to do what was right, trying to perform for her, make her proud of him, or at least trying to please her. She liked that. Therapy 101 had been her idea, and she was pleased with the result.

"You know," she said, trying to sound nonchalant, "with helping Loose so much lately, it sort of makes me think about Mom a lot."

Uncle Doug suddenly began to paint. "And?"

"I guess I've sort of been trying to fill her role with my dad." She fussed with things on the table. Admitting this made her a little uncomfortable. "Maybe I've even been mothering you a little." She looked at him to see his reaction. "But she was my Dad's wife not his mother. She was your sister. She was only a mother to me." She paused. "I guess I was trying to give you two what I was missing. But anyhow, I like being a big sister better, and that's what I feel like I am to Loose. It's more my style, more appropriate for a girl my age. It even feels more natural."

"I would suppose so," Uncle Doug said. He opened his arms. "Come here." He gave her a quick one-armed hug. He seemed to be doing that more and more lately, hugging her,

310

becoming more comfortable with intimacy. "Don't worry about it. Big sisters have to be motherly once in a while too."

"Most definitely." Terra smiled, stepping back up to the canvas. Using the edge of her putty knife, she finished up her laser beams.

"How is Loose?"

Terra watched as Uncle Doug painted the fine blue lines in the heart of the flames. He was getting into it now, enjoying the process. She smiled, once again thinking that these painting sessions were her favorite times with her uncle.

"He's working really hard at school. And he loves the apartment. He still spends a lot of time in his van, though. Tonight, he's probably down at the Saint Anthony's. You want to go visit?"

"That sounds like a wonderful idea."

"Maybe Angel will be working there tonight," Terra said.

"Oh, I really don't think so." A sad expression ran across his face, but he didn't explain himself further.

Changing the subject, she said, "I take my driver's test next week. I really appreciate you helping with all the practice lessons."

"Are you ready for it?"

"Well, I could always use a little more practice."

"Ah, well, by all means. We'll just have to do that. One more lesson coming right up."

37

Inside the BMW 3.0 CS coupe, on their way to Saint Anthony's, with Doug riding shotgun and Constant in the back, Bug tuned the radio to a college station that was playing some kind of post-punk pop. She cranked it up and Doug reached over and turned the radio off.

"Concentrate on your driving," he said.

She smiled and turned the radio back on, but she turned the volume down low. "Better?"

"Much. Now stop bouncing around so much and watch the road."

"Nag, nag, nag. The music helps me get into driving in traffic."

"You get much more into it, and we'll be piled into it. Don't wait so long to begin stopping. Ease into it sooner."

"Yes, Master," Bug said imitating Igor from some old Frankenstein movie. She moved through traffic like a taxi driver, jerking her way through acceleration and braking, swerving in and out of lanes. Doug wasn't sure if he should compliment her on her confidence or get out and walk the rest of the way.

"I don't think you want to drive quite so aggressively on your test. Let's just practice exactly as if you were taking your test. Why don't you pull up here and try parking."

"I thought I'd park in the lot around the corner," she whined.

"I think you should practice parallel parking."

"They don't make you parallel park anymore."

"You're kidding. That's just about the only kind of parking there is in the city." He twirled his walking stick with both hands.

"It's not on the test."

Maybe there were too many accidents during the tests and the DMV didn't want the liability anymore. *But officer, the instructor made me do it.*

"Are you sure?" Doug had the feeling that she had told him this before.

"Positive."

"That's weird."

"So are you." This was a line she used on him a lot.

To which he gave his normal retort, "But not as weird as you."

"That's true," she responded quickly.

They entered Saint Anthony's with Constant leading the way as if he was king, this was his castle, and these homeless people were his subjects. Watching him, Doug smiled. The place seemed more crowded than usual. So many hungry people.

Across the room Doug noticed Loose encircled by a group of children younger than he. Loose was telling them a story of when he had been camping with his parents. Doug assumed that none of these children had ever been camping, for their eyes were lit in astonishment.

"And within a couple of hours the sun had heated the water in the black plastic bag enough so that it could be used for a shower," Loose said.

"But," said one of the older boys in the circle, "you could just bathe in the lake if you wanted, right?"

"Well, yeah. The water in the lake was certainly warm enough."

A younger girl chimed in. "So you wouldn't even need a place to stay. You could just live outdoors and live off the fish in the lake."

"But on a tropical island you could live there all year round," said another.

"Yes," said Loose, "but you couldn't drink the water." Loose looked up from the group and noticed Doug.

He dismissed himself from the other children and came over to Doug holding his palms outward to ward off whatever Doug might be thinking. He said, "I've already finished my homework so that this won't interfere."

"I wasn't going to say a word," said Doug. "I like seeing you teaching the kids. Maybe you can work for the school once we get it up and running. A teacher's assistant of some sort."

"That would be great," said Loose. He obviously knew about the project, so Doug assumed they'd talked about it before.

"I got a notice from the school the other day. The authorities want me to come and see them," Loose said with sadness in his voice. "Do you think they're gonna try to put me in a foster home?"

"I'll come with you. We'll deal with this."

"That would be great!"

Doug realized that, if push came to shove, he could have Loose come live with him. That wouldn't be easy, now that the authorities were involved, though. He would probably have to petition the courts for custody and that would most likely get complicated.

Doug noticed Bug talking to Marcia over by the serving line. He went over to ask about Angel with Loose following closely behind. But before he could ask, Marcia spoke.

"Angel was supposed to work this evening. She didn't even call in sick. That's not like her."

"So you haven't heard?" asked Doug.

"Heard what?" Marcia responded.

"About her mother."

"I knew she was sick. Is she gone?"

"Yes. Sometime last night."

"She called you?"

"No."

"Don't you think she needs your support?"

"Yeah, I suppose I should head on over there, huh?"

"Ya think?" Sarcasm dripped from her words.

Doug thought that the reason he had not run immediately to Angel's side was that she hadn't called him. He was uncertain of their relationship. But how dumb was that. He didn't need to be her lover to be supportive. And even Marcia thought he should be with her, which meant that everyone knew they were close.

And then it occurred to Doug that Marcia had called her "Angel." No one else had ever called her by that name. She had told him that herself.

Doug's phone vibrated. He looked at the screen and saw that it was Angel's number.

Suddenly Doug very much wanted to be by her side.

"Hello," he said, tentatively.

"Could you come over?" she asked.

"Absolutely."

"Mama…"

"I know."

"Thank you."

"I'll be there as fast as I can." He hung up.

"Bug, I gotta go. You want a ride home?" Doug noticed that she didn't seem to mind that he had mistakenly called her by her nickname in public. She simply nodded in reply.

"Was that Angel?"

"Yes."

"And her mother just died?"

"Yes."

"So why aren't you with her already?"

"I know. I'm going now."

37

"Do you mind if I leave Constant here while I run over to Angel's?" Doug asked Hunt. Bug and the dog were in the front room sitting on the couch together watching TV.

"Constant is always welcome here. You know that." Hunt splashed some paint on a canvas with his bare hand.

"Hey, do you remember when you were describing quantum flux to me?"

"Sure, yeah, sometime before the concert."

"And you said something about every action creating multiple realities."

"Different choices setting off parallel universes. Sure, I remember."

"What if there weren't other universes? What if there was just one? And what if the past of this universe changes to validate every decision we make?"

"You mean like if I just popped you one in the face for no reason? By the time I was done hitting you, the past would have changed so that you had given me a reason to hit you."

"Something like that, yeah."

"Zamyatin or Orwell wrote something about that – that those who control the present control the past. But I don't think this is what he meant. He was talking about the ones in power being allowed to write the history books any way they want."

"No, that isn't quite the same."

"Well, if what you suggest were happening, I highly doubt if anyone would notice."

Doug smiled and said nothing. He had no way to prove if coming off his medication had made him aware of the phenomenon, or if doing so had just made him hallucinate the whole thing. Though he chose to believe the former, he doubted he'd ever be able to convince anyone else.

Then it occurred to Doug that the past wasn't changing because of just anyone's decisions; it was only changing according to his. The past was validating *his* decisions. Somehow he was unique. And this thought made him smile. That's why Charlie had reached out to him. She had known all along that he was different, that he was special.

Hunt noticed his hand was dripping paint, so, after splashing it at the canvas one more time, he went to the corner sink to rinse. Doug stood and watched with a smile still spread across his face.

38

Evangelina was working on the funeral announcement. It was hard to keep it short as she thought of all the things she wanted to say about Mama. All the memories twirled around inside her, bringing tears to her eyes. She could do this; she had to. Surely her sisters weren't up to the task.

There were so many things to get done. She had already made an appointment at the funeral parlor. She had given them the information and they would coordinate with the hospital. And she needed to schedule the funeral to be able to finish this announcement.

The announcement, a summary of Mama's life – as if mere words could do this – was an impossible task. She could write a book and it wouldn't be enough.

She wrote yesterday's date at the top of the page. July 25, 2008: the day her mama died.

She grabbed another tissue from the box and blew her nose, adding it to the pile already stacked there on the kitchen table. There was the picture of her mother Evangelina had chosen for the newspaper propped against a bunch of bananas. She stared at it and thought about how beautiful Mama had been.

Had been? There it was again, past tense, a reminder that it was over. She'd never see her Mama again, never rub her feet, never hear her laugh. Never, ever again. It seemed so unreal somehow, a bad dream that perhaps she might wake from. This was the day she hadn't wanted to face since she had heard of Mama's condition more than a year and a half ago.

She placed her face in her hands, sobbing silently. She heard a knock at her front door and remembered that she had called Doug. She didn't realize how much she wanted to see him until this moment.

Two more tissues tossed on the pile, she gathered herself and made her way to the door.

Doug stood there solemnly. She had wanted so much to be strong, to handle this all on her own. Now that he was here, though, she knew how much she needed him. She threw her arms around him, burying her face in his shoulder. It felt like forever since she had been in his arms, but it was only yesterday that he had visited her at the hospital. He'd gone home and she hadn't called him to say that Mama had passed. That was silly of her; this was what she needed.

All the self-control she had gathered came crashing down in a heartbeat. She gripped him with all her strength and hung on for dear life. Angel eventually felt Doug walking her backwards, closing the door behind him, but still she couldn't let go. And she couldn't stop crying.

"Hey, now," he whispered, stroking her hair with one hand, the other arm firmly grasping her shoulders. Hers were around his back, hands clutching his shoulder blades. She didn't want to let go, couldn't.

He was the only person in the world who could give her a reason to live right now. He was her future. She could feel it here in his arms. It was the only thing at this moment she was sure of. And that assurance – that semblance of joy mixed with her sorrow – made her cry even harder. She was a mess.

She leaned back, still hanging on, and looked deep into his eyes, those beautiful blue eyes. The love there was obvious for all the world to see. She rested her head on his chest, felt her body relaxing, her heart slow down. She breathed a sigh into his shirt. She wiped her face there and looked up at him and smiled. It wasn't much of a smile, but it was real. She sniffled and placed her head back down.

He patted her back. "That's better." He gave her a squeeze.

She took him by the hand and led him to the kitchen. He looked at the table and then at her. He held her chin in one hand and gave her a kiss.

She offered him the best smile she could. "There's just so much to do and I'm…not functioning all that well."

"You're doing fine," he said, squeezing her shoulder. "What can I do to help?" His touch was enough reassurance. Just his being here made such a difference.

"I have an appointment at the funeral parlor in about an hour."

"We'll go together, if that's okay."

She nodded again and kissed his hand on her shoulder.

He placed his other hand on the announcement she had been working on. He looked into her eyes. He said, "You keep working on this, and I'll start a list of all the things we need to do."

Evangelina liked his use of the word, "we." Together they could get this done. She sniffled once more, drew in a deep breath, and sat down, handing him his own pen and a piece of paper. He joined her at the table. She hadn't wanted her sisters to help her; she had wanted to do this alone. But this was different; she found relief here in his company. She smiled again, a little wider this time, but without looking at him. He used the back of his hand, softly sliding it along her cheek and the line of her jaw. She closed her eyes. This was something Mama used to do. She leaned into it like a cat being stroked. The gesture told her that everything was going to be all right. Opening her eyes, she kissed his hand once again. She smiled at him. Then she started to write.

39

A week after the funeral, on Beideman Street in the Western Addition neighborhood of San Francisco, where Doug's first project had taken place, Doug held Angel's hand as they stared at Charlie's home. Beideman ran only one block between O'Farrell and Ellis streets, parallel to Scott and Divisadero on the edge of the Fillmore district. The project had changed. What Doug remembered as modern condos were now refurbished three-storied Victorians beautifully remodeled and painted in dazzling color. Each building was trimmed differently, looking like something Hunt might have painted. It felt like Disneyland or maybe some photo from Argentina.

Doug stooped to pick up an empty soda can; the street was clean without it. He tossed it toward the front door to pick up later.

Angel smiled at him.

A wren watched the two of them from a branch of a large tree in the park on the corner. A wooden jungle gym was there for the kids.

"I think I'm going to move out of my place on Forrest View and move back here," she said, nodding at 55 Beideman, the building adjacent to the park. She had already mentioned that the mortgage had been paid off. Her mother had lived here a long time. This was where Angel had grown up, little Evangelina. That thought alone made Doug feel younger, like a teenager in love.

"This will be a nice place to live. I'll help you move."

Constant ran over to the park, found a stick, and brought it back. He wasn't about to give it to Doug, but he teased Doug with it. Doug and Angel followed the dog to the park. A squirrel took to the tree trunk and the wren took off to the sky.

"Even when I was a kid, the park was here," reminisced Angel. "Most of the street was empty lots, but the park was the same."

"I know," said Doug.

"Yes, I know. You were the one who trucked the Victorians here. Mama loved you for it. She was so proud of you. I guess she never told you that."

Doug's memory was solid about the way things had happened before the past changed. Yet, memories emerged that coincided with the way things were after the change. Doug could remember how they had built the foundations for the houses and then trucked them over on flatbeds in the middle of the night. It had been surreal to watch.

"Oh, she thanked me. She left me a note in the package you gave me."

"I'm glad, because she talked about you a lot. She thought you were wonderful."

Doug let go of her hand and leaned against the side of the Jungle Gym.

326

"Speaking of kids," Doug said.

Angel smiled and waited.

"I was thinking of adopting Loose. I haven't talked to him about it yet."

"That's wonderful. He'll be thrilled. It will do you a world of good too. Kids are a good way for parents to face their own problems."

"You think?"

"It's like going back to the basics, to what makes us tick. You see yourself in everything they do."

"I was wondering if I might be too old."

Constant came up to Doug and nudged his leg with his snout. Doug patted the dog's head. Constant stared at the squirrel in the tree. It was the only tree in the park, so the little rodent had no other branches to jump to.

"Early thirties seems when most people are having kids these days," Angel said. "I definitely don't consider myself too old."

"I didn't mean that," defended Doug.

"I know you didn't." She ruffled the fur around Constant's neck. From her purse she handed Doug a picture, the one she took the night Loose and he had dyed their hair in the bathroom at Loose's new apartment. It showed the four of them together, laughing. Doug was amazed that the trip to Great America had still happened with how much of the past had changed. It was such a good memory.

"Speaking about the package Mama sent you, I was thinking that she might have had an ulterior motive for doing so."

"Yeah?" The memory of the empty box was receding, as if it had always held the thank you note. But the empty box had been symbolic in a way, empty space begging to be filled, pure potential.

"Yes. I think she wanted to bring us together."

"That's a nice thought."

"It's one I want to keep."

Doug nestled her into his arms, dropping his walking stick to the ground. "Me too."

Yes, he thought, *she set us off on a great adventure, and this is only the beginning.*

Doug made up his mind then and there while he held her. He was definitely going to adopt Loose. It was the right thing to do.

The ground began to shake as he held tightly to Angel. He heard Constant begin to whimper.

At that moment then, in his heart, he knew that, for whatever reason, the universe had chosen him as the pivotal point of what was and what might have been. All that was required of him was to identify the next right thing to do.

He closed his eyes and thought about all the changes tomorrow might bring.